ICEBONES

MAMMOTH: Book Three

Stephen Baxter

Copyright © Stephen Baxter 2001

All rights reserved

The right of Stephen Baxter to be identified as the
author of this work has been asserted by him in accordance
with the Copyright, Designs and Patents Act 1988.

This edition published in Great Britain in 2002 by
Gollancz
An imprint of the Orion Publishing Group
Orion House, 5 Upper St Martin's Lane,
London WC2H 9EA

A CIP catalogue record for this book
is available from the British Library

ISBN 0 57507 298 9

Printed in Great Britain by
Clays Ltd, St Ives plc

To David and Sarah Oliver
and
Colin Pillinger and the *Beagle 2* team

The Sky Steppe — c. AD 3,000 (MARS)

The Ocean of the North
(VASTITAS BOREALIS)

The Fire Mountain
(OLYMPUS MONS)

The Cracked Land
(NOCTIS LABYRINTHUS)

The Gouge
(VALLES MARINERIS)

The High Plains
(SOUTHERN UPLANDS)

The Footfall
(HELLAS)

PROLOGUE

There is a flat, sharp, close horizon, a plain of dust and rocks. The rocks are carved by the wind. Everything is stained rust brown, like dried blood, the shadows long and sharp.

This is not Earth.

Though the sun is rising, the sky above is still speckled with stars. And in the east there is a morning star: steady, brilliant, its delicate blue-white distinct against the violet wash of the dawn. Sharp-eyed creatures might see that this is a double star; a faint silver-grey companion circles close to its blue master.

The sun continues to strengthen. Now it is an elliptical patch of yellow light, suspended in a brown sky. But the sun looks small, feeble; this seems a cold, remote place. As the dawn progresses the dust suspended in the air scatters the light and suffuses everything with a pale, salmon hue.

At last the gathering light masks the moons. Two of them.

On this world, a single large ocean spans much of the

northern hemisphere. There are smaller lakes and seas: many of them circular, confined within craters, linked by rivers and canals. Much of the land is covered by dark green forest and by broad, sweeping grasslands and steppe.

But ice is gathering at the poles. The oceans and lakes are crawling back into ancient underground aquifers.

The grip of the ice persisted for billions of years. Now it comes again.

Soon the air itself will start to snow out.

This is the Sky Steppe.

This is Mars.

The time is three thousand years after the birth of Christ.

The rocky land rings to the calls of the mammoths. But there is no human to hear them.

ONE

MOUNTAIN

THE STORY OF THE LANGUAGE OF KILUKPUK

This is a story Kilukpuk told Silverhair, at the end of her life.

All this happened a long time ago, long before mammoths came to this place, which we call the Sky Steppe. It is a story of Kilukpuk herself, the Matriarch of Matriarchs, who was born in a burrow in the time of the Reptiles. But at the time of this story the Reptiles were long gone, and the world was young and warm and empty.

Kilukpuk had been alive for a very long time. She had become so huge that her body had sunk into the ground, turning it into a Swamp within which she dwelled.

But she had a womb as fertile as the sea. And every year she bore Calves.

Kilukpuk was concerned that her Calves were foolish.

Now, in those days, no Calves could talk. Oh, they made noises: chirps and barks and rumbles and snores and trumpets, just as Calves will make today. But what the Calves chattered to each other didn't *mean* anything. They made the noises in play, or without thinking, or from pain or joy.

Kilukpuk decided to change this.

One year Kilukpuk bore three Calves.

As they suckled at her mighty dugs, she took each of them aside. She said, 'If you want to suckle, you must make this sound.' And she made the suckling cry. And then, when the Calves were no longer hungry, she pushed them away.

The next day all the Calves were hungry again, and Kilukpuk waited in her Swamp.

The first Calf was silent, for she had forgotten the cry Kilukpuk taught her. And so she received no milk.

And she died.

The second Calf made the suckling cry, but made many other noises besides, for she thought that the cry was as meaningless as any other chatter. And so she received no milk.

And she died.

The third Calf, observing the fate of her sisters, made the suckling cry correctly. And Kilukpuk gathered her to her teat, and suckled her, and that Calf lived to grow strong.

When she grew up, that Calf had three Calves of her own. And all of them were born knowing the suckling cry.

Now Kilukpuk gathered the three Calves of her Calf. She said, 'If you ever lose your mother, you must make this sound.' And she made the lost cry. And then she pushed the Calves away.

A few days later, the playful Calves lost their mother – as Calves will – and Kilukpuk waited in her Swamp.

The first Calf was silent, for she had forgotten the cry

Kilukpuk taught her. And so she stayed lost, and the wolves got her.

And she died.

The second Calf made the lost cry, but made many other noises besides, for she thought that the cry was as meaningless as any other chatter. And so she stayed lost, and the wolves got her.

And she died.

The third Calf, observing the fate of her sisters, made the lost cry correctly. And Kilukpuk gathered her up in her trunk and delivered her to her mother, who suckled her, and that Calf lived to grow strong.

And when she grew up, that Calf had three Calves of her own. And all of them were born knowing the suckling cry, and the lost cry.

And the next generation of Calves were born knowing the suckling cry, and the lost cry, and the 'Let's go' rumble.

And the next generation after that were born knowing the suckling cry, and the lost cry, and the 'Let's go' rumble, and the contact rumble.

And so it went, as Kilukpuk instructed each new generation. Calves who learned the new calls were bound tightly together, and Kilukpuk's Family grew stronger.

Calves who did not learn the new calls died. And still Kilukpuk's Family grew stronger.

That is how the language of mammoths and their Cousins came about. And that is why every new Calf is born with the language of Kilukpuk in her head.

Yes, it was cruel, and Kilukpuk mourned every one of those Calves who died. But it is the truth.

The Cycle is the wisdom of uncounted generations of

mammoths. Nothing in there is false. For if it had been false, it would have been removed.

Just as the foolish Calves who would not learn were removed, by death.

THE AWAKENING

Icebones was cold.

She was trapped in chill darkness. She couldn't feel her legs, her tail, even her trunk. She could hear nothing, see nothing.

She tried to call out to her mother, Silverhair, by rumbling, trumpeting, stamping. She couldn't even do that. It was like being immersed in thick cold mud.

And the cold was deep, deeper than she had ever known, soaking into the core of her body, reaching the warm centre under her layers of hair and fat and flesh and bone, the core heat every mammoth had to protect, all her life.

Perhaps this was the aurora, where mammoths believed their souls rose when they died.

. . . But, she thought resentfully, she was only fifteen years old. She had never mated, never borne a calf. How could *she* have died?

Besides, much was wrong. The aurora was full of light, but

there was no light here. The aurora was full of the scent of growing grass, but there was no scent here.

And things were changing.

She had been – *asleep* – and now she was awake. *That* had changed.

She recalled a time before this darkness, when she had been with Silverhair. They had walked across the cold steppe of the Island, surrounded by the Lost and their incomprehensible gadgetry, perturbed and yet not harmed by them. She recalled what her mother had been saying: 'You will be a Matriarch some day, little Icebones. You will be the greatest of them all. But responsibility will lie heavily on you . . .' Icebones hadn't understood.

With her mother, then, on the Island. Now here. *Change*. A time asleep. Now, awake in the dark. Change, change, change.

Everyone knew that in the aurora nothing changed. In the aurora mammoths gathered in the calm warm presence of Kilukpuk, immersed in Family, and there was no day or night, no hunger or thirst, no *I*: merely a continual, endless moment of belonging.

This was *not* the aurora. I am not dead, she realised. My long walk continues.

But with life came hope and fear, and dread settled on her.

She made the lost cry, like a calf. But she couldn't even hear that.

Thunder cracked. Light flashed in sharp lines above and below her. She felt a shuddering, deep in her belly, as if the ground itself was stirring.

She tried to retreat, to rumble her alarm, but still she could not move.

The close darkness receded. Great hard sheets of blackness, like dark ice, fell away. She was suddenly immersed in pink-red light.

And now the feeling returned to her legs and trunk, belly and back, all in a rush. It was like being drenched suddenly in ice water. She staggered, her legs stiff and remote. She tried to trumpet, but her trunk was heavy, and a thick, briny liquid gushed out of it, like sea water.

When her nostrils were clear she took a deep, shuddering breath. The air was cold and sharp – and *thin*. It made her gasp, hurting her raw lungs. Her weak eyes prickled, suddenly streaming with salty water. But she rejoiced, for she was whole again, immersed in her body, and the world.

But it was not the world she had known.

The sky was pink, like a dawn, or a sunset.

She was standing on a shallow slope. She ran her soft trunk tip over the ground. It was hard smooth rock, blue-red. Its surface was rippled and lobed, as if it had melted and refrozen.

This broad plain of rock descended as far as she could see, all the way to the horizon. She must be standing on the flank of a giant mountain, she thought. She turned to look up towards the summit, and she saw a great pillar of black smoke thrusting up to the sky, billows caught in their motion as if frozen.

Her patch of rock, soiled by her watery vomit, was surrounded by sheets of dense blackness that lay on the ground. When she touched this black stuff, she found it was hard and cold and lacking in scent and taste, quite unlike the rock in its chilling smoothness. And the sheets had sharp, straight edges. It was the crust of darkness that had contained her when she had woken from her strange Sleep, and it filled her with renewed dread.

She stepped reluctantly over the smooth black sheets, until she had reached the comparative comfort of the solid rock. But the rock's lobes and ridges were hard under her feet, and every time she took a step she had a strange, dream-like sensation of floating.

Nothing grew here: no herbs, no trees. There was nothing to eat, not so much as a blade of grass.

The air stank of smoke and sulphur. The sun was small and dim and shrunken. The ground shuddered, as if some immense beast buried there were snoring softly in its sleep.

I am in a strange place indeed, she thought. Her brief euphoria evaporated, and disorientation and fear returned.

A contact rumble reached her, resonating deep in her belly. *She was not alone*: relief flooded her.

She turned sharply. Pain prickled in her knees and back and neck, and in the pads of her feet.

A mammoth was approaching – a Bull, taller than she was.

As he walked his powerful shoulders rose and fell, and his head nodded and swayed, his trunk a tangible weight that pulled at his neck. His underfur was light brown, but yellow-white around his rump and belly. His tough overlying guard hairs were much darker, nearly black on his rump and flanks, but shading to a deep brown flecked with crimson on his fore-quarters. The hairs that dangled from his trunk and chin and feet were paler, in places almost white. His tusks curled before him, heavy and proud. He walked slowly, languidly, as if dazed or ill.

She could see him only dimly, through air laden with mist and smoke. But she could smell the deep warmth of his layered hair, feel the steady press of his footsteps against the hard ground.

He was *mammuthus primigenius*: a woolly mammoth, as she was.

She didn't know him.

The two of them began to growl and stomp, facing each other and turning away, touching tusks and trunks, even emitting high, bird-like chirrups from their trunks. The moist pink tip of his trunk reached out and explored her mouth, scalp and eyes. She ran her own trunk fingers through his long guard hairs, finding the woolly underfur beneath.

In this way, touching and singing and listening and smelling, the two mammoths shared a complex, rich exchange of information.

'. . . Who are you? Where are you from?'

'My name is Icebones—'

'Do you know where the food is? We're all hungry here.'

She stumbled back, confused. He was hard to understand, his sounds and postures and gestures a distortion of the language she was used to, as if he had come from a different Clan, not related to her own. And his manner was strange – eager, clumsy, more befitting a callow calf than a grown Bull.

She realised immediately, *He is frightened*.

Discreetly she probed the area of his temple between his eyes and his small ears where he would secrete musth fluid, if it was his time. But she found nothing.

'I don't know anything about food.'

He growled. 'But you came out of *that*.' He probed at the black sheets around her.

She didn't know what to say to him.

Baffled, disturbed, she stepped forward, ignoring the continuing stiffness in her legs, and walked down the featureless slope. The Bull followed her, demanding food noisily, like a calf pursuing his mother.

She reached a shallow ridge. She paused there, raised her trunk and sniffed, studying the world.

She saw how this Mountain's vast shadow spilled across the rocky plains below. Looking beyond the shadow to where the land was still sunlit, she saw splashes of grey-green – steppe, perhaps, or forest. And beyond that she saw the broad shoulders of two more vast, shallow mountains, pushing above the horizon, mighty twins of the Mountain under her feet, made grey and colourless by distance and mist. Close to the horizon thin clouds glowed, bright blue, stark against the pink sky.

There was a moon in the sky. But it was not *the* Moon, which had floated above the night lands of the Island. This moon was a small white disc, and it was climbing into the smoky sky as she watched – *visibly moving*, moment by moment, with a strange, disturbing speed. As it climbed, approaching the sun, it turned into a crescent, a cup of darkness, that finally disappeared.

And then the moon's shadow passed over the sun itself, a dark spot like a passing cloud.

Icebones cringed.

With her deep mammoth's senses she could hear the songs of the planet: the growl of earthquakes and volcanoes, the howl of wind and thunder, the angry surge of ocean storms, all the noises of earth, air, fire and water. And she could tell that this world was small, round, hard – and strange.

She raised her trunk higher, trying to smell mammoths, her Family, Silverhair. She could smell nothing but the stink of sulphur and ash.

Wherever she was, however she had got here, she was far from her Family. Without her Family she was incomplete –

for a mammoth Cow could no more live apart from her Family than a trunk or leg or tusk could survive if cut off the body.

The Bull continued to pursue her.

She turned on him. 'Why are you following me? I am not in oestrus. Can't you tell that? And you are not in musth.'

His eyes gleamed, amber pebbles in pits of wrinkled skin. 'What is *oestrus*? What is *musth*?'

She growled. 'My name is Icebones. What is your name? Where is your bachelor herd?'

'Do you know where the food is? Please, I am *very* hungry.'

She came closer to him, curiosity warring with her anger and confusion. She explored his face with her trunk. How could he know so little? How could he not have a *name*?

And – where *was* she? This strange place of pink mountains was like nowhere she had ever heard of, nowhere spoken of even in the Cycle, the mammoths' great and ancient body of lore . . .

Nowhere, except one place.

'*The Sky Steppe*. That's where we are, isn't it?' The Sky Steppe, the Island in the sky where – according to the Cycle – mammoths would one day find a world of their own, far from the predations and cruelty of the Lost, a world of calm and plenty.

But this place of barren rock and smoky air didn't seem so plentiful to her, and nor was it calm.

The Bull ignored her questions. 'I'm hungry,' he repeated.

She turned her back on him deliberately.

She heard him grunt and snort, the soft uncertain pads of his footsteps recede. She felt relief – then renewed anxiety.

I'm hungry too, she realised. And I'm thirsty. And, after all, the strange, infuriating Bull was the only mammoth she had seen here.

She turned. His broad back, long guard hairs shining, was still visible over a blue-black ridge that poked like a bone out of the hard ground.

She hurried after him.

Walking was difficult. The hard ground crumpled into folds, as if it had once flowed like congealing ice, and great gullies had been raked out of the side of the Mountain.

Her strength seemed sapped. She struggled to climb the ridges, and slithered on her splayed feet down slopes where she could not get a purchase. The air was smoky and thin, and her chest heaved at it.

She found a gully that was roofed over by a layer of rock. She probed with brief curiosity into a kind of cave, much taller than she was, that receded into the darkness like a vast nostril. Perhaps all the gullies here had once been long tubular caves like this, but their rocky roofs had collapsed.

In one place the ground had cracked open, like burned skin, and steam billowed. Mud, grey and liquid, boiled inside the crack, and it built up tall, skinny vents, like trunks sticking out of the ground. The air around the mud pool was hot and dense with smoke and ash, making it even harder to draw a breath.

Grit settled on her eyes, making them weep. She longed for the soft earth of the Island in summer, for grass and herbs and bushes.

But the Bull was striding on, his gait still languidly slow to her eyes. He was confident, used to the vagaries of the ground where she was uncertain, healthy and strong where she still felt stiff and disoriented. She hurried after him.

And now, as she came over a last ridge, she saw that he had joined a group of mammoths.

They were all Cows, she saw instantly. She felt a surge of relief to see a Family here – even if it was not *her* Family. She hurried forward, trumpeting a greeting.

They turned, sniffing the air. The mammoths stood close together, and the wind made their long guard hairs swirl around them in a single wave, like a curtain of falling water.

There were three young-looking Cows, so similar they must have been sisters. One appeared to be carrying a calf: her belly was heavy and low, and her dugs were swollen. An older Cow might have been their mother – her posture was tense and uncertain – and a still older Cow, moving stiffly as if her bones ached, might be *her* mother, grandmother to the sisters – and so, surely, the Matriarch of the Family. Icebones thought they all seemed agitated, uncertain.

Icebones watched as the Cow she had tagged as the mother lumbered over to the Bull and cuffed his scalp affectionately with her trunk . . . *And the mother towered over the Bull.*

That didn't make sense, Icebones thought, bewildered. Adult Bulls were taller than Cows. This Bull had been much taller than Icebones, and Icebones, at fifteen years old, was nearly her full adult height. So how could this older Cow tower over *him* as if he was a calf?

There was one more Cow here, Icebones saw now, standing a little way away from the clustered Family. This Cow was different. Her hair was very fine – so fine that in places Icebones could see her skin, which was pale grey, mottled pink. Her tusks were short and straight, lacking the usual curling sweep of mammoth tusks, and her ears were large and floppy.

This Cow was staring straight at Icebones as she approached, her trunk held high as she sniffed the air. Her posture was hard and still, as if she were a musth Bull challenging a younger rival.

'I am Icebones,' she said.

The others did not reply. She walked forward.

The mammoths seemed to grow taller and taller, their legs extending like shadows cast by a setting sun, until they loomed over her, as if she too was reduced to the dimensions of a calf.

Icebones felt reluctant, increasingly nervous. Must everything be strange here?

She approached the grandmother. Though she too was much taller than Icebones, this old one's hair was discoloured black and grey and her head was lean, the skin and hair sunken around her eyes and temples, so that the shape of the skull was clearly visible. Icebones reached out and slipped her trunk into the grandmother's mouth, and tasted staleness and blood. She is very old, Icebones realised with dismay.

She said, 'You are the Matriarch. My Matriarch is Silverhair. But my Family is far from here . . .'

'*Matriarch*,' said the grandmother. '*Family*.' She gazed at Icebones. '*Silverhair*. These are old words, words buried deep in our heads, our bellies. I am no *Matriarch*, child.'

Icebones was confused. 'Every Family has a Matriarch.'

The grandmother growled. 'This is my daughter. These are her children, these three Cows. And *this* one carries a calf of her own – another generation, if I live to see it . . . But we are not a Family.' She sneezed, her limp trunk flexing, and blood-stained mucus splashed over the rock at her feet.

Icebones shrank back. 'I never heard of mammoths without names, a Family that wasn't a Family, Cows without a Matriarch.'

One of the three tall sisters approached Icebones curiously. Her tusks were handsome symmetrical spirals before her face. Her legs were skinny and extended. Even her head was large, Icebones saw, the delicate skull expansive above the fringe of hair that draped down from her chin.

She reached out with her trunk and probed at Icebones's hair and mouth and ears, just as if Icebones was a calf. 'I know who you are.'

Icebones recoiled.

But now the others were all around her – the other sisters, the mother, the Bull.

'We were told you would come.'

'I am thirsty. I want water.'

'My baby is stirring. I am hungry.'

The strange, tall mammoths clamoured at her, like calves seeking dugs to suckle, plucking at the hair on her back and legs, even the clumps on her stubby tail.

She trumpeted, backing off. 'Get away from me!'

The other – the Ragged One, stub-tusked, pink-spotted – came lumbering over the rocky slope to stand close to Icebones. 'You mustn't mind them. They think *you* might be the Matriarch, you see. That's what they've been promised.'

Now the Bull-calf came loping towards her, oddly slow, ungainly. He said to Icebones, 'Show us how to find food. That's what Matriarchs are supposed to do.'

I'm no Matriarch, she thought. I've never even had a calf. I've never mated. I'm little older than you are, for all your size . . . 'You must find food for yourself,' she said.

'But he can't,' the Ragged One said slyly. 'Let me show you.'

And she turned and began to follow a trail, lightly worn into the hard rock, that led over a further ridge.

Confused, apprehensive, Icebones followed.

The Ragged One brought her to a shallow pit that had been sliced into the flank of the Mountain. At the back of the pit was a vertical wall, like a cliff face, into which sockets had been cut, showing dark and empty spaces beyond.

And, strangest of all, on a raised outcrop at the centre of the levelled floor stood a mammoth – but it was not a mammoth. It, he or she, was merely a heap of bones, painstakingly reassembled to mimic life, with not a scrap of flesh or fat or hair. The naked skeleton raised great yellow tusks challengingly to the pink sky.

Icebones recognised the nature of this place immediately: the harsh straight lines and level planes of its construction, the casual horror of the bony monument at the centre. 'This is a place of the Lost,' she said. 'We should get away from here.'

The Ragged One gazed at her with eyes that were too orange, too bright. 'You really don't understand, do you? The Lost aren't the problem. The problem is, *the Lost have gone.*' She circled her trunk around Icebones's, and began to tug her, gently but relentlessly, towards the shallow, open pit.

Icebones walked forward, one heavy step after another, straining to detect the presence of the Lost. But her sense of smell was scrambled by the stink of the smoky air.

'Where were you born?'

'On the Island,' Icebones said. 'A steppe. A land of grass and bushes and water.'

The Ragged One growled. 'Your Island, if it ever existed, is long ago and far away. *Here* – this is where I was born. And my mother before me – and her mother – and hers. Here, in this place of the Lost. What do you think of that?'

Icebones looked up at the cavernous rooms cut into the wall. 'And was a Lost your Matriarch? Did the Lost give you your names?'

'We had no Matriarch,' the Ragged One said simply. 'We had no need of Families. We had no need of names. For we only had to do what the Lost showed us, and we would be kept well and happy. Look.' The Ragged One stalked over to a low trough set in the sheer wall. A flap of shining stone dangled before it, like the curtain of guard hairs beneath the belly of a mammoth. The Ragged One pushed the tip of her trunk under the flap, which lifted up. When she withdrew her trunk, she held it up before Icebones. Save for a little dust, her pink trunk tip was empty.

Icebones was baffled by this mysterious behaviour. And she saw that the trunk had just a single nostril.

The Ragged One said, 'Every day since I was born I came to this place and pushed my trunk in the hole, and was rewarded with food. Grass, herbs, bark, twigs. *Every day*. And from other holes in this wall I have drawn water to drink – as much as I like. But not today, and not for several days.'

'How can food grow in a hole?'

The old grandmother came limping towards them, her gaunt head heavy. 'It doesn't grow there, child. The Lost put it there with their paws.'

'And now,' the Ragged One said, 'the Lost are gone. All of them. And so there is no more food in the hole, no more water. *Now* can you see why we are frightened?'

The old one, with a weary effort, lifted her trunk and laid it on Icebones's scalp. 'I don't know who you are, or where you came from. But we have a legend. One day the Lost would leave this place, and the great empty spaces of this world would be ours. And on that day, one would come who would lead us, and show us how to live: how to eat, how to drink, how to survive the heat of the summer and the cold of the winter.'

'A Matriarch,' Icebones said softly.

The grandmother murmured, 'It has been a very long time – more generations than there are stars in the sky. So they say . . .'

'But now,' the Ragged One said, 'the Lost are gone, and we are hungry. Are you to be our Matriarch, Icebones?'

Icebones lifted her trunk from one to the other. The grandmother seemed to be gazing at her expectantly, as if with hope, but there was only envy and ambition in the stance of the Ragged One.

'I am no Matriarch,' Icebones said.

The Ragged One snorted contempt. 'Then must we die here——?'

Her words were drowned by a roar louder than any mammoth's. The ground shuddered sharply under Icebones's feet, and she stumbled.

Dark smoke thrust out of the higher slopes of the Mountain. The huge black column was shot through with fire, and lumps of burning rock flew high. The air became thick and dark, full of the stink of sulphur, and darkness fell over them.

'Ah,' said the Ragged One, as if satisfied. 'This old monster is waking up at last.'

Flakes of ash were falling through the muddy air, like snowflakes, settling on the mammoths' outer hair. It was a strange, distracting sight. Icebones caught one flake on her trunk tip. It was hot enough to burn, and she flicked it away.

A mammoth trumpeted, piercingly.

Icebones hurried back, trying to ignore the sting of ash flakes on her exposed skin, and the stink of her own singed hair.

She met a mammoth, running in panic. It was one of the three sisters, and the long hairs that dangled from her belly were smouldering. 'Help me! Oh, help me!' Even as she ran, Icebones was struck by the liquid slowness of her gait, the languid way her hair flopped over her face.

The injured one, confused, agitated, ran back to the others. Icebones hurried after her and beat at the Cow's scorched and smouldering fur with her trunk.

The others stood around helplessly. The mammoths, coated in dirty ash, were turning grey, as if transmuting into rock themselves.

At last the smouldering was stopped. The injured Cow was weeping thick tears of pain, and Icebones saw that she would have a scarred patch on her belly.

Icebones asked, 'How did this happen to you . . . ?'

There was a predatory howl, and light glared from the sky. The mammoths cringed and trumpeted.

A giant rock fell from the smoke-filled sky. It slammed into the floor, sending smaller flaming fragments flying far, and the ground shuddered again. Beneath a thin crust of black stone, the fallen rock was glowing red-hot.

With a clatter, the patiently reconstructed skeleton of the long-dead mammoth fell to pieces.

'*That* is how I was burned,' the injured sister said resentfully.

More of the lethal glowing rocks began to fall from the sky, each of them howling like a descending raptor, and where they fell the stony ground splashed like soft ice.

The mother lumbered up. 'We have to get out of this rain of rocks,' she said grimly.

'The feeding place,' gasped the injured sister.

'No,' growled the mother. '*Look*.'

Icebones peered through curling smoke and the steady drizzle of ash flakes. A falling rock had smashed into the place of feeding, breaking open the thin wall as a mammoth's foot might crush a skull.

The Ragged One was watching Icebones, as if this was a trial of strength. She said slyly, 'The Lost have abandoned us. Must we all die here? Tell us what to do, Matriarch.'

Icebones, dizzy, disoriented, tried to think. Did these spindly mammoths really believe she was a Matriarch? And whatever they believed, what was she to do, in this strange upside-down world where it rained ash and fiery rock? Surely Silverhair would have known . . .

The grandmother, through a trunk clogged with ash and dirt, was struggling to speak.

Her daughter stepped closer. 'What did you say?'

'The tube,' the old one said. 'The lava tube.'

The others seemed baffled, but Icebones understood. 'The great nostril of rock . . . It is not far.' I should have thought of it. Silverhair would have thought of it. But I am not Silverhair. I am only Icebones.

She waited for the grandmother to give her command to proceed. But, of course, this old one was no Matriarch. The mammoths milled about, uncertain.

'We must not leave here,' said the burned sister. 'What if the Lost return? They will help us.'

At last her mother stepped forward and slapped her sharply on the scalp with her trunk. 'We must go to the lava tube. Come now.' She turned and began to lead the way. The others followed, the Bull pacing ahead with foolish boldness, the three sisters clustered together. The Ragged One tracked them at a distance, more like an adolescent Bull than a Cow.

As they toiled away into the thickening grey murk, Icebones realised that the grandmother was not following.

She turned back. To find her way she had to probe with her trunk through the murk. The smoke and ash was so thick now it was hard to breathe.

The grandmother had slumped to her knees, and her belly was flat on the ground, guard hairs trailing around her. Her eyes were closed, her trunk coiled limply before her, and her breath was a shallow laboured scratch.

'You must get up. Come on.' Icebones nudged the old one's rump with her forehead, trying to force her to stand. She trumpeted to the others. 'Help her!'

The grandmother's rumble was weak, deep, almost inaudible over the shuddering of the rocky ground. 'Let them go.' She slumped again, her breath bubbling, her body turning into a shapeless grey mound under the ash.

Icebones feverishly probed at the old one's face and mouth with her trunk. 'I will see you in the aurora.'

One eye opened, like a stone embedded in broken flesh and scorched hair. 'There is no aurora in this place, child.'

Icebones was shocked. 'Then where do we go when we die?'

The old one closed her eyes. 'I suppose I'll soon find out.' Her chest was heaving as she strained at the hot, filthy air. She raised her trunk, limply, and pushed at Icebones's face. 'Go. Your mother would be proud of you.'

Icebones backed away. She was immersed in strangeness and peril, far from her Family – and now she was confronted by death. 'I will Remember you.'

But the grandmother, subsiding as if into sleep, did not seem to hear, and Icebones turned away.

It was the greatest volcano in the solar system. It had been dormant for tens of millions of years. Now it was active once more, and its voice could be heard all around this small world.

And, across the volcano's mighty flanks, the small band of mammoths toiled through fire and ash, seeking shelter.

Chapter Two

THE SONGS OF THE WORLD

The blazing rocks continued to fall from the sky, splashing against the stolid ground.

The rocky tube shuddered and groaned. Sometimes dust or larger fragments of the inner roof came loose, and the mammoths, huddled together, squealed in terror. But the tube held, protecting them.

The darkness of night closed in. Still the ash snow fell thickly. The cave grew black. The mammoths tried to ignore the hunger and thirst that gnawed at them all.

Sometimes, in the darkness, Icebones heard the others snore or mumble. Icebones felt weariness weigh on her too. But she was reluctant to fall back into the dark, having emerged from that timeless, dreamless Sleep so recently.

She felt compassion for these wretched nameless ones – but at the same time her own fear deepened, for it was apparent that there was nobody here who could help *her*, no Family or Matriarch or even an experienced, battle-scarred old Bull.

She wished with all her heart that Silverhair was here.

The morning came at last, bringing a thin pinkish light that only slowly dispelled the purple-black of night. But the ash continued to fall, and there was a renewed round of rock falls.

The mammoths were forced to stay cooped up together in the lava tube, bickering and trying to avoid each other's dung, which was thin and stinking of malnourishment.

By mid-afternoon, thirst drove them out. They had to push their way through ash which had piled up against the mouth of their long cave.

The world had turned grey.

A cloud of thick noxious gas continued to pump out of the summit of this immense Fire Mountain, and a grey-black lid of it hung beneath the pink sky, darkening the day. Ash drifted down, turning the rocky ground into a field of grey smoothness over which the mammoths toiled like fat brown ghosts, every footfall leaving a crater in fine grey layers.

Everything moved slowly here, Icebones observed. As she walked her steps felt light, as if in a dream, or as if she was wading through some deep pond. When she kicked up ash flakes they fell back with an eerie calmness. Even the guard hairs of the mammoths rippled languidly.

Trying to ignore the strangeness, Icebones walked with exaggerated caution. If she must be called a Matriarch, she should fulfil the role. 'The ash hides the rock's folds and crevices,' she said. 'You must be careful not to injure yourselves.' She showed the others how to probe at the ground ahead with their trunks, feeling out hidden traps.

But the Ragged One stalked alongside her, her posture stiff and mocking. 'So you know all about ash. You know better than I do, after I have spent my whole life here on this Fire Mountain.'

'No,' said Icebones evenly. 'But I have seen how snow covers the ground. And the dangers are surely alike.'

The Ragged One growled. '*There*,' she said. 'There are dangers in this place you have never imagined.'

Icebones saw that a new river was making its way down the broad flank of the Mountain. It was a river of fire.

Glowing red, it flowed stickily and slowly, like blood. It was crusted over by a dark brown scum that continually crumbled, broke and congealed again. Flames licked all along the length of the flow, and wispy yellow smoke coiled. In one place the flow cut through a frozen pond, and a vast cloud of yellow-white steam rose with a harsh hissing.

Icebones could smell the burning stench of the molten rock river, feel its huge rumble as it churned its way down the slope, cutting through layers of ancient rock as if they were no more substantial than ice. 'We were fortunate,' she said softly. 'If that rock river had chosen to flow a little more to the east—'

'It would have overwhelmed our lava tube,' said the Ragged One. 'Yes. We would have been scorched, or buried alive, or crushed . . .'

'It is a shame the rock flow is destroying the pool. We could have drunk there.'

The Ragged One snorted. 'In your wisdom you will find us more water.'

Icebones, irritated, walked up the rocky slope. 'Very well. Let's find water.'

Reluctantly the Ragged One followed.

Icebones came to an area where the ash was a little less thick. She walked back and forth across the rock, stamping, scraping exposed outcrops with her tusks and slapping them with her trunk, listening hard.

The young Bull approached, ungainly on his oddly elongated legs. 'What are you doing?'

Feeling like a foolish infant – she had to remind herself that this towering Bull was only a calf himself – she said, 'I'm looking for water.'

'There is no water here.'

'Yes, there is. But it's deep underground. Can't you hear it?'

Comically, he cocked his small ears. 'No,' he said.

'Listen with your belly and feet and chest.' She stamped again. 'The ground here is hard and it rings well. And the water that flows deep makes the rock shudder . . .' To Icebones, the rumble of the deep water was a distinct noise under the frothy din of the surface world, like the far-off call of a thunderstorm, or the giant crack of a distant glacier calving an iceberg.

The Bull raised his trunk, as if to smell the deep-buried water. He rammed his tusks against the hard, rippled rock, but they rebounded, and he yelped with pain.

'We must find a place where the water comes closer to the surface.' She walked down the hillside, pausing to stamp and listen, tracking the path of the underground river.

The others followed, the Bull with eagerness, the rest with incomprehension or resentment, but all driven by their thirst.

She came to a place where a vast pipe thrust out of the ground. It stalked away over the rocky slope on spindly legs, like some immense centipede. The pipe was as wide as three or four mammoths standing side by side, and its surface was slick and white, like a tusk.

The pipe was obviously a creation of the Lost. But its

purpose did not interest her – for she could hear water running through it.

She began to probe at the ground just above the pipe. The rock was shattered here; underneath a surface layer of dust there was fine rubble. And, when she dug into this with her trunk, she could smell water.

The Bull could smell it too. 'Let me drink! Give me the water!'

Icebones growled. 'I am not your Lost keeper, here to nurse you. The water is here, but you must work for it.' She trumpeted to the others. 'Come, now. Watch what I do.'

She bent her head and cleared away surface debris with brisk swipes of her tusks. Then she stood square and began to dig her way into the rubble with her trunk.

The Ragged One snorted sceptically, but the others crowded closer.

Icebones soon grew tired, but she ignored her discomfort and kept digging.

Perhaps half a trunk's length deep the rubble began to turn into sticky, half-dried mud, and she gratefully sucked out the first droplets of water.

After that the others quickly settled to work around her. They grumbled and complained as they scraped their tusks or caught their sensitive trunk fingers on sharp rock fragments. But the scent of water lured them on, and soon their complaints turned to a murmur of mutual encouragement.

Icebones could sense warmth rising from the ground here. Perhaps that had something to do with the rivers of rock which had gushed from this Mountain; perhaps that deep warmth had kept the underground water from freezing here.

At last Icebones dug deep enough to find soil soaked to mud.

She had to kneel on her front legs to reach. With her trunk tip she hollowed out a chamber deep beneath the ground. She let the hole fill with seeping water, which she sucked out in a great trunk load and emptied into her mouth. The water was hot, a little salty, and it fizzed oddly in her throat — but it was delicious.

The others, working less expertly, were slower, but her success drove them on. At length they were all pumping out muddy, brownish water and filling their mouths.

Working together at the rock face was the nearest this strange, fractured bunch had come to behaving like a Family, Icebones thought. She allowed herself to relish this moment of immersion: the shuffling of feet and the scrape of tusk on rock, the soft rustle of the mammoths' thick hair, and the myriad small sounds, farts and hums and squeals and rumbles, that emanated from the mammoths' immense torsos as they drank.

When she had drunk her fill, Icebones walked away from the others.

The rock beneath her feet came in layers, she found, exploring it with her trunk: layers of red overlying grey, grey overlying blue, blue overlying black. Here and there this stratified rock was pocked by craters, huge circular scars.

Perhaps all of this vast Mountain was made up of layer after layer of hardened rock, vomited from the summit over many years.

When she urinated, the rock and dust fizzed and hissed where her water splashed it. She sniffed at this new peculiarity, baffled and disturbed. The very dust was strange here.

She found a steep-sided ridge and climbed it stiffly, the mild exertion making her gasp for air. The ash had drifted away from the top of the broad ridge, leaving hard exposed rock.

Standing on the ridge, she was suspended between purple sky and a land that glowed red.

The flank of the Fire Mountain swept away beneath her. The sun was setting behind her, already hidden by the Mountain — she was looking east, then — and the sky was a stark dome of bruised purple, showing a few stars at the zenith. The Mountain thrust out of the belly of this world, as if some monstrous planetary calf were struggling to be born. And, on the eastern horizon, she saw those other rocky cones, mountains almost as vast, their sunlit faces glowing red.

There was a layer of clouds *beneath* her. The clouds were tall thunderheads, flat and smooth and black beneath, topped by huge pink-white mounds, and they sailed like icebergs on some invisible sea of thicker, moister air. I really am very high, she thought.

Below the clouds, on the deeper land beneath, she saw swathes of pale green and grey: the mark of life, grasslands or steppe. Raising her trunk she thought she could smell water, far away, far below.

We must go there, she thought, down to that plain. For we surely cannot stay here, on this barren slope.

She could see the giant water-bearing pipe, at the roof of which the mammoths still dug for water. When she climbed a little higher she saw that more pipes thrust out of the bulk of the Mountain and spread around it across the rocky land. They were thin lines that shone pink in the last of the sunlight.

In a way this great structure was magnificent, she thought, the huge shining trunks stretching straight and far, farther than many mammoth trails. But she wondered if that was why this old Fire Mountain had come to life. The Lost were always thirsty for water. Perhaps, like a greedy mammoth who drains the ground beneath her feet, the Lost had sucked away too much of the water which had gathered here, disturbing the Mountain.

Now the light was fading fast, and the immense shadow of the Fire Mountain stretched across the land. Soon she could hear calls, rising from the hidden depths of the landscape, drifting on the thin, cold air. They were clearly the voices of predators – wolves, perhaps, or cats – marking out their killing territories. Though the predators' calls made her tense and alert, there was something reassuring in the thought that she and her motley band of mammoths were not the only living things in this strange, cold world.

As the light faded further, she heard more subtle sounds: the hiss of wind over mountains and forests and steppe, the deep, subtle murmur of an ocean, the groan of glaciers and the crackling of ice sheets, the murmur of liquid rock within the Fire Mountain, the deeper churning of this world's hot core. When she stamped her feet, she could hear washes of sound echoing back and forth through the deep foundations of the land.

The sunset and the dawn were the times sound carried best. And so she listened, with every aspect of her being, her ears and belly and chest, to the deeper sounds, the songs of the world. And gradually she built up an image, in sounds and echoes, of the spinning rocky ball to which she clung.

This was a small, cold world. It was made of rock, rock that was hard deep into its being – unlike that other world, the world of her birth, whose rocky skin was laid thin over a churning liquid body, like thin ice on a pond.

But the cold here would suit mammoths, she thought. And the hardness of the rocks made the world's songs easy to hear.

The world was round, like a ball of dung. But it was a misshapen ball. To the north it was flattened, as if a massive foot had stamped down there, cracking and compressing the rock across half the world. The giant pit made by that stamping was, she sensed, filled with water, a world-girdling ocean. The southern lands were higher, but they, too, had been struck a series of immense, damaging blows. One of those slamming impacts had been so powerful it had punched a great pit into the hide of the world – and the impact had caused a re-bounding upthrust of rock *here*, in the lands beneath her feet. The huge Fire Mountain itself stood over that rock mound.

This world was a small, swollen, battered place, she saw, born in unimaginable violence, bruised by ancient blows from which it had never healed.

And the world was dying.

She could hear water freezing over, or flowing into deep basins, or seeping into the ground. She could hear the crack of ice spreading over that vast northern ocean. Even the air was settling out. She could hear its moan as it pooled, cooling, like water running downhill, reaching at last the lowest places of all – like that immense punched-in depression on the far side of the world.

The world was growing cold, and its air and water were shrivelling away – and, she supposed, all life with them . . .

And it was not the world where she had been born. The songs of this small world and the songs of that other place – massive, liquid, alive – were unmistakably different.

But how could that be? How could there be a place *here* that was not *there*? It was beyond her imagination.

And – *why* had she been brought here?

She recalled the Island, her Family. It was as if she had been with them yesterday, listening to Silverhair's patient account of how, when she was no older than Icebones now, the Lost had found the Island and nearly killed them off, the last of all the mammoths. All her life, Silverhair had told Icebones she would one day be a Matriarch. And she had steadily coached her daughter in the wisdom of the mammoths, teaching her the songs of the Cycle, imparting a deep sense of blood and land . . .

Yes, one day I will be a Matriarch, Icebones thought. I have always accepted my destiny. But not here. Not now. I am not ready!

But, ready or not, what was she to do next?

She sucked the thin, dry air through her trunk, felt its cold prickle in her lungs, smelled the lingering tang of ash. Alone, longing for the warmth of her Family, she began to sing: 'I am Icebones. My Matriarch was Silverhair, my mother. And her Matriarch was Owlheart. And her Matriarch was Wolfnose . . .'

She called with deep rumbles. She sensed a fluttering of skin over her forehead, the membranes stretched tight over the hollows in her skull that made her voice's deepest sounds. And she stamped, too, a rhythmic thumping that sent acoustic pulses out through the hard rocky ground.

Icebones. Icebones . . .

She gasped and turned around, trunk held high. But she was alone.

Her name had come not through the air, but as deep sound through the hard rock of the ground.

She stamped out, 'I am Icebones, daughter of Silverhair. Who are you?'

Long heartbeats later came a reply. *I am strong and my tusks are powerful. More powerful than my brother's. Are you in oestrus? Are you with calf? Are you suckling?*

Icebones snorted. It was a Bull, then: intent only on rivalry with his fellows and on mating with any receptive Cow – just like all Bulls, who, some Cows would say, are calves all their lives.

'I am not in oestrus. Where are you?'

It is a cold place. By the shore of a round sea. There is little to eat. Snow falls. There are few of us. Predators stalk us.

She raised her trunk and sniffed the air. She could smell only the rock, the thin, dry air and her own dung. There was no scent of Bull – and an adult Bull in musth, dribbling from his temple glands and trickling urine, emitted a powerful scent indeed. 'You must be far away, very far.'

But my tusks are long and powerful, almost as long as my . . .

His last word was indistinct.

'And you have no need of a name?'

Names? None of us have names.

She snorted. 'I will call you Boaster.'

The steppe is sparse. We walk far to graze. Once we were many, like daisies on the steppe. Now we are few.

'We must find each other,' she said immediately, rapping her message into the deep rock.

A Family of Cows, with no adult Bulls, could not prosper: without Bulls to impregnate the Cows, it would be extinct within a generation. And likewise an isolated bachelor herd without Cows would soon die, unable to reproduce itself. It was a deeper layer of peril, she realised, lurking beyond the dangers of the fires that belched into the air.

Yes. I am ready for you, Icebones. I have no need to wait for musth. But now his words were becoming indistinct. Perhaps he was walking over softer ground, or a storm on that northern ocean was making the rocks too noisy. . . . *Follow the water,* she caught. . . . *Water and the thick warm air . . . the lowest place . . .*

And then he was gone, and she was alone again.

The light was ebbing out of the sky now. The sun had long vanished behind the Mountain, and an ocean of shadow was pooling at its base, obscuring those stretches of steppe and forest, turning them grey and lifeless. The stars were emerging through a great disc of blackness that spread down from the zenith towards the horizon, revealing a huge, clear sky.

There was a presence beside her, a trunk pulling at hers. Eager for company, she clung to it gratefully. But she felt sparse, stiff hair on that trunk, and tasted bitterness.

It was the Ragged One. 'You must come back. The others want you.'

'Why?'

'They want to Remember the old one. As you told them they should.'

Icebones told the Ragged One of the Bull she had spoken to.

The Ragged One seemed to understand little. 'The Bulls were brought here, to the Mountain, to us. And if one of them was in musth, and one of us in oestrus, there would be a mating. That was all we needed to know about Bulls.'

'And you would sing the Song of Oestrus?'

But the Ragged One knew nothing of that. 'Once there were many of us. Many like you, many like *me*. The Lost did not mean to keep us for ever. They were making the world, you see. They were covering it with oceans and steppe and forests. One day there would be room for us to roam, in Clans. But then the Sickness came . . .'

She described an horrific illness among the mammoths. It would begin with blood in urine. Then would come waves of heat and cold, and growths that would sprout from mouth and feet and anus. Finally, after a suffusion of great pain, there would be death.

'And if one caught it, all would fall.' She turned to Icebones, growling. 'I know you think we have been kept by the Lost, that we are like calves. But we heard the mammoths calling to each other, all over this quiet world, Icebones. We heard the cries of the carnivores too, as they broke through fences no longer maintained by the Lost. We heard their joy at the ease of the kills they made, and later their disappointment at how little meat remained.

'And one by one those distant mammoth voices fell silent.

'Can you imagine how that was? Perhaps you should indeed teach us to Remember. Perhaps that is why you have been sent among us – to Remember all who died.'

Icebones was horrified. But she said, '*We* aren't dead yet. On this Mountain there is no food, and precious little water. We must go down to the plains.'

The Ragged One snorted. 'You are a fool. The world is growing cold, yes. *Because the Lost have gone*.'

Icebones was baffled. 'Where did they go?'

'They went up, into the sky,' the Ragged One said. 'And that is where *we* must go. Not down. *Up*.' She said this decisively, and stalked away stiff-legged.

The Remembering was simple.

Icebones had the mammoths help her dig out the body of

their grandmother. It had been scorched and dried by its immersion in the ash. Much of the hair was blackened and curling, and the skin was drawn tight. The eyelids, gruesomely, had fallen open, and the eyes had become globes of cloudy, fibrous material, sightless.

Icebones said, 'Watch now, and learn.' She scraped at the bare ground with her tusks. Then she picked up a fingerful of grit and ash and dropped it on the grandmother's unresponding flank.

The mother reached down, picked up a loose rock, and stepped forward to do the same.

Soon they were all using their trunks and feet to cover the inert body with ash, dust and stones – all save the Ragged One, who stayed on the edge of the group, unwilling to participate, and yet unable to turn away.

As they worked, Icebones felt a deeper calm settle on her soul. The Cycle said this was how the mammoths had always honoured their dead.

Silverhair had told her of a place on the Island called the Plain of Bones, where the ground was thick with the bones of mammoths – of Icebones's ancestors, who had walked across the land for uncounted generations before her. She wondered how many mammoth bones lay beneath the hard rocky ground of this small new world.

Chapter Three

THE SKY TRAIL

At dawn the world glowed its brightest red. It was as if the dust and the rocks caught the red light of the rising sun and hurled it back with vigour. Even the mammoths' hair trapped the all-pervasive red light, their guard hairs glowing as if they were on fire. On the plains far below, pools or rivers looked jet black, and the green of life was scattered, irrelevant in this mighty redness.

Icebones longed for a scrap of blue sky.

It was apparent that the mammoths, lacking any better idea, were prepared to go along with the Ragged One's scheme. Though Icebones felt nothing but dread at the very notion of pursuing Lost, she had no better suggestion either.

When the light was adequate, the Ragged One simply set off up the flank of the Mountain. The others followed only haphazardly, paying no attention to each other, with none of the calm discipline of a true Family.

Icebones took a place at the back of their rough line.

The Mountain's slope was shallow, and the mammoths climbed steadily. With their strong hind legs mammoths were well suited to climbing – though descending a slope was always harder, as that meant all a mammoth's weight was supported by her front legs.

Here and there mosses, lichens and even clumps of grass protruded from cracks in the hard red-black ground. Icebones pulled up grass tufts, wrapping her trunk lips around the thin-tasting goodies. But the grass was sparse and yellowed, struggling for life.

And there was no water to be found, none at all. She could tell from the rock's deep echoes that the groundwater was buried deep here, far beneath a lid of rock much too thick and hard for any mammoth tusk to penetrate.

The dung of the other mammoths was thin and watery. These mammoths had built up a reserve of fat from the ambiguous generosity of their Lost keepers. But it had clearly been a long time since they had fed properly.

As for herself, Icebones had no real idea how long it had been since she had last tasted the Island's lush autumn grass. What a strange thought that was . . . We must find proper grazing soon, she thought.

At length the mammoths reached something new. A line of shining silver stood above the rust-red rock, running parallel to the line of the slope. It stood above the ground on legs like spindly tree trunks.

The line swept down from the humped slope of the Mountain, down towards the hummocked plain below, down as far as Icebones could see until it dwindled to a silvery thread invisible against the red-blue clutter of the layered rock.

Icebones felt cold, deep inside. A thing of clean surfaces and hard sharp edges, this was clearly the work of the Lost.

But the others showed no fear – indeed they seemed curious, and they walked around the skinny supports, probing with pink trunk tips.

The Ragged One came to Icebones. 'This is the south side of the Fire Mountain. The sunlight lingers here. You see the green further below, smell the tang of the leaves? The Lost grew vines there. But now the vines are dying.'

Icebones asked, 'What would you have us do?'

'This is the path the Lost took to the sky,' the Ragged One said simply. 'We must follow it. That way we will find the Lost again.'

Paths worn by mammoths in the steppe were simple trails of bare and compacted earth. This shining aerial band looked like no path Icebones had ever seen. She said starkly, 'Perhaps the Lost don't want you to find them. Have you thought of that? If they wanted you, they would have taken you with them.'

The Ragged One growled and clashed her stubby tusks against Icebones's. 'You should crawl back into the cave of darkness you came from. I will lead these others. When we find the Lost we will be safe.' And she turned her back on Icebones and stalked away, trunk folded beneath her face.

Icebones, fighting her instincts, trailed behind.

As day followed day, the mammoths climbed the endless shallow slope, following the Sky Trail. They grew still more weary, hungry, thirsty, and their joints ached, the soft pads of their feet protesting at the hard cold rock beneath them. Icebones learned to concentrate on each footfall, one after another, letting her strength carry her upward even when it

43

seemed that there was too little air in her aching lungs to sustain her.

The sky above was never brighter than a deep purple-red, even at midday. In the morning there would be a thick blanket of frost that turned the ground pink-white, covering the living things. But as the sun rose the frost quickly burned off, faster than they could scrape it up with their trunks. Even here, life clung to the rock. Grass was sparse, but moss and lichen coated the crimson rock. But as they climbed higher the last traces of ground cover evaporated.

Soon there was only the rock, red and hard and unforgiving. It was as if the land's skull was emerging from beneath a fragile skin of life.

And the higher they climbed, the more the world opened out.

This Fire Mountain was a vast, flattened dome of rock. A sharp cliff surrounded its circular base, with walls that cast long shadows in the light of the dipping sun. Icebones could follow the line of the strange shining Sky Trail down the slope. It passed through a cleft in that forbidding base cliff and strode on into the remote plain, until it dwindled to invisibility amid the thickening green of vegetation.

The land beyond the Fire Mountain was rough and broken, ribbed with sharp ridges. Though littered with patches of green and glinting with water, it would surely be difficult country to cross.

Further away still, she glimpsed an immense valley running almost directly east. The valley was heavily shadowed by this swollen land of giant Fire Mountains, but it ran to the horizon, vanishing in the mist there.

And to the north she saw a gleaming line of ice, flat and pure.

The ice spanned the world from horizon to horizon, and she knew she was seeing an ocean, thick with pack ice: it was the ocean whose presence she had sensed, the ocean that had pooled in the great depression that had shaped the northern hemisphere of this world.

It was a vast landscape of shaped rock, red and shadowed grey, pitted with shallow craters – and only thinly marked by the green of life.

There was nothing for Icebones here.

This is not my world, she thought. And it never could be. Why had she been taken from her home, stranded on this alien ball of rock with all its strangeness, where insane moons careened across the sky? Who had done it – the Lost? What twisted cruelty had caused them to plunge her into this strange madness . . . ?

There was a flurry of movement above her. She stood still, raising her tusks suspiciously.

She found herself facing a goat. An ibex, perhaps. It carried proud antlers, and was coated with thick white wool. Its chest was immense, swelling in the thin, dry air. The ibex appeared to have been digging into a patch of black ice with one spindly hoof.

The goat seemed to be limping. The skin over one of its feet was blackened.

'Frostbite,' Icebones said. It was a dread fear of all mammoths. 'That goat has been incautious. It may lose that foot, and then the stump will turn infected, if it lives that long.'

'No,' growled the Ragged One. 'The frostbitten skin will harden and fall away, leaving new pink skin that will quickly toughen.'

'No creature can recover from frostbite.'

'You cannot,' said the Ragged One. '*I* cannot. But this goat can. It is not like the creatures you have met before, Icebones. Just as this is not the world you knew.'

Icebones watched the goat hobble away, and she wondered if the clever paws of the Lost had made these disturbing changes, even in goats.

The mammoths approached the goat's abandoned ice patch. This had been a pond, Icebones found. In places the ice was clear, so that she could see through it to the black mud at the bottom. On the shallow bank around the pond she found dead vegetation, fronds of grass and pond plants, deep brown and frozen to the mud. When she touched the plants she could taste nothing but icy dirt.

Once it was warm here, she thought, even at this great height. But this world has grown colder, and the pond froze, right down to its base.

The pregnant Cow mewled, 'Nothing can live here. This is no place for us.'

The Ragged One rumbled deeply. 'We should get on.'

But all the mammoths were weary and agitated. Icebones could smell blood and milk in the pregnant Cow's musky scent. Her sisters clustered close around their mother, reluctant to move further. The Bull stomped back and forth, agitated.

'This is foolish,' said the mother, with a sharp slap of her trunk on the ground. 'Enough. We are cold and tired, and it is hard to breathe. We should not climb further.'

The Ragged One regarded them with contempt. She said simply, 'Then I will go on alone.' And she turned her back and, with trunk held high, stood beneath the shining Sky Trail.

'Wait,' Icebones called.

The Ragged One snorted. 'Will you make me stop? You are no Matriarch.'

Icebones said, 'I will come with you. It is not safe for you to go alone. But,' she said carefully, 'if we do not find the Lost, you will come down with me.'

The Ragged One rumbled, hesitating.

Icebones took a step forward, trying to conceal her reluctance to continue this futile climb. The others were watching her sombrely.

The Ragged One proceeded up the slope. Icebones followed.

After a few paces Icebones looked back at the others. Already they were diminished to rust-brown specks on the vast, darkling hillside.

They had long risen far above the sounds of life: the rumbling of the mammoths, the call of birds, the rustle of the thin breeze in the sparse grass. Here there was to be heard only the voice of the Mountain itself. Occasionally Icebones would hear a deep, startling crack, a rattle of distant echoes, as rock broke and fell and an avalanche tumbled down some slab of crimson hillside.

The Sky Trail, ignoring the toiling mammoths beneath it, strode on confidently towards the still-hidden summit of the Mountain.

The ground was complex now, covered by many ancient lava flows: this Mountain had spewed out liquid rock over and over. In places the rock flows had bunched into broad terraces, perhaps shaped by some underlying feature in the mighty slope. The walking was a little easier on the terraces, though the steps between them made for a difficult climb, and Icebones did not relish the prospect of the return.

There were many craters, on this shoulder of rock. Some of them were vast pits filled with sharp-edged rubble, while others were dents little larger than the footfalls Icebones might make in a field of mud. Some of the larger craters were filled with hard, level pools of fresh rock, and rivers of frozen rock snaked from one pit to another.

Ice had gathered in scattered pocks in the twisted rock face, black and hard, resistant to the probe of her tusks.

These scattered pockets grew larger until they merged, filling shallow depressions between low ridges. Soon Icebones was forced to walk on ice: hard, ridged, wind-sculpted ice, it creaked under her feet as it compressed.

If anything this was worse than the rock. On this pitted surface there was no food, no liquid water to drink – nothing but the ice, its deep cold ever willing to suck a mammoth's heat from her. And the air was thinner and colder than ever, and Icebones's lungs ached unbearably with every step she took.

She heard grunting. The Ragged One was working at a patch of ice with sharp scrapes of her tusks. Her hair, frosted white, stuck out at random angles from her body.

Icebones lumbered up the slope to join her. To her surprise she saw that a tree had grown there. It had a thick trunk that protruded from the ice, and its branches, almost flat against the ice, were laden with a kind of fruit – a black, leathery berry, broad but flaccid, about the size of a mammoth's foot pad.

She asked, 'Is it a willow?' But she knew that no willow could grow on ice.

'Not a willow,' the Ragged One said, panting hard. 'It is a breathing tree. Help me.'

Icebones saw that the Ragged One had been trying to prise

some of the broad black fruit out of the ice. Icebones bent to help, lowering her tusks.

One of the fruit popped out of its ice pit, and the Ragged One pulled it to her greedily. Icebones watched curiously as she used her trunk fingers to pull a plug of a hard, shell-like material from the husk of the fruit, and pushed her trunk into a dark, pulp-filled cavity revealed beneath. The fruit quickly collapsed, shrivelling as if thrown on a fire, but the Ragged One closed her eyes, her pleasure evident. Then she cast aside the fruit and began to prise loose another.

'Is it good to eat?'

'Just try it,' said the Ragged One, not sparing attention from her task.

On her first attempt Icebones punctured the fruit's skin, and it deflated quickly with a thin wail. But with her second try she got her fruit safely out of the ice. When she plunged her trunk tip into the soft pulpy cavity, she was startled by a gush of thick, warm, moist air. It was unexpected, remarkable, delicious. She closed her mouth and tried to suck all the air into her lungs, but she got a nostrilful of odourless fruit pulp, and sneezed, wasting most of the air.

She found another fruit and tried again.

For a time the two mammoths worked at the tree, side by side.

The Ragged One poked at an empty skin. 'The tree breathes in during the day, drawing its warmth from the sun and the rock, and it makes the air thick and wet. And at night the fruit breathes out again. In, out, like a sleeping mammoth – but each fruit takes only one breath a day.

'The breathing tree was the first tree that grew here. That is the legend of my kind. The breathing tree makes the air a little warmer and sweeter, so that grass and bushes and birds and ibexes and *we* can live here.'

This meant nothing to Icebones. A *breathing tree*? A fruit that could make a dead world live . . . ?

'Your kind? Where are your kind now?'

The Ragged One's trunk lifted towards Icebones, its mottled skin ugly beneath sparse hair. 'Gone. Dead. I am alone. And so are you. I am not like the others. *They* are all calves of the calves of Silverhair, the last of the mammoths of the Old Steppe.'

Icebones stopped dead. '*Silverhair*?'

'Have you heard of her?'

'She was my mother.'

The Ragged One snorted. 'You are her calf? She *suckled* you?'

'Yes!'

'Then where is she?'

'I don't know,' said Icebones miserably. 'Far from here.'

The Ragged One said slowly, 'Listen to me. Silverhair was the mother of all the mammoths of this Sky Steppe. She was the mother of their mothers, and the mother of their mothers before them . . . and on, back and back. Silverhair has been bones, dust, for a very long time. So how can she have borne *you*, who are standing here before me? You must have slept in your box of darkness for an age, squat one.'

Icebones, bewildered, tried to comprehend all this. *Was it possible?* Could it really be that she had somehow slept away the generations, as calf grew to mother and Matriarch and fell away into death, over and over – as her mother's calves grew to a mighty horde that covered this world – while she, daughter of their first ancestor, had stayed young and childless?

'If what you say is true,' she said, 'you must be a daughter of Silverhair too.'

'Not me,' said the Ragged One, discarding the emptied husk of the last fruit. And she strode on without explanation.

Icebones felt a deep, unaccountable revulsion towards the Ragged One. But she hurried after her, following the pale shadow of the Sky Trail.

Within a few steps, all the warmth and air she had garnered from the breathing tree had dissipated, and she was exhausted again.

Icebones marched grimly on through her hunger and thirst, through the gathering pain in her lungs and the aching cold that sucked at the pads of her feet.

At first she was not even aware that the Ragged One had stopped again. It was only when she made out the other's grim, mournful lowing that she realised something was wrong.

The Sky Trail had fallen.

Icebones walked carefully over hard ridges of wind-sculpted ice.

Although those mighty legs still cast their gaunt, clean shadows over the Mountain's slope, the silvery thread of the path itself had crumbled and fallen. It lay over the icy rocks like a length of shining spider-web. When she looked back down the Mountain's flank she saw how the path dangled from the last leg to which it was attached, lank and limp as a mammoth's belly hairs.

The fallen Sky Trail lay in short, sharp-edged segments, shattered and separated. When she probed at the wreckage with her trunk it was cold, hard and without taste or odour, like most of what the Lost produced.

The Ragged One was standing beside a great pod, long, narrow, like a huge broken-open nut. It seemed to be made of the same odourless, gleaming stuff as the Sky Trail itself.

And it contained bodies.

Icebones recognised them immediately. The stubby limbs, the round heads and hairless faces, all enclosed in complex, worked skins. *They were Lost.* And they were dead, that much was clear: there was frost on their faces and in their clouded eyes and opened mouths.

The Ragged One stood over the silent, motionless tableau, probing uselessly at faces and claw-like paws with her trunk. The wind howled thinly through the structure of the leg towers around her.

Icebones said, 'They have been dead a long time. See how the skin of this one is dried out, shrunken on the bone. If not for the height here, the wolves and other scavengers would surely—'

'They were trying to leave,' the Ragged One blurted. 'Perhaps they were the last. And they died when they spilled out of the warmth of their pod on to this cold Mountain.'

'Where were they going?'

'I don't know. How can I know?'

'We should Remember them,' Icebones said.

But the Ragged One snapped harshly, 'No. It is not their way.'

The shrunken sun was approaching the western horizon, and its light was spreading into a broad pale band across the sky. The light glimmered from the ice line of the distant ocean, and the tangled thread of the wrecked Sky Trail, and the tusks of the mammoths. Soon it would be dark.

Icebones said, 'Listen to me. The Lost are gone or dead, and we cannot follow them. And we cannot stay on this Fire Mountain.'

The Ragged One growled and stamped her feet, making the hard rock ring.

Icebones felt immensely tired. 'I don't want to fight you. I have no wish to lead. *You* lead. But you must lead us to a place we can live. You must lead us down from this Mountain of death. Down to where the air pools, like morning mist in a hollow.'

The Ragged One stood silently. Then she said reluctantly, 'You don't understand. I am afraid. I have lived my whole life on this Mountain. I have lived my whole life with the Lost. I don't know how else life can be.'

Impulsively Icebones grabbed her trunk. 'You are not alone. We are all Cousins, and we are bound by the ancient Oath of Kilukpuk, one to the other . . .'

But the Ragged One had never heard of Kilukpuk, or the vows that bound her descendants, whether they climbed the trees or swam the ocean or walked the land with heavy tusks dangling. She pulled away from Icebones's touch.

Still suffused by that deep physical revulsion, Icebones nevertheless felt oddly bound to this pale, malformed creature. For all her strangeness, the Ragged One seemed to have more in common with Icebones than any of the other mammoths here. Only the Ragged One seemed to understand that Icebones was truly *different* – had come from a different place, perhaps even a different time. Only the Ragged One seemed to understand that the world had not always been the same as this – that there were other ways for mammoths to live.

And yet the Ragged One seemed intent on becoming Icebones's enemy.

The Ragged One dropped her head dolefully, emitting a slow, sad murmur. She was clearly unwilling to leave these sad remains, all that was left of the Lost.

Alone, Icebones trudged further up the shallow slope.

The ice thinned. Higher up the slope it began to break up and dissipate altogether, as if she had come so high that even the ice could not survive, and there was only the bare rock. The texture of the rock itself was austere and beautiful, if deadly: it was a bony ground of red and crimson and orange, with not a scrap of white or green, no water or life, not an ice crystal or the smallest patch of lichen.

From here she could see that the eastern flank of the Mountain was a swathe of smooth crimson rock, marked here and there by the black cracks of gullies, or by narrow white threads that were frozen streams. But to the west she saw the white stripes of huge glaciers spilling down towards the lower plains from great bowls of ice.

The ground flattened out to afford her broadening views of the landscape: that gleaming white of ocean ice, the grey-green land below, the Fire Mountain's twin sisters. The land had been distorted and broken by the vast uplift that had created the volcanoes here. In places the rock was wrinkled, covered with sharp ridges that ran around the base of the Mountain, and even cracked open like dried-out skin. The greatest crack of all, running directly to the east away from the Mountain, was that immense valley that stretched far to the horizon, extending around the curve of the world.

And soon she could see the caldera at the very summit of this Mountain-continent, the crater from which burning rock had so recently gushed. It was no simple pit, but a vast walled landscape of pits and craters. On its complex floor molten rock pooled, glowing bright red. The far side of the caldera was a long flat-topped cliff marked by layers, some black, some brown, some pinkish red. Immense caverns had worn into the softer rock, between harder, protective layers.

It was a pit big enough itself to swallow a mountain.

She stood there, listening to the quiet subterranean murmur of the Mountain. The sky faded to a deep purple and then a blue-black above. In that huge blueness, even though the sun still lingered above the horizon, stars swam. The ground under her feet was red-black, cracked and smashed, as if it had been battered by mighty feet, over and over.

She felt humbled by the immensity of this rock beast. The Lost had stolen the water that had lain frozen in its interior, and by doing so had woken its ancient rage. But the Lost's puny devices were no more than scrapes on the Mountain's mighty ancient bulk, the bite of an insect on a mammoth's broad flank.

She returned, carefully, down the slope to where the Ragged One still stood beside the wreckage of the Lost seed pod.

Chapter Four

THE DESCENT

The sky was crossed – not by one abnormal moon – but *two*.

The twin moons climbed rapidly in the daylit sky. But without warning they would wink into darkness, as if entering some huge mouth. Or, just as unexpectedly, they flickered into brightness in the middle of the night sky. One of them, which moved more rapidly, had a lumpish shape, like a rock or a bit of dung, not like a real Moon at all. But the other moon was, if anything, stranger still: just a pinpoint of light, like a meandering star.

The moons were eerie, unpredictable, and utterly strange. Icebones felt disturbed every time she glimpsed them.

It took days for the two of them to climb back down to the other mammoths.

One cold dawn, longing for company, Icebones stepped away from the Ragged One, who browsed fitfully, still half-asleep.

Icebones stamped hard. 'Boaster! Boaster . . . !'

I hear you, Icebones. It is bright day here.

High on this Fire Mountain it was not yet morning. The pinkish light of the dawn had turned the Mountain's bulk into a deep black silhouette above her, and she could see the spreading plain at the foot of the Mountain as a jumble of shadows, lifeless, intimidating.

This Boaster and his companions must be far away, far around the curve of the world. She felt a twinge of regret. It seemed impossible that she would ever meet her immodest friend.

She said, 'It is cold and dry.'

Here the land is flat but it is frozen. I am tall and strong, but even my great weight leaves no foot marks, and my heavy tusks will not scratch the ice. Nothing lives. Nothing but the carnivores, who stalk us. Their bellies brush the ground, for the pickings are easy for them in this harsh land . . . We seek deeper places.

Yes, she thought, with new determination. Yes, that is what we must do.

Boaster said now, *Yesterday there was a duel. Neither Bull would back down. One was gored, the other's head was crushed.*

'Were they in musth?'

Yes, both in musth, in deep musth.

With no Cows, the rivalry battles in that isolated bachelor herd were futile, so must be all the more savage. Frustrated, the Bulls were fighting themselves to death.

But now Boaster was saying, *Be wary, little Icebones. Even as an infant I was mighty. My calf will weigh you down, like a boulder in the belly. Are you in oestrus yet?*

No, she thought. Not yet. And when she probed that deep oceanic part of herself, she detected no sign that oestrus was near. She felt well enough. Perhaps it was simply not her time.

When I am in musth, my dribble smells sweet. It will make you wonder, before I mount you.

'If I permit you . . .'

They talked on, as the planet turned.

Icebones and the Ragged One returned, weary, to the group.

It seemed to Icebones that in just a few days the air had grown distinctly colder. And it was clear to all the mammoths that they couldn't stay here.

But to Icebones's dismay the mammoths bickered about what to do.

The mother wanted them to descend from this high Mountain shoulder. Perhaps they should make for the sea, the mother suggested, for there at least they would find water.

Icebones kept her counsel. To descend was in accord with her own instincts. She knew that the seas around the Island had been salty – no use for drinking – but perhaps here the seas were different, like so much else.

The pregnant sister kept apart. Obsessed and worried about the dependent creature growing within her, she had turned inward. The Cow needed the support and guidance of her Family as at no other time in her life. But such support was not forthcoming, for her relatives did not know how to give it.

Sometimes the infant kicked and murmured, and Icebones knew it was enduring bad dreams of its life to come.

Like the Ragged One, the other sisters seemed intent on seeking out the vanished Lost. The older of them – a tall, vain creature with tightly spiralling tusks – demanded they roam around the Mountain. Her younger sister, dominated by the vain one, rumbled eager agreement. It was the younger who had been scorched by the Mountain's falling rock, and she still bore a pink, hairless patch of healing skin.

As for the Bull, he seemed intent only on adventure. He charged back and forth across the bleak rock slope, trumpeting and brandishing his tusks, in pursuit of imaginary enemies and rivals.

Icebones growled her frustration. In a true Family at a time of decision making, all would be entitled to their say, but all would know their place. A good Matriarch would listen calmly, and then make her decision – or rather, speak the Family's decision for them.

In a Family everybody knew what to do, from instinct and a lifetime's training. Here, it seemed, nobody knew their roles, or how to behave. And as Icebones listened to the bickering she heard a deeper truth: without the cocoon of Lost which had protected them all their lives, these mammoths were bewildered, all but helpless, and very, very afraid.

She drew the mother aside. 'You must lead them.'

The mother raised her trunk sorrowfully and probed at Icebones's scalp hairs. Her scent was rich and smoky, like the last leaves of autumn. 'You want me to be a Matriarch.'

'You must make them into a Family. A Family is always there – from the day you are born, to the day you die . . .' Icebones recalled wistfully how her own mother, Silverhair, had been with her as she grew up, with her for every heartbeat of her young life. 'And without a Family—' Without my Family, she thought, I am not complete. She quoted the Cycle. 'In the Family, I becomes We.'

The mother said wistfully, 'We don't have Families here. The Lost saw to that.'

Icebones said harshly, 'The Lost are gone now. I saw them

59

up on that mountainside – the last of them, their dried-out corpses. They cannot help you. You are the mother of these squabbling calves. Tell them what you have decided, and then lead them.'

The mother seemed dubious. But she stood before the younger mammoths and slapped the ground with her trunk.

The sisters and the Bull turned, rumbling in soft alarm.

The mother said, 'We must go down to the lower places. There will be warmth, and grass to eat. We will go to the shore of the great northern sea, and drink its water.'

For a frozen moment the mammoths fell silent. The sisters regarded their mother. The Bull pawed the ground and growled softly.

The Ragged One stood aloof, head turned away, the thin wind raising the loose hairs of her back. She said: '*Which way?*'

Icebones saw the mother was hesitating. It wasn't a trivial question: Icebones had seen from the summit that this dome-shaped Mountain was surrounded by a scarp of tall, impassable cliffs. But she knew there was a way through.

She stepped up to the mother. As if she was addressing a true Matriarch, she said respectfully, 'If we follow the Sky Trail down the Mountain, we will find a way through the cliffs.'

The mother, with relief, replied, 'Yes. We will follow the Sky Trail. It will be many days' walk. The sooner we begin, the sooner we will reach the sea.' And she stepped forward with confidence.

Grumbling, resentful – but perhaps inwardly relieved that somebody was taking the lead – her daughters fell in behind her. Icebones took the rear of the little line, while the Bull ran alongside, keeping his separation from the group of Cows, as a growing Bull should.

At least we are trying, Icebones thought. And, wherever I die, at least it will not be here, on this dismal rocky slope.

As the little group made its way down the Mountain, following the strange straight-line shadow of the shining Sky Trail, the Ragged One followed them, distant, silent.

The rock beneath their feet was unyielding. Sometimes, when the land was gouged and scarred by ancient flows of molten rock, they had to detour far from the Sky Trail.

The only water was to be found in hollows where rain or snow had gathered. Most of these puddles were frozen to their bases, but as they descended they found a few larger ponds where some liquid water persisted beneath a thick shell of ice. Gratefully the mammoths cracked the ice lids with their tusks or feet and sucked up the dirty, brackish water.

But the taller, spiral-tusked sister complained about the foul stink of the pond water compared to the cool, clean stuff the Lost used to provide for them.

At night, when the shrunken sun had fallen away and the cold clear stars emerged from the purple sky, they mostly kept walking, their trunks seeking out water and scraps of vegetation. They would pause only briefly to sleep, and Icebones encouraged them to gather close together, the pregnant one at the centre, so that they shared and trapped the warmth of their bodies.

It was very disturbing to Icebones to walk over new land: land where there were no mammoth trails, no memories in her head, nobody to lead. It was the mammoths' way to learn the land, to build it into their memories and wisdom, and to teach it to their young. That way the land's perils could be avoided and its riches sought. That learning had never happened here.

And it troubled her that every step she took was into strangeness – and unknown danger.

After a few days they reached the terminus of the Sky Trail. The shining line sank into a kind of cave, a place of hard straight lines and smooth walls. Icebones shrank from it. But the others clumped forward eagerly and explored every cold surface and every sharp straight edge, as if saying goodbye.

They walked on.

Below the Sky Trail terminus, the rock was just as barren and sparse of life as it had been at higher altitude. But Icebones felt her spirits lift subtly, as if the looming Sky Trail, the mark of the Lost, had been weighing on her spirit.

The Bull came to walk with her. His coat was glossy and thick, and he held his growing tusks high. 'Why must we call you Icebones?'

'Because it is my name.'

He thought about that. 'Very well. But why not Boulder, or Snowflake, or Pond?'

'My mother said I was heavy and cold in her womb. As if she'd swallowed a lump of ice, she told me. And so she called me Icebones. A name is part of a mammoth—'

'I have no name,' he said.

'I know.'

'Will you give me a name?'

Intrigued, she asked, 'What kind of name?'

'I am strong and fierce,' he said, illustrating this with a comically deep growl. 'I will be a brave hero, and I will mate all the Cows in the world. Silverhair was brave and strong. Perhaps my name should be Silverhair.'

She snorted her amusement. 'That was the name of my

mother. She was indeed brave and strong. But you are a Bull, and you need the name of a Bull.'

'I don't know the names of any Bulls.'

'The Cycle tells of the bravest and strongest Bull who ever lived. His name was Longtusk. He lived long ago, in a time when the steppe was full of mammoths. He lived alone among the animals, and he even lived among the Lost – for it is the fate of Bulls, you know, to leave their Families and travel far. But then at last he found his Clan and led them on a great journey, to a place where they could live without fear. In the end he gave his life to save them.'

The Bull trumpeted his appreciation. 'I would like to be called Longtusk,' he growled. 'But I am no hero. Not yet, anyway.'

She pondered. 'Your voice is deep and carries far, like the thunder. Longtusk had a faithful companion called Walks With Thunder. *Thunder*. There. That shall be your name.'

'Thunder, Thunder!' The towering Bull, with his spindly legs and thin, immature tusks, ran after the Cows to tell them his exciting news.

The next morning, the Cow with the spiral-shaped tusks came up to Icebones, trailed, as always, by her smaller sister. The older one said diffidently, 'That fool of a Bull says you have given him a name.'

'He has found his name,' Icebones said.

The Cow snorted. '*I* have no need of a name – not from a mammoth. The Lost liked me, you see. They used to admire my tusks and my long hair. Their cubs would brush my belly hairs with their paws, and I would let the older ones climb on my back while I walked.'

Icebones tried not to show her revulsion.

'They would talk to me all the time,' said the Cow. 'Not the way a mammoth talks, of course. They had a funny jabber they made with their mouths, and they didn't use their bellies or feet or foreheads at all. But you could tell they were talking even so.' She walked oddly as she said this, as if showing off her hair and fine muscles for an invisible audience of Lost. 'So I am quite sure the Lost had their own name for *me*.'

Icebones stayed silent, watching her.

At length the Cow said, 'But if you *were* to give me a name – a mammoth name, I mean – what would it be?'

Most mammoth names reflected a deep characteristic of their holder: an attribute of her body, her smell or taste or noise – even her weight, like Icebones's. Few were to do with the way a mammoth *looked*: Silverhair, yes, for that lank of grey on her forehead had been such a startling characteristic. But Icebones knew that sight was the most important sense of all for the Lost. And so for this one, the way she had looked in the eyes of the Lost was the key to her character.

'Your name will be Spiral,' Icebones said. 'For your tusks twist around in spirals, the one like the other.'

'*Spiral*.' The Cow wandered away, admiring her own tusks.

Her sister made to follow Spiral as usual, but she hesitated. 'Icebones, what about my mother?'

It is not my place to name these mammoths, Icebones thought. I am not their Matriarch, or their mother. But if not me, who? She thought of the smell of the older Cow, her tangy, smoky musk. 'Autumn,' Icebones said impulsively. 'For she smells of the last, delicious grass of summer.'

The Cow seemed pleased. 'And my other sister, the one with calf?'

'I would call her Breeze—'

'For her hair is loose and whips in the wind, like the grass on a windblown steppe!'

'Yes.' This little one isn't so bad, Icebones thought, when she gets away from her foolish sister. 'Will you tell them for me?'

'Yes, I will.'

'And what about you?'

'Me?' The Cow was transfixed, as if she hadn't imagined such an honour could be applied to her. 'You choose, Icebones.'

Icebones probed at the young Cow's mouth, and tasted sweetness. 'Shoot,' she said at last. 'For you taste of young, fresh grass.'

The Cow seemed delighted. 'Thank you, Icebones . . . But what about *her*?'

She meant the Ragged One, who grazed alone as usual, irritably dragging at grass tufts and willow tips, her rough hair a cloud of captured sunlight around her.

'She is the Ragged One,' said Icebones. 'No other name would suit.'

But the little Cow had already scampered away, after her sister.

They approached the lip of the Mountain-base cliff. The wall was heavily eroded, and very steep – what they could see of it; none of them cared to approach the edge.

At last Icebones found a steep gully that cut deep into the ground. Its floor was strewn with boulders and frost-shattered rubble, as if a river had once flowed there. It would not be an easy route, but this cleft, cutting deep into the rock behind the cliffs, offered a way down to the plains below.

Cautiously, reluctantly, the mammoths filed into the gully.

The rock that made up the walls was grey-red and very hard, its surface covered with sharp-edged protruding lumps, speckled with glimmering minerals of green and black. Moss grew in cracks in the walls and over some of the loose rocks. The wind tumbling off the Fire Mountain's broad flanks poured through this gap, and mercilessly sucked out the mammoths' heat. Icebones could hear the rumbles of complaint echoing back from the tall, sheer walls.

A pair of birds flew up and down the gully, graceful, large-winged. Perhaps they were swallows.

The mammoths found a place where the rocky floor was broken by small crevices, which provided shelter for succulent grass clumps and even herbs. The mammoths fell on this feast and ate greedily.

Leaving the feeding mammoths, Icebones came to a broad ledge that led out to the face of the cliff itself. She walked along the ledge, curious, probing at the smooth rock with her trunk . . . and the cliff face opened out around her.

She realised that looking down from the Mountain's summit she had had no real idea of the vast size of this cliff. Seen from here, there was *only* the cliff: a wall of blue-red rock that rose above her and out of sight, and fell away beneath her to a blur of red tinged with grey-green that might have been the ground. There was cloud both above her *and* below: a layer of pink-grey cirrus far above, and a smooth rippling sea below.

The world was simple: cloud above and below, and this hard vertical cliff face, like an upturned landscape.

She spotted a waterfall, where an underground river burst out of the rock face into the air. But the water fell with an eerie slowness, as if the air was too thick to allow it to pass, and it broke up into myriad red-glimmering droplets that dispersed in the air. This was a waterfall that would never reach the ground, she realised.

. . . And then it struck her how *high* she was here, higher than clouds, higher than birds – and how unprotected. Mammoths were plain animals, unused to heights. Vertigo overwhelmed her, and she inched back along the ledge towards the others, and safety.

As they neared the base of the gully, it began to broaden and flatten, its eroded walls diminishing. But its floor was littered with rocks. The mammoths had to work their way past boulders which towered over them, and under their feet was a litter of loose rock, scree and talus that sometimes gave way under an incautious step. But the big rocks were pitted and carved by the wind, and many of the looser small rocks underfoot were worn smooth by wind or water also.

Icebones was the first to break out of the gully, and walk beyond the cliff. She stepped forward carefully, relishing the openness around her. Sandpipers fled from her, screeching in protest.

She found herself walking over dwarf willows, a flattened, ground-hugging forest that crunched under her feet. A red-black river meandered sluggishly across a ruddy plain. Two cranes stood by the river, still and watchful, as many creatures of the steppe habitually were. As she approached a longspur, it sat as still as a stone on its nest of woven grass, watching her with black eyes. She could see the bird's eggs, which glowed with a smooth pink light.

Away from the river small lakes stood out, purple-black. In the larger ponds Icebones could see a gleam of green: cores of ice that survived from the last winter, and would probably persist to the next.

In the shimmering, complex light, this land at the foot of the cliff was a bowl of life. She saw more willows and sedges, their green vivid against the underlying crimson of the rock. And even the bare outcropping rock was stained yellow or orange by lichen.

It was a typical steppe. It was a place of stillness and watchfulness, for the land was ungenerous. But, unlike the bare wall of the Mountain, this land was *alive*, and Icebones felt her soul expand into its familiar silence.

She turned and looked back towards the cliff. Its base was fringed by conifer forest. Compared to the mammoths grazing at their bases, these trees grew very tall, Icebones saw immediately: they were slender, but they soared fifty, even a hundred times the height of a mammoth, so that their upper branches were a blur of greenery.

But the trees, huge as they were, were utterly dwarfed by the wall of rock that banded the base of the Fire Mountain.

Bright red, extensively fluted and carved by the wind, the tremendous cliff soared high above the broken ground. The columns and vertical chasms of its face glowed a deep burnt orange in the light of the setting sun. The gully the mammoths had climbed down was a black crack, barely visible.

So immense was its length that the cliff looked like a flat, unbending wall, marching from horizon to horizon. The cliff was a wall that cut the sky in half, and it was oppressive, crushing: like a wall of time, she thought, separating her from her Family, like death, which would one day part her from everything she knew and loved.

★

The mammoths stayed at the base of the cliff for a night, grazing and resting.

The sun, easing west, passed over the cliff's rim not long after midday, and shadows spilled over the ground. The cliff turned purple-red, and the air immediately started to feel colder. Although the day was only half gone – a glance at the bright pale pink sky told Icebones that – here at the foot of this mighty barrier it was already twilight. She noticed now how spindly the conifer trees were, as if they were straining for the light they could never hope to reach.

And in the dawn, with the sky barely paled by the rising sun, the light caught the top of the cliff, so that a great band of orange rock shone high in the sky directly above her. It was like a smeared-out rocky sun, and it actually cast a little light – though no warmth – over the night-darkened plains at the cliff's base.

It was a relief to walk away from the cliff's brooding mass, and out of its pool of shadow.

Chapter Five

THE OCEAN OF THE NORTH

The mammoths worked their way steadily northwards, seeking the ocean.

The going was slow, for the land, folded and broken, was covered by lobes and ridges and collapsed rocky tunnels, and the mammoths were frequently forced to turn away from their northern heading. Icebones was acutely aware that every diversion lengthened the journey they must complete.

But she was not aware of any change of the season. The last she recalled of the Island it had been autumn — but that fading memory seemed to have no relevance here. The mammoths were not shedding any winter coat, so she supposed it must be late summer or autumn. But she sensed no drawing-in of the nights, no gathering cold. Perhaps even time ran slowly here, slow as falling water, slow as coagulating blood.

The days wore away.

*

At length the mammoths reached a new land.

It was an ocean of dust: a flat red plain, a line of ice close to the northern horizon, a dome of pinkish sky in which the small sun sailed. Where bare rock was exposed, it was dark and tinged with blue or purple, sheets of it eroded almost flat.

The higher land they were leaving, to the south, curved in a great arc, a coast for this sea of dust. The 'shore' was littered with gravel bars and drifts of red dust.

There were structures on this higher ground – blocky, straight-edged shelters that were obviously the work of the Lost.

The mammoths looked around these buildings desultorily. They were boxes pierced by straight-edged holes. Dust had drifted up against the walls of the buildings, and had filtered inside, covering their inner floors with a fine red carpet. The mammoths' broad feet left shallow cone-shaped tracks in the dust, which flowed quickly back where they had disturbed it. Near the buildings a stand of trees poked out of the bright red ground. They might have been oaks. But they were clearly long dead, their bare branches skeletal and gaunt and their trunks hollowed out, and any last leaves that had fallen had long been buried or driven away by the wind.

The Ragged One had walked a little way further to the north, on to the dust plain. She was probing at something black and ropy on the ground. It was clearly dead, and it crumbled and broke.

'See this?' she said to Icebones. 'Seaweed. Once the sea covered all this dust and sand. But now the sea is far away. Look – you can see where the shore used to be.'

Icebones made out rippled ridges in the sand, the footprint of the vanished sea.

'And look at this.' The Ragged One walked a little deeper into the plain. She came to a set of smooth, rounded shapes that protruded from the dust. She blew on the shapes with her trunk and exposed wood, scuffed and pitted by windblown sand.

'More work of the Lost,' said Icebones.

'Yes.' The Ragged One dug her tusks under one of the objects and, with a heave, flipped it on its back, sending dust flying. It was like a bird's nest, sculpted in smooth wood. 'The Lost would sit in such things as these, and float upon the water. As was their right. For they made these floating things – *and they made the ocean itself*, brought the water here to cover the land, brought the fish and worms and even the seaweed to live here. But now the world is drying like a corpse – the water has gone—'

'And so have the Lost.'

'Yes. And so have the Lost.' The Ragged One ran her trunk tip longingly over the eroded lines of the stranded boat. The red dust had stained the pale ivory of her tusks a subtle, rusty pink.

Icebones felt a sudden surge of sympathy for her. She reached out and wrapped her trunk around the head of the other, ignoring the now-familiar stale stink. 'Come,' she said. 'We must cross this dried-out seabed. If we start, the others will follow.'

Briefly the Ragged One closed her eyes, rumbling a kind of contentment at Icebones's touch. Then, sharply, she pulled away. 'Yes. We must go to the water.'

Side by side, Icebones and the Ragged One began to plod across the bone-dry plain.

★

The land remained utterly flat, a beach left stranded by a last fatal tide. When Icebones walked, windblown dust would billow around her, as if dancing in memory of the waters that had once washed over this place.

When she walked over more compact dust or exposed rock, she felt her footsteps ring through the rocky foundation of this ancient sea. And she could tell that this plain, overlaid by the shrunken sea to the north, encompassed the whole top half of this world, a wasteland that stretched all the way to the north pole and down almost to the equator. It was remarkable, enormous, intimidating, and by comparison she was like a beetle crawling across the textured footprint of a mammoth.

If the water was gone, then this had become a sea of light.

Broad, shallow, wave-like dunes crossed from horizon to horizon. As the sun descended, the low light shone brightly from the west-facing slopes of the dunes, and shadows lengthened behind them, so that Icebones was surrounded by bands of shining ochre light. And when she looked at the soft ground at her feet she saw how each dust grain shone grey or red, as if defying the dying of the light.

Here and there rocks littered the surface. Some of the rocks were half buried by dust, and their buried edges were generally sharper than those exposed to the erosion of wind and rain. She learned caution where she stepped, not wishing to cut her foot pads. Sometimes the remnants of living things clung to an exposed rock: fronds of dried-up, blackened seaweed, or small white shells.

The dust was thick and clinging, but it had its uses. All the mammoths were plagued by ticks and lice – Icebones suspected the Lost had groomed them, keeping them clear of such parasites – and she had to show them how to rub dust and dirt into their skin to scrub away the irritants.

It seemed very strange to have to teach a calf's skills to a tall old Cow like Autumn.

But there was nothing to drink here, nothing to eat. The dust clogged her trunk and throat, sucking out the moisture, making her even more thirsty. The dust stank, of blood and iron.

As they continued to walk steadily north the character of the ground changed. In places the land shone, coated with fine flat sheets of some white, glittering substance. When she tasted this, she found it was salt, another relic of the vanished sea.

Soon her footfalls were breaking through an upper layer of dust, exposing frosty, damp mud, rust-coloured. There was water here, not far beneath the surface.

And now there was vegetation, grass sprouting out of the dirty red mud. It was nothing but tough dune grass. But the mammoths, who had eaten nothing for half a day, fell on the wiry yellow stuff as if it was the finest browse.

Gulls hopped among the spindly grass tufts or circled overhead, their caws thin and clear in the cold, still air. Icebones thought the gulls seemed huge – their bobbing heads rose higher than her own belly hairs – much larger than any birds she recalled from the Island.

At last the land sloped down sharply, forming a beach strewn with rust-red gravel and littered with scraps of dusty frost.

The mammoths stepped forward cautiously.

Beyond the beach, just a few paces away, water lapped, black and oily. It was a half-frozen ocean. Here and there ice sheets clung to the beach. Further out floes of ice drifted on the water, colliding with slow, grinding crashes. Some of the ice was stained brown, perhaps where floes had been flipped over by bears or seals, exposing the weeds that crusted their lower surface. Stretches of exposed water made a complex pattern of cracks and scrapings like the wrinkled skin of a very old mammoth, shaped by wind and current. The exposed water was as black as night. Here and there traces of fog and even windblown snow curled tiredly.

Birds wheeled exuberantly. She spied huge-winged kitti-wakes, fulmars and jet-black guillemots. Every so often one of them would plunge into the dark water, seeking plankton or cod.

There was more life here, crowded close to this shore, than anywhere else Icebones had seen on this small world.

She heard an angry screeching. There was a bloody carcass on the ice – perhaps it was a seal, or even a bear cub. Petrels soared over it trailing arched wings, their tails fanned out to ward off rivals. Landing on the ice, they tucked their heads right inside the corpse, emerging with their heads and necks gleaming bright red, only their pale, angry eyes showing white.

The light of the pinkish sky turned the ice rust red, the exposed water a deep purple-black. The sea rolled with huge, languid waves, much taller and slower than anything on the oceans around the Island. The ice seemed to moan and wail like a living thing, as, riding the ocean's tremendous waves, it warped and cracked.

In this setting even the mammoths looked strange, trans-formed: they were stolid blocks of fur and fat, their tusks shining red-pink, their bodies surrounded by crimson-glowing haloes where the sunlight caught their guard hairs.

This was not like the coast of the Island. To Icebones this rust-red shore was a strange and alien scene indeed.

She spotted a bear, swimming through a lead of open water.

His head was white as bone, and he cut steadily through the black water, trailing a fine wake behind him. He reached an ice floe and, in a single powerful lunge, pulled himself out of the water, his back feet catching the lip of the ice without hesitation. He shook himself, and water flew off his fur in a cloud of spray.

The bear turned and glared at the mammoths with small black eyes.

His fur caught the light, so that subtle reds and pink-whites gleamed from his guard hairs. Icebones saw that his hips were wider than his shoulder, his long neck sinuous, so that he was a wedge of muscle and power that faced her with a deadly concentration. And he was huge, she saw: much larger than any bear she ever saw off the coast of the Island.

He crossed to the other side of his floe, his great clawed paws swinging, and slid back into the water, silently.

She was in a hunting ground. Her underfur prickled, and she raised her trunk suspiciously.

She stepped down to the water's edge. A few paces from the sea, petrels had dug their burrows into the unfrozen earth. When Icebones trod on a burrow inadvertently, collapsing it, a soft-plumed adult bird blinked up at her in silent protest.

Icebones let the sea water soak into the long hairs that dangled over her feet. The water itself was cold and sharp.

She sucked up a cautious trunkful and dipped her trunk tip into her mouth. It seemed to fizz, oddly, making bubbles in her nostrils, as if air dissolved in it were struggling to escape.

It was a bitter brine.

And in the air that blew off the face of the ocean, soft but very cold, she could smell salt.

Of course this tremendous world sea would be full of salt,

just like the ocean that had surrounded the Island. This Ocean of the North was nothing but sour undrinkable brine, all the way to the pole of the world.

She sensed in their hunched postures that the other mammoths knew this as well as she did. It was as she had expected, but she felt disappointed nonetheless.

As if to put on a brave swagger, the Bull, Thunder, trumpeted and charged forward into open water. Spray danced up around his legs, quickly soaking his fur, and ice crackled against his chest. 'Come on,' he yelled. 'At least we can get rid of this foul dust for a while!' And he plunged his trunk into the water and sprayed it high in the air.

Shoot ran after the Bull into the deeper water, lumbering and squealing. The little Cow stumbled, immersing her head, but she came up squirting water from her trunk brightly. 'It's cold! And it gets deep, just here. Watch out—'

'Thunder. Call me Thunder!' And the Bull rapped his trunk into the water, sending spray over the Cow. Vigorously, Shoot splashed back.

Haughty Spiral stayed close to her mother and sister Breeze, watching the antics of the others with disdain.

Droplets of brine, caught on the wind, spattered into Icebones's face and stung her eyes.

A flash of motion further from the shore caught her eye. It had looked, oddly, like a tusk – but it had been straight and sharp, not like a mammoth's ivory spiral. There it was again, a fine twisted cone that rolled languidly through the air. And now she saw a vast grey body sliding through a dark lead of open water, turning slowly. She heard a moan, and then a harsh screech, accompanied by a spray of water. Perhaps this was some strange whale.

The Ragged One came to stand beside Icebones. 'The water is foul,' she rumbled. 'I suppose you will tell us now you always knew it would be like this.'

'This is not my world,' Icebones said levelly. 'I know nothing of its oceans.'

The Ragged One growled.

'This is not the time to argue,' Icebones said. 'We cannot stay here. That much is obvious.' She turned, trunk raised, seeking Autumn.

But there was a sharp trumpet from the water.

All the mammoths turned.

Shoot was floundering, hair soaked, struggling to keep her head above the water. Icebones could see the black triangle of her small mouth beneath her raised trunk.

But the trumpet had come not from Shoot, but from Thunder. The Bull was splashing his way out of the water as fast as he could, trunk held high, eyes ringed white with panic.

Now there was a surge behind Shoot, like a huge wave gathering.

Abruptly a mass burst out of the water, scattering smashed ice that tumbled back with a clatter. Icebones glimpsed a blunt head with a smooth, rounded forehead, and that strange twisted tusk thrust out through the upper lip of the opened mouth, on the left side. The tusk alone would have dwarfed Icebones. But even the head was small in comparison with a vast body: grey and marbled, marked with spots and streaks, grey as dead flesh, with small front flippers, and a crumpled ridge along its back. When the whole of that body had lifted out of the water, the flukes of its powerful tail beat the water with great slaps.

By Kilukpuk's mercy, Icebones thought, bewildered.

The whale fell back into the water, writhing, with a vast languid splash. Shoot was engulfed, and Icebones wondered if she had already been taken in that vast mouth.

But when the water subsided, Icebones saw that Shoot was still alive, gamely trying to swim in the churning water. 'Help me!' she called, with high, thin chirps of her trunk.

Without thinking further, Icebones rushed into the water. She ran past Thunder, who stood shivering on the shore. But the Ragged One ran with her.

Icebones slowed when the water reached her chest and soaked into her heavy hairs, and the sea-bottom ooze clumped around her feet. The Ragged One, taller and with longer legs, was able to make faster progress, and she reached Shoot first.

The whale made another run. Water surged. A school of silver fish came flying from the water before splashing back, dead or stunned. Fulmars and kittiwakes fell on this unexpected bounty, screeching.

The Ragged One had wrapped her trunk around Shoot's, and was hauling her towards the shore. Icebones hurried to the Cow's rear, half-swimming in the rapidly deepening water, and rammed at Shoot's rump with her forehead.

The whale lunged out of the water, and that huge twisted tusk was held high above the mammoths, ugly and sharp.

For a heartbeat Icebones found herself peering into the whale's ugly purple mouth. Its lips barely covered its rows of cone-shaped teeth. Its eyes were set at the corners of the mouth – and, though a dark intelligence glimmered there, Icebones saw that the eyes could not move in their sockets.

In its way it was beautiful, Icebones couldn't help thinking: a solitary killer, stripped of the social complexity of a mammoth's life, its whole being intent only on killing – beautiful, and terrible.

The whale fell back.

As they struggled on towards the shore, with her head immersed in the murky, icy brine, Icebones rammed at Shoot's backside with increased urgency.

But the snap of jaws around her did not come. At last the mammoths found themselves in shallower water, beyond the reach of those immense teeth.

Shoot's sisters hurried to her and ran their trunks over her head and into her mouth, cherishing her survival. Shoot, shaking herself free of water, showed no signs of injury from her ordeal, though the whale's teeth must have missed her by no more than a hair's-breadth.

The Ragged One stood with Icebones by the edge of the suddenly treacherous sea. The whale's tusk broke the surface and cruised to and fro, as if seeking to lure an unwary mammoth back into the water, and where it passed, sheets of ice were cracked and lifted and brushed aside.

'If the Lost created this ocean,' Icebones said, 'why would they put in it such a monster as that?'

'Perhaps they didn't,' the Ragged One said. 'Perhaps it has cruised the waters of this world ocean, eating all the smaller creatures, devouring its rivals, growing larger and larger as it feeds – devouring until nothing was left to challenge it . . . A monster to suit a giant ocean. If the Lost were here they would surely destroy it.'

'But they are not here.'

'No.'

'You did well,' Icebones said.

The Ragged One slapped the water with her trunk, irritably. Evidently she did not welcome Icebones's praise. 'This is not your world,' the Ragged One growled. 'Just as you said.'

Thunder was strutting to and fro, raising and lowering his tusks, his posture an odd mixture of aggression and submission.

Icebones approached him cautiously. 'Thunder?'

'Don't call me that!' He scuffed the dusty beach angrily. 'Shoot was threatened, and I ran from danger. I am not Thunder. I am not even a Bull. I am nothing.'

'I know that the heart of a great Bull beats inside you. And you are part of this Family, just as much as the others.'

'I have no Family. I was taken from my mother when I was a calf.'

'Taken? Why?'

'That is what the Lost do. What does it matter?'

'It matters a great deal. A calf should be with his mother.'

'I have no Family,' he repeated. 'You despise me.'

'You followed your instinct,' she said harshly. '*The mammoth dies, but mammoths live on.* That's what the Cycle says. There are times when it is right to sacrifice another's life to save your own.'

The Bull growled bitterly, 'Even if that's true, *you saved Shoot*, where I failed.'

She reached out to him, but he flinched, muttering and rumbling, and stalked away.

She sought out Autumn. The tall, clear-eyed Cow was standing alone.

'The Bull-calf blames himself,' Autumn said. 'But *I* led us here, to this vile and useless sea.'

'How could you have known? You have lived all your life on your Mountain. It was a worthwhile gamble—'

'Because I led us here my daughter was nearly killed, and we will all starve or die of thirst. If some new monster does not burst out of the ground to devour us first.'

Icebones grabbed her trunk. 'You must lead us.'

Autumn probed at Icebones's face. 'Don't you understand? I was the Matriarch, for a few brief days, and I have killed us all.' And she stumbled away.

The Ragged One, standing alone by the shore, was remote, withdrawn as ever, still mourning her failure to find the Lost on the mountain summit. Thunder and Autumn were both immersed in their private worlds of self-loathing and anger. Breeze was standing at the water's edge, lost in herself, her swollen belly brushing the languid waves. Shoot was pursuing her sister, regaling her with lurid tales of her encounter with the monster from the sea, while Spiral trotted haughtily away.

None of them will lead, Icebones realised, dismayed. They will stay here on this desolate beach, sulking or fretting or boasting, as the sun rises and falls, and we grow still more thirsty and hungry.

No, Icebones thought. I am not prepared to die. Not yet.

She drew herself up to her full height, and emitted a commanding rumble, as loudly as she could.

The other mammoths turned towards her.

Silverhair, be with me now, she prayed.

'You will pay attention to me,' she said.

A flock of ivory gulls, startled by her call, lifted into the air on vast translucent wings.

She kept her voice as deep and loud as she could — although, before these towering mammoths, she felt small and inferior, a squat, noisy calf.

'You were right in your first guesses, when I emerged from my cave of Sleep. I am indeed a Matriarch. On the Old Steppe, where I lived, I was Matriarch of a Family of many mammoths, despite my youth. I led them well, and I was loved and respected.'

The Ragged One said slyly, 'If this is so, why didn't you say so before?'

'I wanted to see if you were fit to join my new Family.' She raised her trunk, as if sniffing them all. 'And I have decided that you are strong mammoths with good hearts. I am your Matriarch. I will listen to you, but you will do as I say.'

Autumn had turned away, and Thunder looked merely confused.

Breeze asked, 'What should we do?'

'We cannot stay here. There is no food, and the water is foul. The world is growing cold, day by day. But the air, like the water, flows to the deep places. There is a place, far from here, which is deeper than anywhere in the world.'

The Ragged One rumbled suspiciously, 'Where is this place?'

And Icebones described the great pit on the other side of the world – a hole gouged by a giant impact, a blow so powerful it had made the rocks rise up here, on the planet's opposite side. 'It is called the Footfall of Kilukpuk,' she said, thinking fast. 'And that is where we will go. There will be pasture for you and your calves. There will even be Bulls for you to run with, Thunder, and for you others to mate with.'

The Ragged One brayed. 'And this wonderful place is on *the other side of the world*? So you have never seen or smelled it?'

It was as if she was articulating Icebones's own doubts.

But Icebones said firmly, 'I will lead you there.' She raised her trunk, sniffing the air. 'We must walk away from the setting sun. We will keep walking east, and in the end we will reach the Footfall. Let's go,' she said, as she had heard her mother say many times to her own Family. 'Let's go, let's go.'

But the mammoths simply watched her, baffled.

So she raised her trunk and trumpeted, and began to walk east, following the line of the old coast, towards a sky that was already turning a deepening purple.

After a few paces she paused and turned. The three sisters, huddled together, were walking after her slowly, tracking her moist footsteps in the dusty sand. A little behind them came Autumn and Thunder, each still distracted, but submissively following the lead Icebones had given.

But now the Ragged One lumbered up to her. 'You cannot make this rabble into a Family just by saying it. And you cannot make yourself a Matriarch.'

'If you wish to stay here,' Icebones said, her voice a deep, coarse rumble, 'I will not oppose you.'

The Ragged One growled, 'If you fail – when you fail – I will be there to remind you of this day.'

I know you will, Icebones thought.

The wind was rising now. She saw that it was swirling over the pack ice, lifting spray and bits of loose ice and snow into a great grey spiral, angry and intimidating. The scavenging petrels left their bloody meals and rose into the sky, cawing angrily, their feathers stained red.

Chapter Six

THE ICE BEETLE

Heading towards the light of the rising sun, they skirted the shore of the giant ocean. There was better forage to be had a little way to the south, away from the barren coast itself, where soil and water had gathered in hollows.

But the landscape, distorted by the volcanic uplift that lay beneath the Fire Mountain, was flawed and difficult. Deep, sharp-walled valleys cut across their path. Conversely, sometimes the mammoths found themselves labouring over networks of ridges that rose one after the other, like wrinkles in aged flesh.

As leader, Icebones was able to impose a rhythm appropriate for a Family on the move. She had the mammoths walk slowly but steadily, all day and most of each night, probing at the ground with their trunks, foraging for grass and herbs and water. At first the others complained, for this was an alien way of life for creatures used to being fed as they needed it. But Icebones knew that this steady progress was better suited to a mammoth's internal constitution. And when after a few days the others got used to the steady, satisfying rhythm, and food passed pleasingly through their systems, the level of complaints dwindled.

But they were not yet a Family.

A Family was supposed to walk in coordination, led by its Matriarch and the senior Cows, all of them watching out for each other, in case of predators or natural traps like mud holes. *This* untidy rabble rambled over the broken ground as if they were rogue Bulls, as if the others did not exist, or matter.

Icebones knew it would take a long time to teach them habits that should have been ingrained since birth, and it seemed presumptuous even to imagine that she, young and inexperienced, was the one to do it. But, she reminded herself, there was nobody else.

So she persisted.

Sometimes Spiral would walk alongside Icebones, with Shoot prancing in her wake. The tall, elegant Cow would regale Icebones with unwelcome tales of her time with the Lost, when they had tied shining ribbons to her hair, or rode on her back, or had encouraged her to do tricks, picking up fruit and walking backwards and bowing at their behest.

This irritated Icebones immensely. 'You are mammoth,' she said sternly. 'You are not a creature of the Lost. You should not boast of your foolish dancing. And you should not ignore your sister. You should watch out for her, as she watches out for you. That is what it is to be Family.'

'Ah, the Family,' Spiral said. 'But what is there for me in your Family, Icebones? I am beautiful and clever and I smell fine, while *you* are small and squat. Will a Family stop you being ugly?'

Icebones reached up and tugged at Spiral's pretty tusks. 'It does not matter what I look like – or what *you* look or smell like. You will not always be healthy and pretty, Spiral. And someday you will have a calf of your own – perhaps many calves – just as your sister is carrying now. And then you too will have to rely on others.'

For a brief moment Spiral seemed to be listening hard, and her trunk tip shyly probed at Icebones's mouth. But then she pulled away, trumpeting brightly, and lumbered off, Shoot as ever trailing her eagerly.

They came to a place where enormous valleys cut across their path. The mammoths climbed down shallow banks and worked their way across rubble-strewn floors.

These tremendous channels were littered with huge eroded boulders, pitted and scoured by water and wind, around which the mammoths had to pick their way. Perhaps water had once flowed from the high southern lands into the basin of the north, cutting these channels and depositing this debris. But those vanished rivers must have been mighty indeed. And these huge channels were clearly very ancient, for many of them were pitted by craters, or even cut through by younger channels.

The great age of the land was obvious, the complexity of its formation recalled in the folded rock around them.

They found a flooded crater, a shallow circular lake in a pit smashed into a channel bottom. The mammoths welcomed this easily accessible pool, though they had to break through layers of ice to reach the dark, cold water beneath.

At the water's circular edge, Icebones found clumps of grass. She would twist her trunk around a clump of stems and kick at its base to dislodge it. After beating the grass against her knees to knock off the dirt, she pushed it into her mouth, and her trunk explored for new clumps as she chewed.

She inspected the ice on the crater pond. Much of it was hard and blue. Mammoths learned about ice. Icebones knew that fresh ice first appeared as a film of oily crystals, almost as dark as the water itself. When it thickened it would turn grey and opaque, and thicken slowly. If it lasted to a second winter it would harden and turn a cold white-blue.

So the ice covering this pool was persisting through the long summer of this strange world. It was another sign that the world was cooling, and the tide of warmth and water and life was withdrawing, step by step.

Spiral lumbered up to her, complaining. 'Icebones, that's not fair. You are taking the best grass!'

Icebones slapped Spiral's cheek with her trunk tip – not hard, but enough to sting, and to make the others turn to listen. 'I am the Matriarch,' she growled. 'I take the first, and the best. Your mother is next. And then the rest of you. It is the way,' The pecking-order she was striving to teach Spiral was part of every Family's internal structure – although no mature Family would stick to it rigidly, with food being apportioned according to need.

Spiral grumbled, 'If this is what it means to be in a Family I would rather the Lost returned.' But she backed away, deferring to Icebones's tentative authority.

Beyond the flooded crater, the ground began to drop in altitude. Though it was still broken and often difficult to negotiate, the soil was richer here, and steppe plants flourished. There were even stretches of forest, conifer trees so tall they seemed to stretch up to the pale pink sky. And there was plenty to eat now: grass, coltsfoot, mountain sorrel, lousewort, sedge, dwarf birch.

Covering ground that was rich in loam and easy under their feet, their stomachs filling up, the mammoths' spirits seemed to lift, and they walked on more vigorously.

Icebones noticed that as they got used to the fodder of the steppe the mammoths' tastes were starting to diverge: Thunder sought out a type of willow with small diamond leaves, while Spiral preferred the sedge. They were starting to forget the rich food the Lost had provided for them, she realised with some relief.

But now Icebones became aware of a dark smudge, like low cloud, on the horizon directly ahead of her, to the east. And she smelled smoke.

Fire ahead. The mammoths drew closer, trunks raised.

Fire was a natural thing, of course — it could be caused by flowing lava, or lightning strikes — but in mammoths' minds fire was primarily a thing of the Lost. *Where there is smoke, there are the Lost* — so went the wisdom of the Cycle.

They walked on, into the thickening smoke.

They came to a shallow crater rim. The smoke was pouring sluggishly into the air from the crater's belly.

It was an easy climb up the crater wall to its narrow crest. But now the smoke was thick, making their eyes stream and filling their nostrils with its stink. The mammoths were agitated, for the scent of fire sparked deep instincts of fear and flight in them all.

The crater was a big one, surrounded by a ring of eroded hillocks that stretched to the horizon. A bank of smoke hung thick and dense over the crater basin.

And the basin was full of trees: fallen, burning trees, with flames licking ponderously. There were so many that they lapped up against the crater walls, and trunks lay thick on the ground like shed pine needles. But each of these 'needles' was the trunk of a great conifer, stripped of its branches.

Autumn growled, 'We can't walk through that. We would suffocate in the smoke, or get trapped beneath the burning trunks, or—'

'You're right.' Icebones raised her trunk, trying to sense the lie of the land despite the distraction of the smoke, and the steady rumble of collapsing, burned-out logs. 'The wind comes this way.' She took a step towards the southern crater rim. 'We will walk around these circular walls. The smoke will blow away from us, not over us.'

'It is out of our way,' the Ragged One pointed out sourly.

Icebones snapped, 'We have no choice. Be careful where you step. Help each other. Let's go, let's go.' And without further discussion she set off, following the narrow ridge that ran around the crater rim.

She didn't look back, but she could tell from their footfalls and rumbles that the mammoths were following her.

The going wasn't difficult, though in places the rim wall broke up into separate eroded hillocks, and they had to climb through narrow gulches or over crumbled rock. But there was no water to be had on this bare rock wall. Soon the air, hot and dry and laden with the stink of wood smoke, burned in her nostrils and throat.

The wind veered and a gust of smoke washed over her, blinding her eyes and flooding her sensitive nostrils, so that she had to work her way over the lumpy ground by touch alone.

When the smoke cleared she saw something moving, dimly visible through the thinning grey veils of smoke.

She stopped dead, trunk raised. She sensed the other mammoths gathering around her, curious, nervous. She could see something shining, like ice, a vast bulk moving. And she could feel how its weight made the ground shudder.

Now it emerged from the smoke.

A vast boxy shape was crawling laboriously up the side of the crater. It was more like a great slab of rock than any living thing. On its back was a kind of shell, like an insect's carapace, but the shell was flat and a pale silvery-grey, and it was liberally covered with caked-dust and dried mud. It would have been big enough for all seven of the mammoths to stand side by side on its back. The beast moved forward, not on legs, but on its underbelly, leaving tracks cut deep in the rock of the crater rim. But those tracks were well worn, Icebones saw. Wherever this strange creature was heading, it had made this journey many times.

'It is like a beetle,' Breeze said. 'With a shell of ice. An ice beetle.'

The ice beetle trailed huge long limbs – far longer but less mobile than a mammoth's trunk. And in a set of shining fingers it grasped a tree-trunk. The tree had been dragged over the dusty plain from a stand of conifer forest. In that forest stood a number of stumps, where trunks had been neatly cut away from their roots.

Icebones could smell, under the dominant stink of the fire, the sap of the tree trunk and the iron tang of the red dust. But she could smell nothing of the beetle, nothing at all.

As the mammoths watched, the ice beetle, in dour silence, hauled the tree-trunk up the side of the steep crater wall. Dust rose up in clouds. Then the beetle spun slowly around and let the tree-trunk fall into the crater, where the flames would soon reach it.

The beetle, its trunk-arms empty, seemed to rest, as if exhausted. Then it roused itself. It swivelled and began to edge its way back down the crater rim wall.

Autumn growled, 'Once mammoths did this. Hauling trees from forests to pits in the ground, where they would be burned and buried. Now, it seems, the Lost have stronger servants even than us.'

'Perhaps it is like mammoth dung,' Icebones mused. 'Where mammoths pass, new life sprouts, for our dung enriches the ground. Maybe the Lost – or at least their servants – are working to build the world, to build life. But why does it continue, now the Lost have vanished?'

'Because it doesn't know what else to do,' the Ragged One said. 'Because nobody told it to stop. Because it is mad, or stupid.'

'Everything about the Lost is a mystery to us,' said Autumn grimly. Spiral made to protest, but Autumn insisted, 'We lived with them, and accepted their gifts of food and water. But we never understood them. It is the truth, daughter.'

As the beetle passed, Shoot reached out tentatively with her trunk tip and brushed the sharp edge of its carapace. 'It is cold. But it is not wet like ice. And it smells of nothing.' She sneezed sharply, sending dust flying. 'It is covered in dust.' She began to blow at the carapace, ridding a corner of dust, and exposing a clean, shining surface.

Spiral stepped forward and joined her. So did Icebones, without being sure why. They blew away the dust, or, where mud was caked, they picked at it with their trunk fingers and brushed it off.

Icebones noticed that Breeze hung back, distracted, evidently uncomfortable from the weight of her calf.

The ice beetle continued to work its way down the hillside, its great body tipping up clumsily. It did not react to the mammoths' attention.

When it reached the level ground outside the crater the beetle began to trundle away, back towards the forest. But now its exposed carapace gleamed silver, free of dust and mud save for a few streaks.

'Do you think it's moving a little faster?' Autumn asked. 'Maybe it needs the sunlight, like a flower.'

'I never saw a flower like *that*,' Icebones said sceptically.

'True, true.'

There was nothing for the mammoths here, nothing but this insane abandoned creature and its endless, meaningless task. Icebones said, 'Let's go.' She took a step forward, meaning to climb down from the crater rim.

But, behind her, Breeze gasped. She had fallen to her knees, her stubby trunk lying pooled and limp on the ground. 'Help me.'

Autumn growled, 'It is the calf. *It is time.*'

Spiral turned to Icebones. 'What must we do? Oh, what must we do?'

Icebones felt her stomach turn as cold as a lump of ice. 'I suppose the Lost helped you even with this.'

Spiral fell back, growling dismally, and Icebones felt a stab of shame.

Autumn said, 'The Lost were with us always . . . But there are no Lost here.'

Close at Icebones's side like a guilty conscience, the Ragged One said softly, 'If not you, who else?'

Icebones gathered her courage and stepped forward. Breeze, still slumped to her knees, was straining, her belly distended. 'You must stand,' Icebones said.

'I can't.'

'Help her,' Icebones ordered.

Briskly Spiral and Shoot stepped forward. They dug their trunks and foreheads under their sister's belly, while Icebones pushed at her rump.

In a few heartbeats Breeze had staggered to her feet, but her legs were shuddering. The two sisters stood close to Breeze, keeping her upright with nudges of their bodies. Even Thunder gently pushed Breeze's rump, rumbling encouragement.

Breeze, panting hard, leaned forward so her back legs were stretched out behind her. Icebones thought she could see the calf moving within its cave of flesh.

Breeze raised her trunk and trumpeted, straining. There was a sudden eruption of blood and water, a stink of urine and milk.

'I can see it!' Shoot called suddenly. 'Look! The calf is coming!'

And Icebones saw it too: in a gush of water and blood, two legs had pushed from Breeze's vagina. Now a small head and the bulk of a little body was squeezed out, wrapped in a clear, shimmering sheet. For a moment it dangled by its hind legs. Then Breeze gave a final heave.

The calf shot out and plopped to the ground.

Shoot and Spiral, suddenly aunts, hurried forward to the baby, which lay wrapped in its blood-streaked sac on the ground.

Icebones stayed with Breeze, who staggered forward. 'You must stay on your feet.'

'It hurts, Icebones,' Breeze said.

'It's all right. Just a little longer. Push hard, Breeze. Push—'

Now the afterbirth emerged, a sodden bloody lump that fell limp to the ground.

Breeze sighed, eyes closing, and she fell to her knees. Thunder curled his trunk over her protectively.

'The calf's not moving,' Shoot wailed. 'Is it dead?'

Icebones pushed past Shoot and Spiral. The calf still lay where it had fallen. 'We have to get it out of the birth sac.' She leaned and tried to catch the membrane with her tusk tips, ripping and pulling it. 'Help me – but do not hurt the calf.'

It seemed to take long heartbeats, but at last they had the amniotic sac free. Shoot hurled the bloody sheet away with an impulsive shake of her head.

Icebones leaned forward to the calf, inspecting it – him! – with her trunk tip. He was a bundle of pale orange fur that was soaked and flattened by amniotic fluid. His legs were spindly stalks, his trunk was a mere thread, and his head was smooth and round, as if not yet formed. He was breathing shallowly, his little chest rising and falling rapidly, and his breath steamed around his face.

Icebones wrapped her trunk underneath the calf, and encouraged Shoot and Spiral to help her. Soon they had him set upright on his skinny, trembling legs. His little eyes opened with a moist pop, and Icebones saw they were bright red. But now he threw back his tiny trunk so it lay on his forehead, and opened his mouth.

'Hungry,' he said, his voice a thin, choked mewl. 'Cold. Hungry. Oh, let me back . . . !'

Chapter Seven

THE CRACKED LAND

The calf made the suckling cry, over and over, as if he had been taught it by Kilukpuk herself.

'He needs milk,' Icebones said. She hurried to Breeze, who still lay on the ground.

Breeze's eyes were closed, and she was breathing hard, obviously exhausted. 'Woodsmoke,' she murmured.

'What?'

'That is what he will be called. For when he was born my head was full of smoke . . .'

'You must come,' Icebones said gently.

'Let me sleep, Icebones . . .'

The calf opened his mouth and wailed, his voice thin and high. 'Cold, cold!'

And now, at last, Icebones was at a loss. 'Without milk he will die,' she said. 'I don't know what to do.'

Autumn came forward, her gait stiff. 'Let me.' And she gathered the little creature in her trunk and guided him forward, pulling him beneath her legs. Blindly, he snuggled at her belly fur until he found the dugs that dangled between her forelegs. Driven by instinct he clamped his mouth to a nipple and began to suckle greedily.

Icebones, astonished, saw thin, pale milk dribble down his cheek. 'Autumn – you have milk. But you are not with calf.'

'It began when I saw how weak Breeze was becoming. I don't know why.' She eyed Icebones. 'You may be Matriarch,' she rumbled softly. 'But you don't know everything, it seems.'

'I know that you are a good mother,' said Icebones. 'For you were there when your daughter, and her calf, needed you most.'

The calf – Woodsmoke – squeaked his contentment, and Autumn rumbled softly.

It was strange, Icebones thought: just heartbeats old, and yet the calf had already achieved something immensely important, by redeeming Autumn, his grandmother . . . Perhaps it was an omen of his life to come.

Spiral and Shoot gathered around their mother protectively, rumbling reassurance. Further away, Thunder stayed with Breeze, stroking her hair with gentle motions of his trunk.

It was a moment of tenderness, of contentment, of togetherness.

But Icebones could not help but look east, trunk raised, towards the difficult country that lay ahead – a country through which she would now have to bring a calf, and a weakened mother.

A wind rose, droning through the clefts in the crater wall, drowning out the reassuring rumbles of the Cows.

★

Further east, the ground rose steadily. The steppe vegetation grew thinner, and any water was frozen over.

Icebones's chest began to ache as she took each breath, as it had not since she was high on the Fire Mountain.

They came to a land covered by vast pits.

The pits were shallow and rounded, and dust pooled deep in them. They were like footprints around a dried mud hole – but these 'footprints' were huge, taking many paces to cross. In some places the pits were overwhelmed by frozen rock flows, as if the pitted landscape had been formed long ago, and then this younger rock poured over it to harden in place.

It was difficult country. But Icebones feared that the terrain further east of here might be more difficult still. Looking that way from the higher ridges, she could see deep shadows and broken walls, hear complex, booming echoes.

And at night she thought she heard the low rumble of some vast animal, echoing from tortuous cliffs.

Difficult, yes. And now they had the calf to consider.

Woodsmoke trotted beside his mother or his grandmother, stumbling frequently. He was still coated with the short under-fur from his birth, topped now by a thin layer of pink-red overfur. His back was round, lacking the slope and distinctive shoulder hump he would develop later in life. Though he had been born with the ancient language of all Kilukpuk's children, there were many things he had to learn. He couldn't yet use his trunk to gather food, or even to drink. For now he was completely dependent on milk, which he drew from his mother's nipple with his mouth – the only time in his life when he would use his mouth directly to feed.

The calf slowed them down: there was no doubt about that. They had had to wait several days at the birthing place while mother and calf recovered, and even now the group could walk no faster than the calf could manage.

But Icebones would not have done without him. Woodsmoke was quickly becoming the focus of the group, this nascent Family. He would run from one to the other, ignorant and uncaring of their obscure adult disputes. Only the Ragged One refused to respond to his unformed charms.

His favourite was his aunt, Spiral.

She would lower her trunk and let him clamber on it or pull it. Or she would lie on the ground and let him climb up over her belly, digging his tiny feet into her guard hairs, determined and dogged, as if she was some great warm rock. In her turn, Spiral would forgive Woodsmoke anything – even when he dribbled urine into her fine coat, of which she was so proud.

Icebones was surprised by this; it showed a side of Spiral she hadn't suspected. Finally, she thought she understood. She sought an opportunity to speak to the Cow.

'Spiral – *you've had a calf of your own*. That's why you're so close to Woodsmoke, isn't it?'

At first Spiral would not reply. She walked along with something of her old haughtiness, head held high, her handsome tusks bright in the cold sunlight. But at length she said, 'Yes. If you must know. I have given birth to two calves. Both Bulls. I watched the calves learn to walk, and I suckled them. But soon, when they were no older than Woodsmoke is now, they were taken away.' She said this flatly, without emotion.

'They were taken by the Lost? What cruelty.'

'They were not – cruel. They were taking the calves to a place that would be better for them.' She shook her head, and her delicate trunk rippled. 'And when my calves were gone,

99

each time, I was stroked and praised by the Lost, and given treats, and—'

'Where are the calves now?'

'Surely they are dead,' she said harshly. 'The Sickness killed so many.'

'You can't know that.'

'It does not hurt.' And she trumpeted brightly, as if joyful. But it was a thin, cold sound.

The little calf came blundering over to Spiral in his tangled, uncoordinated way, seeking to play. But she pushed him away with a gentle shove of her trunk. 'I have no need of *him*,' she snapped.

Icebones brought him back. 'I know,' she said carefully. 'But he needs you.'

And, tentatively, Spiral wrapped her trunk around the little calf's small, smooth head.

The pits in the ground became deeper and more fragmented, and began to merge. Soon Icebones was walking through a deepening gully. The walls grew steadily steeper around her, and the floor, littered with broken rocks, tilted downwards sharply. Soon Icebones's front legs were aching, and her foot pads and trunk tip were scratched raw by the hard-edged rocks.

The gully gave way to a more complex landscape still, a place of branching chasms and tall cliffs. It was the cracked land she had sensed from afar, and dreaded.

Icebones found herself walking through a flat-bottomed valley so deep and sheer-walled that she was immersed in cold shadow, even though she could see a stripe of pinkish day-light sky far above her. The walls, steep above her, were heavily eroded. They were made of layers of hard red-grey sandstone and blue-black lava, and here and there they had slumped tiredly into landslides.

In some places the walls had collapsed altogether, leaving spires and isolated mesas, so that she wandered through a forest of rock, carved into eerie, spindly shapes by the endless wind.

In the weak light the mammoths were rounded, indistinct forms, shuffling gloomily. The ground was littered with sand dunes and rock from the crumbled walls, so the going was difficult and slow. They were all unhappy: mammoths were creatures of the open steppe, and it was against their instincts to be enclosed by high walls.

But the chasm was short. Soon it opened out – but only into a branching array of more deep gorges, separated by tall, sharp-edged walls. Icebones stamped her feet and rumbled. But the walls of this increasingly complex maze sent back only muddled and confusing echoes.

The nights were the worst. The stars and disconcerting moons crossed the sky, but the mammoths were stranded in a deep shadowed darkness.

Icebones tried to keep them moving. But because of the calf's weariness that proved to be impossible, and they were forced to endure the dark huddled closely around Breeze, while her calf napped peacefully in the forest of her legs.

In the darkest night, Icebones heard deep, brooding rumbles. All the mammoths heard it, she thought, but none would speak of it, as if fearful of making it real.

In the daytime Icebones, weary and befuddled, strove to keep moving east.

This maze of chasms was a pattern of grooves cut deep into the land, as if by the claws of some great predator, so that the plain high above their heads was cut into sunlit islands, each separate from the others.

Spiral said, 'I have become a creature of the ground like a lemming, able only to peer up at the sunlight above.' And her grumble was joined by the others.

It was as if it was somehow Icebones's fault that they were having such difficulties. It was utterly unfair, of course. But then, she thought gloomily, nobody had promised her that being a Matriarch was anything to do with fairness.

'I will tell you stories from the Cycle.'

That met with a general groan.

But Icebones said, 'The Cycle is our story – *your* story. This Cracked Land is difficult. But the Cycle is full of stories of mammoths who faced difficulties, for it is the times of hardship that shape us.' And she began to tell them the story of Longtusk. 'It is said that when Longtusk was a calf the mammoths roamed free, great Clans of them, all across the northern steppes. But Longtusk's Family was forced to flee, northwards, ever north, for the Lost were encroaching from the south, breeding and squabbling and building . . .'

The mammoths still grumbled, but the noise was subdued, and suffused by the soft pads of their feet, the growls of their bellies, gentle burps and farts. Even the little calf trotting at Icebones's side listened intently. Woodsmoke was still too young to understand much of what she said. But he was responding to the rhythm of her language, as she hoped they all would.

The Ragged One continued to keep apart.

'At last,' Icebones went on, 'the mammoths had nowhere else to go. The land gave way to a great frozen ocean where nothing could live but seals and other ugly creatures. It seemed that soon the mammoths would be overwhelmed by the Lost.

'But Longtusk found a way. There was a bridge of land that spanned the ocean, from one great steppe to another. And, on the far side of the bridge, there were no Lost – only open steppe, where the mammoths could grow and breed and live. So Longtusk gathered the mammoths of his Clan, and said to them—'

Something dropped before her, huge and heavy and dark. It opened a cavernous mouth and screamed. She glimpsed rows of sharp teeth.

Without thinking she lunged forward – she felt the rasp of fur on her tusks, the squelch of soft flesh breaking – and the creature screamed louder yet.

And then, in an instant, it was gone, leaving her with the stink of blood in her nostrils, and the echo of that deadly scream rattling from the walls around her.

She stood there, shaking like a frightened calf.

The mammoths had scattered. The calf had been left alone, and he was turning back and forth, little trunk raised, mewling pitifully. 'Scared . . . scared . . .'

Icebones said, 'We must stay together. That – thing – was probably after the calf.'

Spiral was stiff with rage and fear. 'Enough of your talk,' she said. 'The Ragged One is right. This is not your world, Icebones. You did not know we would meet such a creature here, did you?'

'If we squabble it will pick us off one by one.' Icebones raised her tusks, which still dripped red blood. 'Is that what you want?'

At last Autumn rumbled, 'She is right. The calf is probably its main target, for he is weakest, and slowest. Breeze, come to him.'

Breeze stepped forward and tucked her calf beneath her legs. Woodsmoke tried to suckle, but Breeze pushed him back. The rest of the mammoths clustered around mother and calf.

'We will go on,' insisted Icebones. 'This warren of chasms will not last for ever. If everyone keeps their trunk high, we will survive.'

They were reluctant, fretful, afraid. But nobody had a better suggestion. And so they began to move forward once more. The calf's mewling was muffled by the legs and belly fur of its mother, and the adult mammoths rumbled uneasily, their deep sounds echoing heavily from the sheer ravine walls.

Thunder walked beside Icebones. 'What do you think it was?'

'Perhaps it was some kind of cat. There are stories of great cats in the Cycle – Longtusk himself fought such a beast. Perhaps it has grown fat by destroying everything else living here, like the whale in the Ocean of the North. But I have never seen a cat, for none lived on the Island. Many of the animals mentioned in the old Cycle stories are long gone . . .'

Icebones saw that the stripe of sky visible far above her head was already fading to a deep orange-pink.

'Soon it will be dark,' the Ragged One said softly. 'And then we will make a story of our own. Won't we, Matriarch?'

They came to another branch in the chasm system. This time Icebones faced three intersecting ravines, each sheer-walled and littered with loose rock, each leading only to further complexity – and each empty, as far as she could see.

We must continue east, she told herself. If we don't achieve that much, everything else is lost. She stepped forward and led them into the central chasm.

There was a bellow. The mammoths stumbled back, trunks raised in alarm.

This time the creature had dropped from above, on to Autumn's back. The mammoth was pawing the ground and trumpeting. She lifted her head in a vain effort to reach her tormentor with her tusks or trunk.

The creature was only dimly visible in the shadows, but Icebones glimpsed hard, front-facing yellow eyes, that black bloody mouth, and claws that gleamed white and dug deep into Autumn's flesh, causing blood to well and drip down her heavy hair.

Autumn blundered against the chasm wall. The cat creature yowled its protest. But it was ripped away from her back, its claws leaving a final set of gouges.

Icebones lunged forward, trumpeting, tusks held high.

The cat raised itself to its full height, yellow eyes fixed on Icebones. It was spindly, but its body was a sleek slab of muscle. It opened its huge mouth and hissed. And it leapt with astonishing agility up the chasm wall.

Again the mammoths were left in sudden silence.

'It lives on the walls,' Shoot said, wondering.

Spiral had her head dipped, her trunk wrapped over her forehead. 'I can't stand it,' she whimpered. 'I am so afraid.'

Icebones herself was shaken to her core. Mammoths were used to facing predators, but as a creature of the open steppe, Icebones had no experience of threats dropping down on her from out of the sky.

She walked up to Autumn. 'Your back is hurt.' She probed with her trunk fingers at the slash wounds. The covering hair was matted with blood. 'We will find mud to bathe your wounds.'

'No,' Autumn growled, pulling back. 'We must get out of this place before dark.'

Thunder said softly, '*Which way?*'

For a terrible moment Icebones realised that she did not know – the chasm looked identical before her and behind her – she had been turned around several times, and the stripe of pink sky above her gave no clues as to the direction of the sun.

The Ragged One was watching her, waiting for her to fail.

At last Icebones spotted a small heap of mammoth dung, still steaming gently, a few paces away. 'That is the way we have come. So we will go the other way – to the east.'

Thunder growled, 'But that is the way the cat went.'

A high-pitched yowl echoed from the chasm walls. The mammoths peered that way fearfully, raising their trunks to sniff the air. 'Where is it?' 'Is it close?' 'I think it came from that way.' 'No, *that* way . . .' But the echoes thrown by the complex walls of the chasm system masked the source of the call – as perhaps the cat intended, Icebones thought.

The Ragged One stood before Icebones. 'It can track us by our dung, and our footprints, and our scent. How can we throw it off? You don't know what to do, do you? You are no Matriarch. You have not told us the truth – not since the moment you woke up inside your cave of darkness. And now you have led us into deadly peril.'

Icebones, desperate, her head full of alarm, thought, Not *now* . . . But she was tired of strangeness, of unpredictable dangers, of dragging this recalcitrant group across a barren rocky world, of the Ragged One's unrelenting hostility.

'All right,' she said sharply. 'You want the truth – then here it is. *I am no Matriarch.* I think my mother intended me to come here to this place and lead you someday . . . but not yet. Not until I was grown, and had calves of my own, and had become a true Matriarch. I don't know what happened – I don't know why I found myself here, now. *I don't want to be here.* But here I am.'

The mammoths rumbled, tense, unhappy.

Thunder reached to her hesitantly. 'You *lied*? But you named us, Icebones.'

She glared at them all. 'Yes, I lied. I had no choice. If I hadn't, you would have died on the shore of that salt-filled ocean.'

Autumn's rumble was tinged with pain. 'Enough of this. It won't make any difference if Icebones is a liar or not if we are all dead by sundown. *Which way?*'

Two chasms led from this point. One was straight, its walls sheer and clean, but the other was a jumble of rocks.

Icebones snapped, 'We go down there.' She meant the jumbled, difficult route.

Autumn growled, 'Are you sure? The other looks much easier.'

The Ragged One said, 'What does it matter? Icebones is a fool. The cat can follow us wherever we go.'

Icebones said, 'You must listen to me. Listen to me because I am Icebones – for who you know me to be, not for who you wish me to be. Go now, that way, as I told you.'

Slowly, sullenly, the mammoths began to move towards the more crowded chasm.

But Icebones called Autumn back. 'Wait, Autumn. Forgive me.' And she dug into the wounds on Autumn's back, breaking open the clots and covering her trunk fingers with blood.

Autumn bore this stoically. Perhaps she understood what Icebones intended.

As the mammoths filed into the crowded chasm, Icebones

set off, alone, into the other, cleaner defile. Where she trod she made sure she left clear footprints in the dust and scattered rock, and even squeezed out a little dung and urine. And she took care to smear Autumn's blood on the rocky walls.

Then she backed out of the chasm, trying to step in the tracks she had already made.

Just as she reached the junction of the chasm, she heard a cold yowl – glimpsed a black form shimmering over the rock above her head – saw yellow predator's eyes. The cat hurtled, black and lithe, into the chasm she had seeded, away from the mammoths.

Quickly she ducked after the others. 'Try not to drop dung for a while – I know that is hard – and try to be quiet . . .'

Thunder asked, subdued, 'How did you know what the cat would do?'

'I hoped that blood would be a stronger lure than the smell of our waste and hair. The other chasm is long, and it will take a while for the cat to explore it. But soon enough it will know that we have tricked it, and come looking for us once more.'

So they proceeded through the shadowed complexity of the chasm, picking their way between huge fallen boulders and over smaller sharp-edged rocks.

Icebones glanced at the Ragged One. But the Ragged One's posture spoke only of resentment and fury. Icebones knew that in the days to come the dynamics of her little band would be even more difficult, and that a final confrontation was yet to come.

After several more days – dismal days, frightening, bereft of food and water – the mammoths emerged at last from the Cracked Land.

With relief they fanned out under a pale, open sky, over a shallow slope of scree and broken rock. There was even food to be had, tufts of grass and scrubby trees growing in the sudden flood of light.

From here they should go south and east, for that was the direction to the Footfall. But when she looked that way, Ice-bones saw that the ground ended in a sharp line, much closer than the horizon, as if there was a dip beyond.

Leaving the mammoths to feed, she walked that way. Soon she had reached the break in the ground – and she recoiled, shocked.

It was a sheer drop.

She was on the lip of a chasm. But this immense feature would have dwarfed the mazy ravines through which she had guided the mammoths.

As if scoured out by a vast tusk, it was a mighty gouge in the land. And it was in her way.

TWO

GOUGE

THE STORY OF THE FAMILY OF KILUKPUK

This is a story Kilukpuk told Silverhair.

Now, as you know, Kilukpuk was born at a time when the world belonged to the Reptiles. The Reptiles were the greatest beasts ever seen – so huge they made the land itself shake with their footfalls – and they were cunning and savage hunters.

In those days our ancestors called themselves Hotbloods.

The Hotbloods were small timid creatures who lived underground, in burrows, the way lemmings do. They had huge, frightened eyes, for they would only emerge from their burrows at night, a time when the Reptiles were less active and less able to hunt them. They all looked alike, and rarely even argued, for their world was dominated by the constant threat of the Reptiles.

The ancestors of every warm-blooded creature you see today lived in those cramped dens: bear with seal, wolf with mammoth.

It was into this world that Kilukpuk, the first of all

Matriarchs, was born. If you could have seen her, small and cautious like the rest, you would never have imagined the mighty races which would one day spring from her loins. But, despite her smallness, Kilukpuk was destined to become the mother of us all.

Kilukpuk had many brothers and sisters.

One was called Aglu. Secretive and sly, his blood runs in the veins of all the creatures that eat the flesh of others, like the wolves.

One was called Ursu. Fierce and aloof, she became the mother of all the bears.

One was called Equu. Foolish and vain, she became the mother of all the horses.

One was called Purga. Strange and clever with paws that could grasp and manipulate, he . . .

Yes, yes, there is a story here, and I will get to it!

Now after the Reptiles had gone, the Hotbloods emerged from their burrows. For a long time they were timid, as if they feared the Reptiles might return. But at last they grew confident, and their calves and cubs and foals grew fat and strong and tall.

And by the time Longtusk was born, much later, a time when the ice crowded down from the north of the Old Steppe, there were many bears and horses and wolves, and many mammoths.

But only mammoths, the Calves of Kilukpuk, had Families.

Now at one time in his life Longtusk lived alone, and he wandered the land. Everywhere he went he won friendship and respect – naturally, since he was the greatest hero of all, and even other, stupid creatures could recognise that.

One spring day Longtusk, wandering the land, happened to come by a snow bank. He saw a bear alone, mourning loudly.

Now a cub of Ursu likes to live alone, in caves she digs out of snow banks with her paws. She will spend her winter in the snow, nursing her cubs, until they come out in the spring to play and hunt.

Longtusk called, 'What is wrong?'

And the bear said, 'My cub has grown sickly and died. My milk was sour, and I could not feed him.'

And Longtusk was saddened. But he knew that if a mammoth's milk soured, she would ask the others of her Family, her mother and sisters and aunts, to suckle the calf for her, and the calf would not die. But the bear lived alone, and had no Family to help care for her cubs.

Longtusk stayed with the bear a day and a night, comforting her, and then he walked on.

In the summer Longtusk, wandering the land, happened to come upon a horse as she cropped a stand of grass. She was mourning loudly.

Now the foals of Equu like to run together in herds, but they have no Matriarch, and no true Family.

Longtusk called, 'What is wrong?'

And the horse said, 'I was running with my brothers and sisters and our foals when we ran into a bank of smoke. It was a fire, lit by the Lost. Well, we turned and ran, as fast as we could. But we ran to a cliff's edge and fell – all but me – and the Lost have taken the flesh and the skin of my brothers and sisters and foals, and I am alone.'

And Longtusk was saddened. But he knew that if Lost hunters tried to panic a mammoth Family, the wisdom of the

Matriarch and her sisters would keep them from falling into such a simple trap.

Longtusk stayed with the horse a day and a night, comforting her, and then he walked on.

In the autumn Longtusk, wandering the land, happened to come upon a wolf as she chewed on a scrap of meat. She was mourning loudly.

Now the wolves run together in packs. But they have no true Family.

Though Longtusk was rightly wary of any cub of Aglu, he approached the wolf. He called, 'What is wrong?'

And the wolf said, 'We were hunting. My brother was injured and he died. My parents and my sister and my cubs fell on him, and I joined them, and we fought over the entrails we dragged from his stomach. But the meat tasted sour in my mouth, and I am still hungry, and my brother is gone, and I am alone.'

And Longtusk was saddened. But he knew that when a mammoth died, her Family would Remember her properly, and those who had to live on were soothed. But when a wolf died he became nothing but another piece of meat between the teeth of his pack.

Longtusk stayed with the wolf a day and a night, comforting her, and then he walked on.

If you are a Cow you are born into a Family, and you live in that Family, and you die in that Family. All your life. A Family must share in the care and protection of the calves. A Family must respect the wisdom of its elders, and especially the Matriarch. A Family must Remember its dead. In a Family, *I* becomes *We*.

All these things Longtusk knew. All these things Kilukpuk taught us, and more.

. . . I know, I know. I have not said what became of Purga, brother of Kilukpuk.

Well, Purga sired clever creatures who climbed and ran and hunted and built and fought and killed. And *they* became the Lost.

But that is another story.

Chapter One

THE BRIDGE

The mammoths spent a night on the lip of the great cliff, huddled under a sky littered with hard, bright stars. Icebones was surrounded by the warm gurgles of the mammoths' bellies, their soft belches and farts. Sometimes she heard a rustle as Woodsmoke scrambled through belly hair and sought a teat to suckle.

But every time sleep approached Icebones imagined she was back in the maze of rock, and that a lithe black creature, all teeth and claws, was preparing to spring out of the air.

It was with relief that she saw the dawn approaching. Finding a stream, she took a trunkful of ice-cold water and tipped it into her mouth. The mammoths were already drifting away in search of the first of the day's forage. The place they had stood for much of the night was littered with dung.

Autumn's wounds still seeped blood that leaked into her ragged guard hairs. Shoot cleaned the wounds of blood and dirt with water, and plastered mud into the deepest cuts.

Breeze encouraged her calf to pop fragments of the adults' dung into his mouth, for it would help his digestion. But his control of his trunk was still clumsy, and he smeared the warm, salty dung liberally over his mouth. He was growing rapidly. His legs, to which tufts of orange hair clung, were spindly and long, and he was already half Icebones's height.

Finished with the dung, Woodsmoke trotted from one adult to another, chirping his simple phrases: 'I am hungry! I am not cold!' – and, most of all: 'Look at me! Look at what I am doing!' Autumn grumbled wearily that it might be better for the nerves of the adults if calves did not speak from the moment they were born. But Icebones knew she didn't mean it.

Icebones walked to the edge of the Gouge.

The canyon was vast, magnificent, austere. It stretched from east to west, passing beyond the horizon in either direction. Its walls, glowing red and crimson and ochre, were nothing but rock, cracked and seamed by heat and frost and wind. Peering down, she saw grey clouds drifting through the canyon, feathery rafts floating on the languid river of air that flowed between those mighty walls.

The wall beneath her was huge, tall enough to dwarf many mountains. Its face was cut into columns and gullies, carved and fluted by water and wind, the detail dwindling to a dim darkness at its base.

But the Gouge's far southern wall was a mere line of darkness on the horizon. She imagined a mammoth like herself standing on that southern wall, peering north across this immense feature. To such an observer, Icebones would be quite invisible.

The Gouge's floor was visible beneath the flowing grey cloud. She made out the ripple of dunes, the snaking glint of a river, and the crowded grey-green of forests or steppe – all very different from the high, frozen plain on which she stood. The Gouge was so deep that the very weather was different on its sunken floor.

Thunder, the young Bull, stood beside her. 'The valley is big,' he said simply.

'Yes. Do you see? It is light *there*, to the east, but it is still dark *there*, to the west.' It was true. The morning sun, a shrunken yellow disc immersed in pale pink light, seemed to be rising from out of the Gouge's eastern extremity. Long, sharp shadows stretched across the Gouge floor, and mist pooled white in valleys and depressions. And, as she looked further to the west, she saw that the floor there still lay in deep darkness, still in the shadow of the world. 'The Gouge is so big that it can contain both day and night.'

Thunder growled. 'It is too big to understand.'

Gently, she prodded his trunk. 'No. Feel the ground. Smell it, listen to it. Hear the wind gushing along this great trench, fleeing the sun's heat. Listen to the rumble of the rivers, flowing along the plain, far below. And listen to the rocks . . .'

'The rocks?'

She stamped, hard. 'You are not a Lost, who is nothing but a pair of eyes. You can hear much more than you can see, if you try. The shape of the world is in the rocks' song.' She walked back and forth, listening to the ringing of the ground. She could feel the spin of the world, and the huge slow echoes that came back from the massive volcanic rise to the east.

And she could feel how this valley stretched on and on, far beyond the horizon. It was like a great wound, she thought, a wound that stretched around a quarter of the planet's belly.

Now Thunder was trotting back and forth, trunk high, eyes half-closed, slamming his clumsy feet into the ground. 'I *can* feel it.' He trumpeted his pleasure. 'The Lost showed me nothing like *this*.'

'The Lost do not understand. This is mammoth.'

Growling, stamping, he stalked away.

Autumn walked up to Icebones. She moved stiffly. 'You are kind to him.'

Icebones rumbled, 'He has a good heart.'

Autumn walked carefully to the lip of the valley. 'It must have been a giant river which carved this valley.'

'Perhaps not a river,' Icebones said. She recalled how she had stood atop the Fire Mountain with the Ragged One, and had seen how the land was uplifted. 'Perhaps the ground was simply broken open.'

'However it was formed, this tusk-gouge lies across our path. Can we walk around it?'

'The Gouge stretches far to the east of here. The land at its edge is high and cold and barren. It would be a difficult trek.'

Autumn raised her trunk and sniffed the warming air that rose from the Gouge. 'I smell water, and grass, and trees,' she said. 'There is life down there.'

'Yes,' Icebones mused. 'If we can reach the floor, perhaps we will find nourishment. We can follow its length, cutting south across the higher land when we near the Footfall itself.'

Autumn walked gingerly along the lip of the Gouge. 'There,' she said.

Icebones made out an immense slope of tumbled rock, piled up against the Gouge wall, reaching from the deep floor almost to its upper surface. As the sun rose further, casting its wan, pink light, the rock slope cast huge shadows. Perhaps there had been a landslide, she thought, the rocks of the wall shaken free by a tremor of the ground.

She murmured doubtfully, 'The rock looks loose and treacherous.'

'Yes. But there might be a way. And—'

A piercing trumpet startled them both. The Ragged One came lumbering up to them.

'I heard what you are saying,' the Ragged One gasped. 'But your trunk does not sniff far, Icebones. There is no need to clamber down into that Gouge and toil along its muddy length.'

Autumn asked mildly, 'Shall we *fly* over?'

The Ragged One snorted. 'We will walk.' And she turned to the west.

When Icebones looked that way she saw a band of pinkish white, picked out by the clear light of the rising sun. It rose from the northern side of the Gouge, on which she stood, and arced smoothly through the air – and it came to rest on the Gouge's far side.

It was a bridge.

Like everything about this immense canyon, the bridge was huge, and it was far away. It took them half a day just to walk to its foot.

The bridge turned out to be a broad shining sheet that emerged from the pink dust as if it had grown there. It sloped sharply upwards, steeply at first, before levelling off. It was wide enough to accommodate four or five mammoths walking abreast.

Icebones probed at its surface with her trunk tip. It was

smooth and cold and hard and smelled of nothing. 'The Lost made this,' she said.

'Of course they did,' snapped the Ragged One. 'Impatient with the Gouge's depth and length, they hurled this mighty bridge right across it. What ambition! What vision!'

'They didn't put anything to eat or drink on it,' Autumn said reasonably.

Thunder stepped forward on to the bridge itself, and stamped heavily at its surface. Where he trod, his dirty foot pads left huge round prints on the gleaming floor. 'It is fragile, like thin ice. What if it is cracked by frost? This bridge was meant for the Lost. They were small creatures, much smaller than us. If we walk on it, perhaps it will fall.'

Icebones rumbled her approval, for the Bull was using the listening skills she had shown him.

But the Ragged One said, 'We will rest the night and feed. We will reach the far side in a day's walk, no more.'

Autumn growled doubtfully.

'No,' Icebones said decisively. 'We should keep away from the things of the Lost. We will climb down the landslide, and—'

'You are a coward and a fool.' The Ragged One's language and posture were clear and determined.

Icebones felt her heart sink. Was this festering sore in their community to be broken open again?

Thunder stepped forward angrily. 'Listen to her. The bridge is not safe.'

'Safe? What is *safe*? Did your precious hero Longtusk ask himself if that famous bridge of land was *safe*?'

'This is not the bridge of Longtusk,' Icebones said steadily. 'And you are not Longtusk.'

The Ragged One stepped back. 'I have endured your

posturing, Icebones, when it did us no harm. But by your own admission you are no Matriarch. And now your foolish arrogance threatens to lead us into disaster. You others should follow me, not her,' she said bluntly.

Autumn, rumbling threateningly, stood by the shoulder of Icebones. 'This one is strange to us,' she said. 'Perhaps she is not yet a Matriarch. But she has displayed wisdom and leadership. And now she is right. There is no need to take the risk of crossing your bridge.'

'Icebones gave me my name,' Thunder said. 'I follow her. *You* are the arrogant one if you cannot tell this bridge is unsafe.' He stood alongside Icebones, and she touched his trunk.

Breeze lumbered towards her mother, her calf tucked safely between her legs. 'You are wrong to divide us. This fighting wastes our energy and time.'

Icebones rumbled, relieved, gratified by their unexpected support. 'Breeze is right. Let us put this behind us—'

'No.' The older sister, Spiral, had spoken. 'We must finish this terrible journey before we all die of hunger, and before another monster leaps out of the sea or sky or ground to consume us. And the quickest way is to take the bridge.'

'*It is not safe*,' Icebones growled.

'So *you* say,' Spiral said angrily. 'But it was made by the Lost. What do you know of the Lost, Icebones? They looked after our every need for a long time – for generations – long before you ever came here.' And, for a moment, behind the gaunt face and the dirty, matted hair, Icebones saw once again the vain, spoiled creature she had first met. 'Shoot? Will you come with me?'

Shoot looked from her mother to her sister and back, dismayed. Then, hesitantly, she stepped up to Spiral.

The Ragged One raised her stubby tusks in triumph. 'We will cross the bridge, we three.'

'No,' Icebones said, gravely anxious. She had not anticipated this turn of events. 'We must not break up the Family.'

'This is no Family here,' said the Ragged One, contemptuous.

'If we stay together we can watch over each other. By splitting us, you endanger us all.'

'If that is so, you must drop your foolish pride and let me lead you, like these two.'

Icebones rumbled, 'I can't. Because you are leading them to their deaths.'

'Then there is nothing more to be said.' The Ragged One turned to face the arcing bridge and stalked away. Spiral followed.

Shoot glanced back at her mother, obviously distressed. But she followed her sister's lead – as, perhaps, she had all her life.

It was another long and difficult night, and it granted Icebones little sleep.

As pink light began to wash over the eastern lands, she walked alone to the edge of the canyon. It was a river of darkness. She listened to the soft chthonic breathing of the rocks beneath her feet, and the gentle ticking of frost, and she strained to hear the rhythm of distant mammoth footsteps.

She called out with deep vibrations of her head and belly and feet: 'Boaster. Can you hear me? It is me, Icebones. Boaster, Boaster . . .'

Icebones. I hear you.

She felt a profound relief, as if she was no longer alone.

We are walking. Every day we walk. The sun is hidden. It rains.

We have come to a huge walled plain covered by something that glitters in the light, even the light of this grey sky. There is nothing to eat on it.

'It is ice.'

No. It is not cold and there is no moisture under my trunk tip.

She shuddered. 'It is a thing of the Lost.'

Yes. There is a great beast, like a beetle, which tends it. The beast wipes away the dust on the floor. My brother challenged the beetle. It turned away.

'Your brother defeated it?'

My brother is brave and strong. But not so brave as me. And he is smaller than me in many ways. Much smaller. For example, his—

'I can guess,' Icebones said dryly. She told him she had decided to head for the basin she had called the Footfall of Kilukpuk. 'But we face many obstacles.' And she told him about the Gouge, and tried to tell him of the mammoths' confusion and dissent.

You think you have problems, he called back. *Imagine how it is for me. All the time I slip up in my own musth dribble, and I trip over my long, erect—*

'You cannot still be in musth.'

Wait until we meet at the Footfall. You will see my musth flow, and you will be awed at its mighty gush. Are you in oestrus yet?

'No,' Icebones said, with a shiver of sadness.

Good, came Boaster's voice, deep-whispering through the rock. *It would be a waste. Wait until we meet at the Footfall. I must go. We have found a dwarf willow and the others are stripping it like wolf cubs, leaving none for me. Be brave, little Icebones. We will meet at the Footfall. Goodbye, goodbye . . .*

Icebones stood alone in the chill, bloody light of dawn, listening to the last of his words wash through the rock.

★

The Ragged One stepped on to the smooth slope of the bridge. She stamped hard on the cold surface, as if testing it under her weight.

The bridge rang hollowly.

More tentatively Shoot followed, and then, at last, Spiral.

Autumn growled, her voice filled with sadness as she watched her daughters walk out into emptiness.

'This is wrong,' Icebones said. 'Wrong, wrong. Mammoths are creatures of the steppe, and the open sky. They are not meant to hover like birds high above the ground.'

But none of the three rebels was listening.

Soon the mammoths had gone so far that they looked like beetles, crawling over the mighty band of the bridge. The sun was still low in the sky, and the three toiling mammoths cast long shadows across the bridge's smooth, pink-lit surface.

Icebones could hear the deep thrumming vibrations of the bridge as it bent and bowed in response to the mammoths' weight.

The Ragged One turned. She trumpeted, her voice dwarfed by the Gouge beneath her. 'You are wrong, all of you. The bridge will protect us. See?' And she raised her foot –

Icebones trumpeted, 'No!'

– and the Ragged One began to stamp, hard, at the shining surface of the bridge.

Icebones heard the cracking long before she could see it. It sounded like pack ice over a swelling sea, or a fragment of bone beneath a clumsy mammoth foot pad.

A spider-web of cracks spread over the pale pink surface. The whole bridge was quivering, and already slivers of it were crumbling off its edges and falling, to be lost far below.

Autumn trumpeted, an ancient, wordless cry, and she ran forward to the edge of the bridge.

Shoot turned back and faced her sister. 'Go back! We must go back!'

But Spiral, last in line, would not move. She stood on the trembling bridge, feet splayed and trunk dipped, as if frozen in place.

'She is terrified,' Breeze said. 'And if she does not move, the others cannot.'

Thunder tossed his head skittishly. 'I will go out there. I will save them.' But there was terror in the white rims of his eyes.

'Your place is here,' Icebones said firmly. 'You must protect these others, and the calf. That is your duty now.'

He tried to hide his relief. 'Yes,' he said. 'That is my duty.'

And my duty, Icebones thought, is to bring the others back – or die trying.

Without thinking about it she stepped on to the cold surface of the bridge. She could feel the deep, dismal resonance of the bridge as it shuddered and shook. The frequent cracks were sharp detonations, carrying clearly to her ears and belly.

She stepped forward gingerly.

Autumn growled, but did not try to stop her.

Soon Icebones had passed beyond the edge of the land, and she could look down into the depths of the Gouge. The rising sun cast deep pink shadows from the layers of cloud, obscuring the brown-grey ground far beneath. She was standing *above* the clouds, she thought, and all that kept her from that immense drop was the fragile thinness of the bridge; her stomach clenched, tight as the jaws of a cat.

At last she reached Spiral. Icebones tugged at her tail until she yelped.

'You must turn around. We have to go back.'

'I can't,' Spiral said, whimpering. The Cow stood rooted as solid as a tree to the thin bridge floor.

Shoot picked her way back along the shuddering bridge. She slapped Spiral's head with her trunk, and even clattered her tusks against her sister's.

At last, under this double assault, Spiral, moaning softly, began to turn. Each footfall was as tentative and nervous as a newborn calf's. Step by step, Icebones led Spiral back towards the cliff top.

They had almost reached the hard, secure rock when there was a harsh trumpet.

Autumn called, '*Shoot!*'

A section of the shuddering bridge had crumbled and fallen away. Icebones could see bits of it falling through the air, sparkling as they spun, diminishing to snowflakes.

And there was nothing beneath Shoot's hind feet.

Shoot fell back, oddly slowly. For a heartbeat she clung to the broken edge of the bridge with her forelegs, and she scrabbled with her trunk. Then she slid back, as smoothly as a drop of water sliding off the tip of a tusk. She wailed, once.

Icebones glimpsed her sprawled in the air, almost absurdly, limbs and trunks and tusks flapping like the wings of a clumsy, misshapen bird. Her fall was agonisingly slow, slow enough for Icebones to hear every whimper and cry, even to smell the urine that gushed into the air around Shoot's legs.

Then she was lost in cloud, and Icebones was grateful.

She heard the trumpeting cry of Spiral, and Autumn's answering wail.

Icebones inspected the crack. It was wide, and getting wider as more chunks of bridge structure fell away like sharp-edged snowflakes.

The Ragged One stood on the far side of the crack, backing away slowly. The damaged bridge was like a great tongue lolling from the remote far side of the Gouge. But as the bridge swung up and down beneath her the Ragged One kept her footing easily.

'You cannot return,' Icebones called.

'I do not choose to return.'

'You will be alone.'

The Ragged One snorted, and stepped back again as more of the bridge fell away. 'I have always been alone. Don't you know that yet?'

'We will meet at the Footfall.'

'Perhaps.' And the Ragged One turned away.

Icebones watched her recede. For all the tragedy and renewed danger her shrunken band would face from now on, a secret part of her was glad that the Ragged One was gone – at least for now.

The bridge trembled and cracked further.

Autumn was still trumpeting, her voice thin and sharp. 'The morning is barely begun. But already my daughter is dead. How can this be?'

The sun rose higher, shining brighter as the blue morning clouds dispersed.

Chapter Two

THE WALK DOWN FROM THE SKY

By midday the mammoths had reached the top of the landslide. Subdued, weary, they scattered in search of forage.

Icebones and Thunder stood at the very edge of the cliff. The Gouge was a river of pink light below them, laced with cloud. The line of the cliff itself was cut back in great scallops, as if some huge animal had taken bites out of it. In one place a broad, deep channel came to an end at the cliff, as if the greater Gouge had simply been cut into the land, leaving the older valley hanging.

The landslide was a great pile of broken rock that fell away into the depths of the Gouge until it disappeared beneath a layer of thin cloud. The slope was pitted by craters, its scree and talus smashed and compressed to a glassy smoothness. Even this landslide was ancient, Icebones realised, old enough to have accumulated the scars of such powerful blows. This was an old world indeed, old upon old.

'We should go *that* way,' Thunder said, looking down at a

point where the landslide slope looked particularly flat and easy. 'And then we can follow that trail.' He meant a rough ridge that had formed in the heaped rubble, zigzagging towards the Gouge floor.

Icebones said, 'But I doubt that any mammoths have walked here before.' Trails made by mammoths had been proven reliable and safe, perhaps over generations. Mammoth trails were part of their deep memory of the world. But there was no memory here. This 'trail' of Thunder's was nothing but a random heaping of rocks. She said at last, 'We cannot move from this place today. The others are not ready for such a challenge.'

'But to lose another day—'

'Your mind is sharp, Thunder. Theirs are crowded by grief. For now, you must continue to study our path. We will rely on you.'

'You are wise,' he said, and resumed his inspection of the path.

That day seemed terribly long – and when it was done, the night seemed even longer.

Autumn had withdrawn into herself once more. Breeze took refuge in the calf, who blundered about oblivious of the greater tragedy around him.

Spiral seemed the worst affected.

At first the tall Cow wailed out her grief loudly. Icebones meant to go to her to comfort her, but Autumn held her back. 'This is how she was with the Lost,' she said harshly. 'When she was hurting, or hungry, or just wanted attention. They would come running to her. We should not go running now. She must bear the burden of what has happened.'

Icebones bowed to the wisdom of the older Cow.

When none of the mammoths responded, Spiral's wails ceased abruptly. She withdrew from the others, seeking out forage in a distracted, half-hearted manner. Then, after a time, she began to make deep, mournful groans, so deep they carried better through the ground than the air, and Icebones saw salty tears well in Spiral's small eyes. At last she was truly grieving, as a mammoth should.

And now Autumn came to her, and wrapped her trunk around her daughter's bowed head.

Icebones, feeling very young, was bemused and distressed by the complexity of the emotions spilling here.

Icebones walked to the edge of the cliff, gathered her courage, and stepped off.

Rubble crunched and compressed under her front feet.

Cautiously she stepped further, bringing her back legs on to the rocky slope. The footing seemed good, and the rock fragments slipped over each other less than she had feared. The surface rocks were worn smooth by dust or water or frost, but some of them were loosely bound together by mats of moss and lichen.

She soon tired, her front legs aching, for it was never comfortable for mammoths to walk downhill. But she persisted, doggedly following the rubble trail Thunder had picked out, listening to the rumbles and grunts of the mammoths who followed her.

The wall of the Gouge loomed behind her. It was striped with bands of varying colour, shades of red and brown, like the rings of a fallen tree. The topmost layer was the thickest, an orange blanket of what appeared to be loose dust. And the wall was carved vertically, marked with huge upright grooves and pillars of rock, perhaps made by rock falls or running water. The grooves cut through the flat strata to make a complex criss-cross pattern. Great flat lids of harder rock stuck out of the wall, sheltering hollowed-out caverns that she climbed past. She made out rustles of movement: birds, perhaps, nesting in these high caves.

This tremendous wall was a complex formation in its own right, she saw, shaped by the vast, slow, inexorable movements of rock and air and water. With its endless detail of strata and carvings and nesting birds, it went on as far as she could see, a vertical world, all the way to the horizon, where it merged in the mist with its remote, parallel twin.

Now she found herself walking into clouds. They were thin, wispy streaks, and they rested on an invisible layer in the air.

She soon passed through the strange cloud lid, into air that was tinged blue, full of mist. The air was noticeably thicker, warmer and moist, and she breathed in deep satisfying lungfuls of it.

The mammoths came to a flat, dusty ledge, still high above the Gouge floor. They fanned out, seeking forage.

Icebones, probing at the ground, found there was vegetation here: yellow and red lichen, mosses, even a little grass. But it was sparse, and the only water was trapped under layers of ice difficult to crack. She knew they must go much deeper before they could be comfortable.

She prepared to move on.

But the calf had other ideas. Woodsmoke reached up to his mother's front leg, lifted his trunk over his fuzzy head, and clamped his mouth to her heavy breast. Icebones could smell the milk that trickled from his mouth. When he was done, he knelt down in his mother's shade and slumped sideways, his eyes closing. His belly rose as he breathed, and his mouth popped open, a circle of darkness.

Time for a nap, it seems, Icebones thought wryly.

The other mammoths gathered around Breeze and her calf. Autumn lifted her heavy trunk and rested it on her tusks. The others let their trunks dangle before them. Only Icebones, in this tall company, was short enough that her trunk reached the ground without her having to dip her head to reach.

The mammoths' bodies swayed gently, in unison. Filled with dust, their thick outer hair caught the pink sunlight, so that each of them was surrounded by a halo of pink-white light.

Immersed in the deep soft breathing of the others, Icebones closed her eyes.

She was woken by a soft, subtle movement.

Spiral had gone to the limit of the ledge, her foot pads compressing soundlessly. Trying not to disturb the others, Icebones followed her.

The afternoon air had grown more clear, and now the deepest world of the Gouge revealed itself. The floor was carved into a series of terraces, and broken up by smaller chasms or chains of hills. And in the deepest section of all she saw the pale glint of water. But it was a straight-line slash that ran right down the length of the Gouge, even cutting through what looked like natural lakes and river tributaries. It was no river but a canal: an artefact of the paws of the Lost.

With trunk raised, Spiral was staring fixedly towards the west. Icebones squinted, trying to make her poor eyes work better.

Over the green-grey floor of the Gouge lay a fine white line.

It crossed the valley from one side to the other, like a scratch through a layer of lichen.

'It is the fallen bridge.'

'Yes,' said Spiral. 'And that is where Shoot lies, crushed like an egg. Should we go back and look for her corpse? That is your way, isn't it? The wolves and birds will have taken the meat and guts and eyes by now. But if the bones are not too scattered—'

'Stop this,' Icebones snapped, with all the Matriarchal command she could muster. 'You must not think of your sister in death. Think of *her*.'

Spiral reached forward with her trunk, as if seeking the ghost of her vanished sister. Hesitantly she said, 'She was – funny. She was loyal. She always stuck by me. Sometimes that would annoy me. Some of the Lost thought she was cuter than me and would give her attention . . .'

'I can see how that would irritate you,' Icebones said gently.

Spiral had the grace to snort, mocking herself. 'She followed me. *Me*. And I betrayed her trust by leading her to her death.'

Icebones groped for something to say. 'Sometimes we have no choice about how we act. Sometimes, *we cannot save even those we love*. That is what the Cycle tells us, over and over.' And that hard fact would be the most unpalatable truth of all for these untutored mammoths, if they ever had to face it.

But Spiral was still distant, wounded, and the Cycle seemed a dusty abstraction.

Icebones thought, Thunder, Autumn, Spiral: all of them suffused by guilt, agonised by the mistakes they felt they had made. It was because they had always been under the care of the Lost. It was because they had never had to act for themselves.

Wisdom must be earned, through pain and loss. That was what these mammoths were struggling to learn.

The mammoths were beginning to stir, blowing dust from their trunks. The calf, revived and excited, bumped against their legs.

They reached a new, steep slope of loose talus. It was more difficult to climb down, but it delivered them to the warmer, moister air more quickly, and they pushed forward with enthusiasm.

Abruptly they emerged on to a broad terrace. Stepping forward stiffly, relieved to be on flat ground again, Icebones immediately felt a soft crackle beneath one foot pad. It was the sprawled-out branch of a dwarf birch. Looking ahead, she could see that the ground was littered with patches of open water.

The mammoths fanned out, emitting grunts of pleasure as they found tufts of grass and clumps of herbs.

Icebones walked to the crumbled lip of the terrace, and found herself in a strange world.

The Gouge's mighty walls ran roughly straight, but they were complex even from this perspective, full of great scraped-out bays separated by knife-sharp ridges. Everywhere she saw landslides: rock skirts, sloping sharply, leaning against the walls. In one place, she saw, a giant landslide had swept right across the wide Gouge floor and come washing up against the far wall.

The walls were so tall they rose up above the clouds. And they were still visible even at the horizon, as if a notch had been taken out of the very planet.

Thin, high cries fell on her like snowflakes. Peering up, she saw geese flying away from the sun in a vast, crowded formation, skimming through the strip of sky enclosed by the walls. The wall itself was pocked with ledges and pits where birds nested: guillemots, murres, kittiwakes and gulls. The birds flew back and forth against the cliff face, their wings flashing bright against the huge wall's brooding crimson.

Below the level of this terrace, the steppe-like terrain gave way to a forest of spruce, pine, aspen: cold-resistant trees so tall they seemed to be straining to reach the sky. And beyond them she saw the glimmer of water. It was the canal, the straight-line cut through the Gouge's deepest part. Alongside the canal more trees grew, but these were fat, water-rich broadleaf trees, oak and elm and maple, basking in the comparative warmth of those depths. She glimpsed a sea of shining black washing along the valley – a herd of migrant animals: bison, reindeer, maybe even horses.

The air over these deeper parts of the Gouge floor shone pink-gold, full of moisture and dust, and the green and blue of water and life overlaid the strong red colour of the underlying rock, making a startling contrast. But the thin scraping of life was utterly overwhelmed by the mighty geology that bounded it. And every sound she heard, every rumble that came to her through the ground, was shaped by those tremendous cliffs.

This was a walled world.

Woodsmoke came running floppily before her, his fuzzy-haired head bobbing up and down, his trunk exploring the ground as he ran. 'Which way? Which way, Icebones? Which way?'

Icebones peered east, away from the setting sun. Her shadow fled along the ground before her, straight along the Gouge floor, a thing of spindly legs and stretched-out body – just like a native-born mammoth, she thought.

She scratched the calf's scalp with her trunk fingers. 'Follow your shadow, Woodsmoke.'

The calf lolloped away, trumpeting his excitement, and his thin cries echoed from the Gouge's mighty walls.

Chapter Three

THE WALLED WORLD

The Gouge's floor was carved by lesser valleys and twisting ridges. Lakes pooled, linked by the cruel gash of that central canal. The lakes were crowded with reeds and littered with ducks and geese. Around their shores forests grew, mighty oaks that stretched up so high their upper branches were lost in mist.

The mammoths would come down to the lakes' gravelly beaches to sip water that was mostly free of salt, even if it fizzed uncomfortably in Icebones's trunk. But the lower ground was softer and frequently boggy, and nothing grew there but bland uninterrupted grasses, or tall coniferous trees, neither of which provided food that sustained mammoths well. They generally kept to higher ground, where grew a rich mosaic vegetation of grass, herbs, shrubs and trees, providing a healthy diet.

They often glimpsed other animals: Icebones recognised reindeer, horses, bison and musk oxen, lemmings and rabbits, and she saw the spoor of creatures who fed off the grazing herds, like wolves and foxes. The smaller animals seemed about the size she recalled from the Island. But the reindeer and horses were very tall, with spindly legs that scarcely seemed capable of supporting their weight.

The long-legged rabbits could bound spectacularly high into the air. But they fell back with eerie slowness, making them tempting targets for diving raptor birds.

For a while an arctic fox followed the mammoths, sniffing their dung. The fox was in his winter coat, a gleaming white so intense it was almost blue. The fox moved with anxious, purposeful movements over a network of trails, undetectable to Icebones. He was no threat to the mammoths, but the fox was an efficient scavenger of food, a hunter of lemmings and eggs and helpless chicks who might fall from a cliff-side nest. Somehow she found it reassuring to see this familiar rogue prospering in this peculiar landscape.

But still, though the Gouge was crowded with life compared to the upper plains from which they had descended, on the higher ground they passed lakes that had dried up, leaving only bowls of cracked mud. Even here, in this strange walled world, the tide of life was inexorably receding.

Icebones inspected one such mud bowl gloomily. It was churned by many hoof marks, and littered with bits of bone, cracked and scored by the teeth and beaks of scavengers. When the water had vanished, animals, dying of thirst, had congregated here to die – and had then provided easy meat for the predators. She tried to imagine the scenes here as adult jostled with adult, fighting for water, maddened by thirst, and the young and old and weak were pushed aside. And she wondered if any of these bits of well-chewed bone had once belonged to mammoths.

She kept these reflections to herself – but she sensed from

Autumn's reflective silence that the older Cow at least understood this.

But meanwhile the walking was steady, the weather on the Gouge floor calm, the grazing good. The mammoths gradually became more confident, their bellies filling, and the steady rhythms of life banished their lingering grief over the loss of Shoot.

The calf helped, of course.

His scrawny little body filled out, becoming almost burly. His newborn's hair was growing out, his underfur thicker, his coarser overfur longer. But his hair was still a bright pink-brown, much lighter than that of adult mammoths. He would gallop on stiff legs, leaving an uneven set of clumsy tracks – only to come to a sudden halt, trunk raised to sniff the air, his low forehead wrinkled with concentration. Or he would scoop up loose grass, suck, sniff, blow out dust, and run about as if trying to explore every detail of the ground they crossed. He picked dust and earth and insects from his thickening coat, and with wide-eyed curiosity he would pop each item into his mouth, more often than not spitting it out again.

He was still dependent on his mother's milk, but Icebones made sure he was happy to be cared for by the others. Spiral, in particular, relished looking after him – so much so, in fact, that Icebones sometimes wondered if she was growing jealous that he wasn't her own.

Though Icebones never spoke it out loud, all of this was a preparation against the dire possibility that Woodsmoke might lose his mother. No mammoth was more vulnerable than a calf without a mother.

But for now, Woodsmoke was secure and happy, and busy

with his exploration of the intriguing world in which he found himself.

One day the calf began to play with a lemming that had, unwisely, not retreated to its burrow as the mammoths' heavy footfalls approached.

'That lemming is not happy,' commented Thunder.

Icebones recalled the Cycle. '*No animal likes to be disturbed.*'

Thunder rumbled deeply. 'You often quote your Cycle. But how do you *know* the Cycle is true?'

She noticed he was walking stiffly. He held his head high, and his legs were stiff, as if sore. Everything about him seemed larger than usual. And, she thought, there was an odd smell about him: something sweet, pervasive, sharp.

He went on, '*You* didn't live in the times of long ago when herds of mammoths darkened the steppe. *You* never met Longtusk or Ganesha or Kilukpuk or any of the rest. Perhaps it is all the murmurings of calves, or foolish old Bulls.'

She bridled at that. No mammoth should speak so disrespectfully of the Cycle, the heart of mammoth culture. But then, she reminded herself, Thunder had been brought up in ignorance. It wasn't his fault, and it was her role to put that right.

'Thunder, you must understand that every mammoth alive today is descended from survivors: mammoths who mastered the world well enough to reach adulthood and raise healthy calves, who grew up in their turn. The Cycle is the wisdom of that great chain of survivors, accumulated over more generations than there are stars in the sky.'

'But *this is a different place.* You say that yourself. Perhaps no mammoths lived here before the Lost brought us. What use is the Cycle to us?'

'While we live, we must not be afraid to *add* to the Cycle. Ganesha taught us that, and Longtusk. The Cycle will never be complete. Not while mammoths live and learn. There is completeness only in extinction . . .'

But she felt that such comfort, embedded in the Cycle itself, was thin.

And perhaps Thunder was right.

This Sky Steppe was itself a part of the Cycle. But whereas the rest of the Cycle was a memory of the past, the Sky Steppe had always been a vision of the *future*: a glittering, succulent promise of days to come.

Sometimes, when this small red world seemed so strange, she wondered if perhaps nothing around her was real. Maybe she was living in a moment embedded in the vision, of a mammoth long dead – Kilukpuk herself, perhaps. *And in that case she was part of that dream too.* She was living thoughts, just a concoction of memories and dreams, with no more life than the reconstructed bones of the mammoth on the Fire Mountain.

But now Woodsmoke brayed and yelled, 'I am a great Bull. I will mate you all, you Cows!' His thin cries and milky scent, and the iron stink of the dust he kicked up, were sharp intrusions of reality into her maundering.

The calf started dancing in a tight circle around the lemming. The little rodent sat as if frozen, clearly wishing this huge monster would go away. Then Woodsmoke made a mock charge, head lowered. The lemming, snapping out of its trance, turned tail and shot across the ground, a muddy brown blur, until it reached a hole and disappeared:

Woodsmoke's mother cuffed him affectionately and tucked him under her belly, where the great Bull was soon seeking out his mother's milk.

Thunder growled. 'That little scrap is mocking me.'

'He is playing at what he will become.'

'But he was threatening a *lemming*.'

'He has to start somewhere. If there were other calves here, he would wrestle with them and stage little tusk-clashes. It is all part of his preparation for the battles he must wage as an adult.'

Thunder growled again. 'Perhaps. But when that wretched calf approaches me, reaching up with his grass-blade trunk to wrestle, I want to throw him out of the Gouge . . .'

Suspicious now, she sniffed at the ground over which Thunder had walked, smelling his urine, which was hissing slightly as it settled into the red dust. And she probed at the thick hair before his ears with her trunk fingers. She found a dark, sticky liquid trickling from his temporal gland.

'Thunder – you are in musth!'

He rumbled deeply. It was the musth call, she realised. Without understanding it he was calling to oestrus Cows, if any had been here to listen. 'I thought I was ill.'

'Not ill.' She stroked the temporal glands on both sides of his head. They were swollen. 'You are sore here.' Gently she lifted his trunk and had him coil it so it rested on its tusks. 'That will relieve the pressure on one side of your face at least.'

'Icebones, what is happening to me? I roam around this Gouge listening, but I don't know what for. The Cows keep their distance from me – even you.'

It was true, she realised. She had responded to his calls without thinking. She said carefully, 'Musth means that you are ready to mate. Your smell, and the rumbles you make, announce your readiness to any receptive Cows. The aggression you feel is meant to be turned on other Bulls, for Bulls

145

must always fight to prove they are fit to sire calves. But here there are no Bulls for you to fight – none save Woodsmoke, and you have shown the correct restraint.'

He growled, 'But there are Cows.'

'None of us is in oestrus, Thunder,' she said gently. 'You will learn to tell that from the smell of our urine. None of us is ready.'

She felt his trunk probe at her belly. 'Not even you?'

'Not even me, Thunder. I am sorry.' Again she was struck by the fact that she had still not come into oestrus, had felt not so much as a single twinge of that great inner warmth in all the time she had been here. 'Don't worry. In a few days this will pass and you will feel normal again.'

He grunted. 'I hope so.'

In fact she suspected that even if one of the Cows were in oestrus, right here and right now, still Thunder would fail to find himself a mate. He was clearly young and immature, and no Cow would willingly accept a mating with such a Bull. If there were other Bulls here he wouldn't even get a chance, of course. For his first few musth seasons Thunder would simply be overpowered by the older, mature Bulls.

He pulled away, grumbling his disappointment. He raised his tusks into the shining sunlit air, and a swarm of insects, rising from a muddy pond, buzzed around his head, glowing with light. 'I feel as if my belly will burst like an overripe fruit. Why, if she were here before me now, I would mate with old Kilukpuk herself—'

'Who speaks of Kilukpuk?'

Thunder brayed, startled, and stopped dead. The voice – like a mammoth's, but shallow and indistinct – had seemed to come from the reaches of the pond ahead of them.

'What is it?' Thunder asked softly. 'Can there be mammoths here?'

Icebones grunted. 'What kind of mammoth lives in the middle of a pond?'

'Kilukpuk, Kilukpuk . . . How is it I know that name?'

And a trunk poked up out of the water, and two wide nostrils twitched. It was short, hairless, stubby, but nevertheless indubitably a trunk.

Icebones stepped forward. The mud squeezed between her toes, unpleasantly thick, cold and moist. 'I am Icebones, daughter of Silverhair. If you are mammoth, show yourself.'

A head broke above the surface of the water. Icebones saw a smooth brow with two small eyes set on top, peering at her. 'Mammoth? I never heard of such things. *Bones-Of-Ice?* What kind of name is that?' The creature sniffed loudly. 'Don't drop your dung in my pond.'

Thunder growled, 'If you don't show yourself I will come in there and drag you out. *Before* I fill up your pond with my dung.'

Thunder's musth-fuelled aggression was out of place, Icebones thought. But it seemed to do the trick.

There was a loud, indignant gurgle. With a powerful heave, a squat body broke through the languidly rippling water.

It stood out of the water on four stubby legs. It had powerful shoulders and rump, and a long skull topped by those small, glittering eyes. It wasn't quite hairless, for fine downy hairs lay plastered over its skin, smoothed back like the scales of a fish. But the whole body was so heavily coated in crimson-brown mud that it was hard to see anything at all.

It was like no mammoth Icebones had ever seen. And yet it

had a trunk, and even two small tusks that protruded from its mouth, curling slightly and pointing downwards. And it gazed at Icebones with frank curiosity, its stubby trunk raised.

More of the hog-like creatures came drifting through the water. They looked like floating logs, Icebones thought, though thick bubbles showed where they belched or farted.

Meanwhile the other mammoths gathered around Icebones and Thunder – all save the calf. Woodsmoke, quickly bored, had splashed into the mud at the fringe of the pond and was digging out lumps of it with his tusks.

Spiral asked, 'What *is* it?'

The creature in the pond said, '*It* is Chaser-Of-Frogs. I am the Mother of the Family that lives here.'

Evidently, Icebones thought dryly, her dignity was easily hurt. '*Mother?* You are a Matriarch?'

Chaser-Of-Frogs eyed Icebones suspiciously. 'I do not know you, Bones-Of-Ice. Do you come from the Pond of Evening?'

She must mean one of the lakes to the west of here, Icebones thought. She said, 'I come from a place far from here, which—'

Chaser-Of-Frogs grunted and buried her snout-like trunk in pond-bottom mud. 'Always making trouble, that lot from Evening. Even though my own daughter mated with one of them. When you go back you can tell them that Chaser-Of-Frogs said—'

Thunder growled and stepped forward. 'Listen to her, you floating fool. We come from no pond. *We are not like you.*'

'And yet we are,' Icebones said, drawn to the pond's edge, trunk raised. She could smell foetid mud, laced with thin dung. 'You have tusks and a trunk. You are my Cousin.'

'Cousin?' The glittering eyes of the not-mammoth stared back at her, curious in their own way. 'Tell me of Kilukpuk. I know that name . . . and yet I do not.'

'It is an old name,' Icebones said. 'Mammoths and their Cousins are born with it on their tongues.' And Icebones spoke of Kilukpuk, and of Kilukpuk's rivalry with her brother, Aglu, and of Kilukpuk's calves, Hyros and Siros, who had squabbled and fought in their jealousy, of Kilukpuk's favourite, Probos, and how Probos had become Matriarch of all the mammoths and their Cousins . . .

Her own nascent Family clustered around her. The log-like bodies in the pond drifted close to the shallow muddy beach, tiny ears pricked, the silence broken only by occasional gulping farts that broke the surface of the water.

'I have never heard such tales,' mused Chaser-Of-Frogs. 'But it is apt. I sink in the mud, as did Kilukpuk in her swamp. I browse on the plants that grow in the pond-bottom ooze, as she must have done. I am as she was.' She seemed proud – but she was so caked in mud it was hard to tell.

How strange, Icebones thought. Could it be that these Swamp-Mammoths really were ancient forms, remade for this new world? Perhaps they had been moulded from mammoths, the way Woodsmoke was moulding lumps of mud.

Only the Lost would do such a thing, of course. And only the Lost knew *why*.

'You mammoths,' said Chaser-Of-Frogs now. 'Tell me where you are going.'

'To the east,' Thunder said promptly. 'We are walking around the belly of the world. We are seeking a place we call the Footfall of Kilukpuk—'

'You will not get far,' Chaser-Of-Frogs said firmly. 'Not unless you know your way through the Nest of the Lost.'

Thunder growled, 'What Nest?'

Chaser-Of-Frogs snorted, and bits of snot and mud flew into the air. 'You've never even heard of it? Then you will soon be running like a calf for her mother's teat.' She sank into her mud, submerging save for the crest of her back and the tip of her trunk.

Then she rose again lazily, as if having second thoughts. 'I will show you. Tomorrow. It is in gratitude for the stories, which I enjoyed. Today I will rest and eat, making myself ready.'

Thunder said, 'You fat log, you look as if you have spent your whole life resting and eating.'

Autumn slapped his forehead. 'She will hear you.'

Chaser-Of-Frogs surfaced again. 'Don't forget. No dung in the pond. Those disease-ridden scoundrels from Evening are always playing that trick. I won't have it, you hear?'

'We won't,' said Icebones.

Chaser-Of-Frogs slid beneath the dirty brown water and, with a final valedictory fart, swam away.

Chapter Four

THE NEST OF THE LOST

The ground stank of night things: of roots, of dew, of worms, of the tiny reptiles and mammals that burrowed through it.

All the mammoths found it difficult to settle. They were deeper into the Gouge than they were accustomed to. The air felt moist and sticky, and was full of the stink of murky pond water. The vegetation was too thick and wet for a mammoth's gut, and soon all of their stomachs were growling in protest.

Icebones could sense the deep wash of fat log-like bodies as the Swamp-Mammoths swam and rolled in their sticky water. Not a heartbeat went by without a fart or belch or muddy splash, or a grumble about a neighbour's crowding or stealing food.

And, as the light faded from the western sky, a new light rose in the east to take its place: a false dawn, Icebones thought, a glowing dome of dusty air, eerily yellow. It was the Nest of the Lost, of course, just as Chaser-Of-Frogs had warned.

Autumn, Breeze and Thunder faced the yellow light,

sniffing the air with suspicious raised trunks. It pleased Icebones to see that they were starting to find their true instincts, buried under generations of the Lost's unwelcome attention.

Not Spiral, though. She started trotting to and fro, lifting her head and raising her fine tusks so they shone in the unnatural light.

As the true dawn approached, Icebones heard the pad of clumsy footsteps. It was Chaser-Of-Frogs.

In the pink-grey half-light the Swamp-Mammoth stood before them, her stubby trunk raised. Her barrel of a body was coated in mud that crackled with frost, her breath steamed around her face, and her broad feet left round damp marks where she passed. 'Are you ready? *Urgh*. Your dung stinks.'

'The food here is bad for us,' Autumn growled.

'Just as well you're leaving, then,' Chaser-Of-Frogs said. 'Go drop a little of that foul stuff in the Pond of Evening, will you? Hey! What's this?'

Woodsmoke had run around to Chaser-Of-Frogs's side and was scrambling on her back. He was taller than she was. He already had his legs hooked over her spine, and he was pulling with his trunk at the sparse hair that grew there. 'I am a Bull, strong and fierce. What are you? If you are a Cow I will mate with you.'

'Get him off! Get him off!' Chaser-Of-Frogs turned her head this way and that, trying to reach him, but her neck was too rigid, her trunk much too small.

Autumn stalked forward and, with an imperious gesture, wrapped her trunk around the calf and lifted him up in the air.

Woodsmoke's little face peered out through a forest of trunk hair. 'I want to mate with it!'

Chaser-Of-Frogs growled and backed away. 'Try it and I'll kick you so hard you'll finish up beyond the next pond, you little guano lump.'

'He's only a calf,' Breeze rumbled.

'I know. I've had four of my own. Just keep him from being a calf around me.'

Icebones said gravely, 'We saw the lights. The Nest of the Lost. We need your guidance, Chaser-Of-Frogs. Please.'

Chaser-Of-Frogs growled again, but evidently her dignity wasn't too badly bruised. She sniffed the breeze. 'Let's go. We must keep up a good pace, for there's nothing to eat in there. But keep this in mind. Whatever you see – *there's nothing to fear.*'

And, without hesitation, she set off across the swampy ground to the east.

Icebones, suppressing her own uneasiness, strode purposefully after her. She could hear the massive shuffle of the mammoths as they gathered in a loose line behind her.

The mammoths followed the bank of the canal. The waterway arrowed straight east, so that the rising sun hung directly over the lapping water, as if to guide their way.

The Gouge here lacked the tidy clarity of its western sections. The walls were broken and eroded, as if they had been drowned beneath an immense, catastrophic flood. The floor terrain was difficult, broken land, littered with huge, eroded rock fragments or covered in steep dust dunes.

But the land close to the canal was levelled: as smooth as the surface of Chaser-Of-Frogs's mud pond.

'I've heard of this place,' said Autumn. 'Once mammoths were bound up with rope, and made to pull great floating things along the length of this shining water.'

Icebones rumbled uncomfortably. She sensed that even Autumn missed something of the certainty of those days, when the Lost ran the world and everything in it.

There was movement on the canal's oily waters. Thunder backed away from the water's edge, perhaps recalling the whale that had come so close to taking Shoot in the Ocean of the North.

But this was no whale. It swam over the surface of the water, a massive straight-edged slab. It had no eyes or ears or trunk or feet. Huge slow waves trailed after it, feathering gracefully.

Autumn growled to Icebones, 'It is obviously a thing of the Lost. And, look – it has a shining shell, like the ice beetle in the crater.'

The huge water beetle drifted to a halt against the canal bank. A straight-edged hole in its side opened up, like a mouth, and a tongue of shining material stuck out and nuzzled against the land. Then the beetle waited, bobbing gently as the waves it had made rippled under it, and its carapace glistened in the dusty sunlight.

Nothing climbed aboard the beetle, and nothing came out of its mouth.

After a time the beetle rolled in its tongue, shut its strange mouth, and pushed its way gently further down the canal. After a time it stopped again, and Icebones saw that once more it opened its mouth, waiting, waiting.

Chaser-Of-Frogs growled, 'Every morning it is the same. This water-thing toils up and down the canal, sticking out its tongue. This is the way of things here. Everything you see will be strange and useless. Nothing will do you harm. Come now.' She stumped on.

They followed, walking beside the shore of the canal, while the waves of the beetle slowly rippled and subsided.

Soon they approached vast spires, slender and impossibly tall, taller than the greatest tree even on this tall planet. The gathering sunlight seeped into the spires, so they were filled with glowing pink light.

As they approached these glittering visions all the mammoths grew perturbed.

When Icebones looked into a spire she was startled to see another mammoth gazing back at her: a somewhat ragged, sunken-eyed, ill-fed Cow staring back at her from the depths of a glimmering pink pool. The mammoth had no smell and made no noise – for it was herself, of course, a reflection just as if she was staring into a pool of still water. But this 'pool' had been set on edge by the strange arts of the Lost, and its strangeness disturbed her, right to the warm core of her being.

Woodsmoke came running from between his mother's legs, trumpeting a shrill greeting. He ran straight into the shining wall and went sprawling, a mess of legs and trunk. Mewling a protest, he got up and trotted back to the wall. He raised his trunk at the mammoth calf he could see there, and the other calf raised its trunk back. With a comical growl, Woodsmoke tried to butt the other mammoth, only to find himself clattering against the wall again.

He might have kept that up all day, Icebones thought, if his mother hadn't come to tuck him between her legs again.

'I am bigger than him. Did you see? My tusks were bigger than his. He was frightened of me. He ran away.'

'Yes. Yes, he ran away.'

There were buildings all around them now, of all sizes and shapes and colours, all characterised by hard, cold straight lines. And there were tall angular shapes, like trees denuded of their branches. These 'trees' had a single fat fruit suspended from their top. Many of the fruit had fallen and smashed, but from others an eerie yellow light glowed, perhaps the source of the light Icebones had observed during the night.

The trails between the buildings were littered with red dust, and as the mammoths passed, their feet left clear round imprints. Many of the buildings showed signs of damage, their walls broken by huge rough-edged holes. In corners of the great avenues there were heaps of debris, branches and dust and bones, smashed up and dumped here as if by some great storm. It was evident that this place had been abandoned for some time.

Icebones was aware of Spiral's growing, silent dismay; she would not find the Lost here.

Suddenly, from all over the Nest, boxy beetles came scurrying.

The mammoths stopped dead, and Breeze trumpeted alarm.

The beetles began to rush from one silent building to another. A mouth would open in the hide of a beetle, and another would open to greet it in the gleaming side of the building, and the beetle would wait – just as the water-beetle had waited by the side of the canal. But nothing came to climb into or out of the beetle, no matter how long it waited. At last the beetle would close itself up again and scuttle off to its next fruitless rendezvous.

As suddenly as it had begun, the swarm of beetles thinned out. The last beetles shut their mouths and hurtled off out of sight.

But now another crowd of toiling beetles hurried between the buildings. These creatures sprouted arms and scrapers and trunk-like hoses, and they swept at the dust, making it rise in billowing red clouds into the air. But the dust would merely settle again once they had passed.

One toiling beetle scurried after the mammoths. It scraped up their dung and placed it into a wide mouth in its own side, and then polished at the floor until no trace of the dung was left. Thunder went up to the beetle and kicked it so hard that he opened up a new mouth in its side. After that, mewling to itself, the beetle moved only in tight circles, endlessly polishing the same piece of ground.

As the sun climbed higher in the sky, they moved away from the spires and scurrying beetles and reached an open area. This abutted the bank of the canal, and it was surrounded by a half-circle of low structures, like a row of wolf's teeth. The floor surface here was hard under their feet, and the light glimmered from it, pink and bright.

Suddenly, all at the same instant, the structures snapped open, revealing black, cavernous interiors. And all the mammoths recoiled, for they smelled the greasy stink of scorched flesh.

From nowhere gulls appeared, cawing. They soared down on huge filmy wings and pecked at the small buildings and the floor around them. Icebones even spotted a fox that came padding silently across the shining floor. The gulls cawed in protest at this intruder.

Spiral cast to and fro, nervous, skittish. 'It is the smell of food.'

'Broiled flesh?' Icebones said. 'What kind of food is that?'

'It is the food of the Lost,' Autumn said grimly.

Breeze said, 'Maybe this is a place where the Lost would come to feed.'

'But if that's so,' Spiral said anxiously, 'where are they?'

'Long gone,' Autumn said. She reached for her daughter.

But Spiral pulled away. Trumpeting, as if calling the small-eared Lost, she ran clumsily from structure to structure.

No Lost came to eat. After a time the structures snapped closed once more, scattering the gulls.

Chaser-Of-Frogs sneezed, and dusty snot gushed out of her trunk. She said brightly, 'All this talk of food is making me thirsty. Come. Let us find water.' Briskly, she turned and began to plod steadily down the canal bank, squat, solid, determined.

Following the canal, they came to a new set of structures, situated at the base of a broad valley. From all over the valley, fat pipes, heavily swathed by some silvery skin, erupted from the ground and converged on this place.

One structure was an inverted wedge of dull grey. It had grilles along its sides, and it was tipped by four giant tubes from which white steam plumed with a continual rushing noise. Icebones saw that water, condensing from the billowing steam, dribbled down the walls. Chaser-Of-Frogs lapped at this with her trunk.

Icebones did likewise, with less enthusiasm. The water was fine, she supposed, but it was too warm, and it tasted of sulphur and iron, and of something else indefinable – *something of the Lost*, she thought.

But she was thirsty, and forced herself to drink her fill.

Soon the others joined her and drank with more apparent enjoyment, for they were more used to accepting water from the Lost than she was.

Chaser-Of-Frogs called, 'Bones-Of-Ice. Come stand here.'

Icebones complied, and, following Chaser-Of-Frogs's urging, leaned gently against a pipe that was almost as tall as she was. The pipe was warm.

Chaser-Of-Frogs barked amusement. 'The pipe contains warm water. The water comes from lodes of warmth buried deep under the skin of the world. And that is what keeps the Nest alive,' she said. 'You see?'

'Not really,' admitted Icebones.

'I do,' said Thunder unexpectedly. 'Didn't Longtusk stamp his feet and draw heat from the ground, to keep his Family alive . . . ?'

Now Chaser-Of-Frogs wandered away from the water plant. Grunting, she began pawing at the ground with her forefeet. With clumsy swipes, the Swamp-Mammoth had soon wiped clear a wide area of the floor.

Icebones saw there were shapes embedded in the shining floor. She leaned down to see better, and blew away more dust with delicate sweeps of her trunk.

She saw leaves, stuck inside the shining floor surface. The leaves were grey and colourless, and they lay in thick sheets, one over the other. She stroked the floor with her trunk, but she touched only the hard, odourless floor surface.

'What do you think of *that*?' Chaser-Of-Frogs demanded proudly.

'They are like no tree I have ever seen.'

'Now look over here.' The Swamp-Mammoth led Icebones to another place, where she swept aside the dust once more.

Here, inside the floor, Icebones saw the shells of animals from the sea – and bones. They were pretty, regular shapes, she thought, sharing a six-fold pattern: six leaves, six stubby limbs, six petals.

Chaser-Of-Frogs said gently, 'These are the bones of creatures who lived here long, long ago – before the Lost ever came here. When you die, Bones-Of-Ice, you will be covered by mud and dust that will squeeze you flat. Until—'

'Until I become like *this*,' Icebones said, awed. 'Where I was born, the bones of mammoths lay thick in the ground. I thought there were no bones here – just as there are no mammoth trails. But I was wrong.'

'These are not the bones of our kind, Cousin. I was not always the Mother of the Big Pond. The Mother before me said that *her* Mother saw the Lost and their toiling beetles dig this strange bone-filled rock out of the Gouge wall – deep down, at its lowest layers. These squashed animals died long ago, you see. And nothing lived after them, so nothing was laid down over them but bare, dead rock, a great thickness of it. And the Lost took the bony rock and put it here.'

'Why?'

Chaser-Of-Frogs grunted. 'Who knows why the Lost do as they do?'

Icebones pondered the meaning of the rock. She pressed, frustrated, at the impenetrable surface, longing to touch and smell the ancient plants, to hear the voices of the animals.

Long ago there was life here. There had been trees, and living oceans, and beasts that roamed the crimson lands. But their world died. The oceans froze over and dried up, and the air cooled, and the last rain fell, and the last snow . . . Now all that was left of them was here, in this rock, compressed flat by time.

Clumsily, self-consciously, Chaser-Of-Frogs turned her

back and pawed at the ground, trying to touch the bones with her hind feet.

'You are Remembering,' Icebones said.

Chaser-Of-Frogs stopped, panting – used to her lethargic life in the mud, she got out of breath easily – and she looked up at Icebones with her small hard eyes. 'Do you think we are foolish?'

'No. I think you are wise.'

Chaser-Of-Frogs eyed her. 'Bones-Of-Ice, I am done here. I am a poor fighter of wolves. I must go back before dark. You will go on. Just follow the canal.'

Suddenly the thought of being without the squat, humorous, courageous Swamp-Mammoth seemed unbearable. Impulsively Icebones twined her trunk around the other's. 'Come with us.'

Chaser-Of-Frogs snorted. 'What for, Cousin?'

'The world is dying – just as it died before, ending the lives of those buried creatures . . .' Icebones explained how she was leading the mammoths to the basin she had called the Footfall of Kilukpuk, the deepest place in the world, where she hoped enough air and water would pool to keep the mammoths alive. 'Come with us.'

'Me?' Chaser-Of-Frogs grunted, self-deprecating. 'Look at me. I can scarcely trudge over an ice-flat plain for half a day before I am exhausted. How could I walk around the world?'

'I'm serious—'

'So am I,' Chaser-Of-Frogs snapped. 'Bones-Of-Ice, I am no fool. I can smell it myself. Every year the line of trees creeps further down the Gouge wall. Every year our ponds shrink, just that bit more. Every year I see more animals migrate one way up the Gouge than come back the other. But look at me, Bones-Of-Ice. I could not contemplate such a trek as yours . . . Not yet, anyhow. I smell wisdom on you, young Bones-Of-Ice, but you have much to learn. You see, my calves are not yet *desperate* enough.'

'I don't see what desperation has to do with it.'

Chaser-Of-Frogs said bluntly, 'A trek to your Footfall pit would kill most of us. That is the truth. And *that* is why we must be desperate before we accept such suffering.'

Icebones was taken aback. 'We will help you.'

'Why should you? You never knew us before. We aren't your kind. We aren't even like you.'

'We are Cousins, and we are bound by the Oath of Kilukpuk.'

Chaser-Of-Frogs grunted. 'My dear Bones-Of-Ice, you have enough to do.' The Swamp-Mammoth waddled away, towards the light of the setting sun. 'I'll tell you what. I will seek out your scent at the Footfall. And if those piss-drinkers from the Pond of Evening get there before me, make sure you save the best pond for me . . .'

The next morning the Lost-made canal, which had guided them eastward for so long, finished its course.

Icebones stood at its head, before a square-edged termination whose regularity made her shudder. From here the canal arced back towards the west, a line of water straight as a sunbeam all the way to the horizon. She glimpsed the Nest of the Lost. In the uncertain light of morning, the fruits of the light-trees were glowing in broken rows. Beetles clanked to and fro once more, opening their mouths for anybody who wanted to ride in them, and the food places opened, sending out thick smells of meat and drink for anybody who cared to call. But nobody came, nobody but the gulls.

There was a flash of light, a distant crack like thunder.

Flinching, Icebones raised her trunk.

The sun was buried in a dense layer of mist and blue ice clouds at the eastern horizon, a band of light framed by the Gouge's silhouetted walls. The sky was clear, the world as peaceful as it ever got. *What storm comes out of a clear sky . . . ?*

Now there was another flash. She peered to the east, where she thought the flash had come from.

The sun was swimming in the sky, sliding from side to side and pulsating in size. A line of light darted down from the sun's disc, connecting it to the ground, like a huge glowing trunk reaching down through the dusty air. She heard a remote sound, deep and complex – like a landslide, or the cracking of a rock under frost or heat.

She blinked her eyes, seeking to clear them of water. When she stared again into the sun she could see its disc quite clearly, whole and round and unperturbed.

She lowered her head, searching for grass and water, trying to forget the strangeness, to put aside her deep unease.

Chapter Five

THE SKUA

They were in difficult country.

The Gouge floor was crumpled into ridges and eroded hillocks, pitted by depressions where water pooled, and littered with vast pocked boulders. Progress was slow, and all the mammoths were weary and fractious.

The Gouge walls were now further apart and badly defined. The nearest wall was a band of deep shadow, striped by orange dawn light at its crest. And it was pocked by huge round holes, as regular as the pits left by raindrops in sand. Inside the holes the wall surface looked glassy, as if coated in ice.

The holes were surely too regular to be natural. Icebones thought they must be the work of the Lost – though what there was to be gained by digging such immense pits in a rock wall, and how they had done it, was beyond her. Sometimes during the day she made out movement in those huge pits, heard the peep of chicks. Birds had made their nests there, high above the attention of the scavengers and predators of the Gouge floor.

One early dawn, Icebones was woken, disturbed. She raised her trunk.

The sun was still below the eastern horizon, where the sky was streaked with pink-grey. The other mammoths had fanned out over a patch of steppe. The only sounds they made were the soft rustle of their hair as they walked, or the rip of grass, and the occasional chirping snore from Woodsmoke, who was napping beneath his mother's legs.

She heard the gaunt honking of geese. Sometimes their isolated barks rose until they became a single outcry, pealing from the sky. Now she saw the birds in the first daylight, their huge wings seeming to glow against the lightening sky.

But it wasn't the geese that had disturbed her.

She turned, sniffing the air. It seemed to her that the light was strange this morning, the air filled with a peculiar orange-grey glow. And there was an odd scent in the breeze that raised her guard hairs: a thin iron tang, like the taste of ocean air.

She looked west, where night still lay thick on the Gouge as it curled around the belly of the world. A band of deeper darkness was smeared across the Gouge floor, and a wind blew stronger in her face, soft but steady.

She felt the hairs on her scalp rise.

Spiral was digging with her trunk under Breeze's belly. 'Let me have him. Let me!' She was trying to get hold of Woodsmoke, who, wide awake now, was cowering under his mother's belly.

'Get away,' Breeze said. 'Leave us alone, Spiral . . .' Breeze pushed her sister away, but she was smaller, weaker. And the calf was becoming increasingly agitated by the pushing and barging of the huge creatures that loomed over him.

Autumn walked to her squabbling daughters, stately and massive. 'What is this trouble you are making?'

The calf, mewling and unhappy, wanted to run to his grandmother, but Breeze kept a firm hold on him with her skinny trunk. 'Make her go away.'

'She is selfish,' Spiral protested. 'He loves me as well as her.'

'Enough,' Autumn said. 'You are both making the calf unhappy. How does that show love . . . ? Breeze, you must let the calf go to Spiral.'

'*No!*'

'It is her right.'

Yes. Because Spiral is senior, Icebones thought, watching.

'But,' Autumn said, 'you must let his mother feed him, Spiral.'

'I can feed him,' Spiral protested.

Autumn said gently, 'No, you can't. He still needs milk. Come now.' Deliberately she stepped between the two Cows, and wrapped her trunk around Woodsmoke's head, soothing him. And, with judicious nudges, she arranged the three of them so that the calf was in the centre.

The two competing Cows stood face to face. They laid their trunks over Woodsmoke's back, soothing and warming him.

After a few heartbeats, now that the tussle was resolved, Woodsmoke snorted contentedly and lay down to nap, half-buried under the Cows' heavy trunks.

The wind picked up further, ruffling Icebones's hair. Far above, a bird hovered, wings widespread. Perhaps it was a skua.

She looked to the west again. The light continued to seep slowly into the sky, but she could see that the band of darkness had grown heavier and denser, filling the canyon from side to side, as if some immense wave was approaching. But she could hear nothing: no rustling of trees or moaning of wind through rock.

Autumn joined Icebones. 'Taste this.' She held up her trunk tip to Icebones's mouth.

Icebones tasted milk.

'I found it on Spiral's breast. She stole it from Breeze, to lure the calf.' Autumn rumbled unhappily. 'Of all of us, I think it is Spiral who suffers the most.'

Icebones wrapped her trunk around Autumn's. 'Then we must help her, as much as we can.'

Icebones knew that Autumn's instinct had been good. In a Family, it was not uncommon for a senior Cow to adopt the calf of another – whether the true mother liked it or not. The whole Family was responsible for the care of each calf, and calves and adults knew it on some deep-buried level. But under the stifling care of the Lost these Cows had never learned to understand their instincts, and were now driven by emotions they probably could not name, let alone understand.

But now Thunder came trumpeting. He was breathing hard, his eyes rimmed by white. 'Icebones! Icebones!' He turned to face west, his trunk raised high.

That wall of crimson darkness had grown, astonishingly quickly. It filled the Gouge from side to side, and towered high up the walls. And now Icebones could hear the first moans of wind, the crack of rock and wood, and she could feel the shuddering of the ground.

Something hovered briefly before the storm front, hurled high in the air, green and brown, before being dashed to the ground and smashing to splinters. It was a mighty conifer tree, uprooted and destroyed as casually as a mammoth's trunk would toss a willow twig.

'By Kilukpuk's eyes,' Autumn said softly.

Icebones trumpeted, 'Circle!'

The adults gathered around Breeze and her calf. Icebones prodded them until they all had their backs to the wind, with Autumn, Thunder and Icebones herself at the rear of the group.

There was a moment of eerie silence. The ground's shaking stopped, and even the wind died.

But still the storm front bore down on them. Its upper reaches were wispy smoke, and its dense front churned and bubbled, like a vast river approaching.

Icebones, pressed between Thunder and Autumn, felt the rapid breathing of the mammoths, smelled their dung and urine and milk and fear. 'Hold your places,' she said. 'Hold your places—'

Suddenly the storm was on them.

Perhaps it had something to do with night and day.

The Gouge was so long that while its eastern end was in day, its western extremity was still in night. Icebones imagined the battle between the cold of night and warmth of day, as the line of dawn worked its slow way along the great channel. Was it so surprising that such a tremendous daily conflict should throw off a few storms?

But the *why* scarcely mattered.

The wind was red–black and solid and icy cold. It battered at Icebones's back and legs. Dust and bits of stone scoured at her skin, working through her layers of hair and grinding at any exposed flesh, her ears and trunk tip and even her feet.

Now a thick sleety snow began to pelt her back. Soon her fur was soaked through with icy melt, and the cold deepened, as if the wind was determined to suck away every last bit of her body heat. The ground itself was shuddering, making it impossible for her rumbles or stamping to reach the others.

She risked opening one eye.

It was like looking into a tunnel lined by soggy snow, rain, crimson dust and rock fragments that drove almost horizontally ahead of her. She could even see a kind of shadow, a gap in the driving storm, cast by the mammoths' huge bulk.

She had seen this vast storm approaching since it was just a line on the bleak horizon. How was it she hadn't heard its howl, or even felt the rumble of its destruction? Perhaps the storm was so violent, so rapid, that it outran even its own mighty roar.

But by standing together the mammoths were defeating the storm, she thought with a stab of exultation. However soaked and battered and cold, they would emerge from this latest crisis stronger and more united as a Family—

There was a noise like thunder, a blow like a strike from Kilukpuk's mighty tusk.

The world spun around, and she was flying, *flying*, through the driven snow and the dust. She could feel her legs and trunk dangling, helpless, not a single one of her feet in contact with the ground, lost in the air like poor Shoot. She could smell blood – no, she could taste it.

But there was no pain, not even fear. How strange, she thought.

A wall, dark red and hard, loomed before her.

She slammed into rock. Pain stabbed in her right shoulder.

She slid down the wall to the ground. Hard-edged rock ripped at her belly and legs and face.

And then she fell into darkness.

She could feel cold rock beneath her belly.

She opened her eyes.

She glimpsed a dim sun through smoky dust, and the round shapes of mammoths, their hair licking around them. A gust battered her face, and she squeezed her eyes shut.

But the storm had diminished.

She was resting on her front, her legs folded beneath her, as a mammoth would lie when preparing to die. She tried to pull her forefeet under her, so she could rise. Pain exploded in her right shoulder, and she stumbled flat again, sprawling like a clumsy calf.

But then there was a trunk under her, strong and supple. 'Lean on me.' Autumn stood over her, a massive silhouette against a crimson sky. 'The storm has gone to find somebody else to torment. But you are hurt.'

High above Autumn, a bird wheeled through dusty red light.

Icebones tried again to stand. The pain in her shoulder betrayed her once more. But this time Autumn's strong trunk helped her, and she managed to stay upright, shakily, her three good legs taking her weight.

The mammoths shook themselves and tugged at their hair, trying to get out the worst of the grit and dust and water. The calf, none the worse for his experience, was trotting from one adult to another, his little trunk held up as he tried to help them groom. Icebones saw that crimson dust had piled up where the mammoths had been standing, making a low dune.

The land showed the passing of the storm. Dust and gravel lay everywhere, and new red–black streaks along the rocky ground showing where the winds had passed. Bushes and bits of trees lay scattered. There was even the broken corpse of a small, young deer, Icebones saw, bent so badly it was almost unrecognisable.

She wondered what damage this storm would have done in the Nest of the Lost. Surely no trace of the mammoths' footsteps in the littered dust would remain.

A shadow arced over the mammoths. Icebones saw that bird still wheeling overhead, wings outstretched. She looked like a skua, hunting a lemming. Perhaps she nested in those great spherical caves in the cliff face. Icebones raised her trunk, but could smell nothing but iron dust and her own blood.

She took a step forward. Pain jarred in her shoulder, making her cry softly.

'Everybody's safe,' Autumn said sternly. 'Everybody but you. Your shoulder is damaged. We will rest here, until your healing begins.'

'We must reach the Footfall—'

'We cannot reach this Footfall of yours at all without you, Icebones. So we will wait, whether you like it or not.'

'I am sorry,' Icebones said softly.

'If you are sorry you are a fool. Maybe we should go back to the ponds. I bet Chaser-Of-Frogs was comfortable in her mud, with only the tip of her trunk sticking out into the storm. What do you think . . . ?'

The bird was descending, Icebones saw, curious despite her pain. Her body was stone grey, her beak bluish, and her wings had white flashes across them. She had webbed feet, spread beneath her, pointing at the ground – webbed, with claws.

She was descending, and descending, and descending. Coming out of the storm, unperturbed by the remnant winds.

Coming straight towards the mammoths.

Growing huge.

The calf was alone, grubbing at a fallen tree.

Icebones roared, 'Watch out!' She tried to run. Her shoulder seared and she fell sprawling, as if her leg had been cut away. Still the mammoths did not look up. And still Icebones tried to stand, pushing herself forward, for the shadow was becoming larger. 'The bird!' she called again. 'The bird . . . !'

A roof of feathers and bone slid over her, rustling, and there was a smell like scorched flesh. She glimpsed a blue–grey beak, and black eyes, flecked with yellow, peered into hers. Those great wings beat once, lazily and powerfully, and air gushed.

Icebones cringed. All the dust-stained mammoths were in the bird's shadow now, standing like blocks of sandstone.

The webbed feet spread, talons reaching out of the sky. The calf ran for his mother, trunk raised, mewling.

The talons closed. Woodsmoke trumpeted as the claws pricked his sides, and blood spurted, gushing over his spiky hair.

The bird screeched, a sound like rock cracking, as she struggled to lift her prey. With every beat of the wings, dust and bits of rock were sent flying, and the ground shuddered. It was a nightmare of noise and dust, shadow and blood, the stink of feathers.

If the skua succeeded in getting off the ground, she would surely carry the calf away to some high, remote nest, where he would be devoured alive, piece by bloody piece, by a clutch of monstrous chicks. Icebones roared her anguish. But, pinned by her injury to the ground, she could do nothing.

Breeze came rushing in, tusks raised, trumpeting, utterly fearless. She got close enough to swipe at the bird with her tusks, and she grabbed a wing with her trunk. The bird screamed and beat her wings, pulling free, leaving long, greasy black feathers fluttering in the air. A beak the size of a mammoth's thigh bone slashed down.

Breeze staggered back, trumpeting. Icebones saw that her back had been laid open. The Cow slumped to the ground, legs splayed.

The bird was flapping harder now, and gushes of rock and dust billowed out from beneath her immense, rustling wings. At last she raised the struggling calf off the ground, and was straining for the sky.

Thunder ran forward. He was waving an uprooted bush over his head, his trunk wrapped around its roots. A cloud of red dust flew around his head.

The skua shrieked and stabbed with her beak, for the bush made Thunder look much larger than he was. He hurled the bush at her head and ran trumpeting into the shadow of her wings, slashing his tusks back and forth.

The bird screeched again – and Icebones knew the Bull had reached flesh.

The skua tried one last time to lift herself. But the calf continued to squirm, and Icebones could see Thunder whirling like a dust devil, striking over and over with blood-stained tusks at the soft feathers of the bird's chest.

At last, with a final angry scream, the bird released Woodsmoke. The calf fell to the ground with a soft impact. The great wings beat, and Icebones saw that Thunder was knocked aside.

But now the bird was rising, diminishing in the sky, becoming a small black speck that wheeled away towards the cliffs.

The calf mewled. His mother rushed to him, uncaring of her own wounds.

They sought shelter under an overhang of rock, a place where no more nightmares could come wheeling down from the sky.

Thunder was sore from heavy bruises inflicted on his flanks by the beating wings of the bird. Breeze's back had been laid open so badly that the white of bone showed in a valley of ripped red flesh, and Autumn laboriously plastered it with mud. The calf had suffered puncture-marks in his side left by the bird's talons, ripped wider by his struggles to get free. Spiral worked with his grandmother to clean them up for him, and to soothe his wailing misery.

All the mammoths were subdued, bombarded as they had been by the storm and the attack of the bird so soon after. Icebones suspected it had been no coincidence. The bird must prefer to hunt after such a storm, when animals, dead or injured or simply bewildered, were most vulnerable to her mighty talons.

Skuas on the Island had fed on rodents, like lemmings, and the chicks of other birds. There had been nothing like this monster. She recalled the birds she had seen nesting in the cliff hollows – but she realised now that she had totally misjudged their size, fooled by the vastness of the cliff. Perhaps such a cliff bred birds of this immense size to suit its mighty scale.

Icebones felt a dread gather in her heart. Perhaps this is how Kilukpuk felt at the beginning of her life, she thought, when she lived in a burrow under the ground, and the Reptiles stalked overhead. But the mammoths had grown huge since those days. Nothing threatened them, for the mammoths were the greatest creatures in the world . . .

But not *this* world, she thought.

As the sun slid down the sky, Icebones limped up to the young Bull. 'Walk with me, Thunder. Let me lean on you.'

Growling uncertainly, he settled in at her right side, and she leaned her shoulder on his comfortingly massive bulk. When they emerged from the shelter of the rock overhang, Thunder raised his trunk higher. 'It is not safe,' he rumbled. 'The bird has blood on her talons now.'

'Yes,' she said. 'And I cannot run fast. But I have you to protect me. Don't I, Thunder?'

'I did nothing,' he growled.

Standing awkwardly, she wrapped her trunk around his. 'You defied your instincts. Mammoths are not used to being preyed upon – and certainly not by a bird, an ugly thing which flaps out of the sky. But you fought her off. You are brave beyond your years, and your strength.'

'I abandoned Shoot when the sea beast threatened. I would not walk on to the bridge after Spiral. You saw my fear—'

'But you saved Woodsmoke. You are what you do, Thunder. And so you are a hero.' He tried to pull away, so she slapped him gently. 'I want you to call somebody now. I cannot, for I cannot stamp . . . There is a Bull I know. He is far from here, but I hope we will meet him someday. He is called Boaster.'

'Boaster?'

'Call him now. Call him as deep and as loud as you can.'

So Thunder called, his massive chest shuddering and his broad feet slamming against the ground.

After a time, Icebones heard the answering call washing through the rock. *Icebones? Is that you?*

'Tell him you are Thunder.'

Hesitantly, Thunder complied.

A Bull? Are you in musth? Keep away from Icebones, for she is mine. For myself, though Icebones calls me Boaster, my relatives and rivals, for obvious reasons, call me Long—

'Never mind that,' said Icebones hastily. 'Tell him what you did today.'

Still hesitant, awkward, Thunder stamped out, 'I killed a bird.'

After a long delay, the reply came: *A bird? What did you do, sneeze on it?*

Thunder trumpeted his anger. 'The bird was vast. So vast its wings spanned this Gouge through which we walk. It descended like a storm and grabbed a calf in its mighty talons . . .'

While Boaster was listening respectfully, Icebones limped away, leaving Thunder standing proud, telling of his deeds to other Bulls – which was just what Bulls were supposed to do.

But as she withdrew she watched the darkling sky.

Chapter Six

THE SHINING TUSK

The character of the landscape slowly changed. The walls became more shallow and broken. It was evident that they were, at last, rising out of the mighty Gouge.

One morning the mammoths found themselves facing a valley that cut across the main body of the Gouge. The valley appeared to flow from the high, dry uplands of the southern hemisphere into the immense ocean basin that was the north, as if from higher ground to lower.

The mammoths clambered down a shallow slope. The light of the rising sun cast long shadows from the rubble strewn on the surface, making the ground seem complex and treacherous.

If walking along the flat ground had been difficult for Icebones, working down a slope like this – where she had to rest her weight on her forelegs and damaged shoulder – was particularly agonising. And even on the floor of the outflow valley, she found she had to tread carefully: a flat surface layer of dust and loose gravel covered much larger rocks beneath, their edges sharp enough to gash a mammoth's foot.

It didn't help that the day seemed peculiarly hot and bright. The rising sun was swollen and oddly misshapen, and the air was full of light.

Icebones knew she should give a lead to the others. But it took all her strength just to keep moving. She plodded on in silence, locked in her own world of determination and pain: *Just this step. Now just one more . . .*

She found a small, deep pond, frozen over. Impatiently she pressed on the ice until it cracked into thick, angular chunks, and she sucked up trunkfuls of cold, black water, ignoring the thin slimy texture of vegetation. Soon she had washed the dust out of her throat and trunk, and was trickling soothing water over her aching shoulder.

The others still bore injuries. Breeze nursed the brutal slashes in her back. The calf was fascinated by his wounds, and his grandmother often caught him picking at the scabs that had formed there.

But the one who slowed them down the most was Icebones herself, to her regret and shame.

Thunder stood very still, listening carefully to the deep song of the rocks, as she had taught him. 'This is a damaged country,' he said.

'Yes.' She forced herself to raise her head.

To the north, the valley branched into a series of smaller channels, like a delta. The waters must once have flowed that way. The valley floor was smoothly carved, textured with sandbars that followed the path of the vanished flood. She saw what must have been an island in the flow, flat-topped, shaped like the body of a fish to push aside the water. To the south, where the water must have come from, the landscape was quite different: littered with blocks and domes and low hills, all of them frost-cracked, water-eroded and streaked with lichen, their outlines softened by layers of windblown dust. But many of these blocks were immense, much larger than any mammoth. It was just like the bottom of a huge dried-up river.

All this was drenched in a pink-white glow, and she could feel the sun's heat on her back. She squinted up, wondering if she would find the sun misshapen again, as she had seen it days before, close to the canal's terminus. But the light was too bright, and it dazzled her. She turned away, eyes watering.

Thunder said, 'There is water under the ground. A great lake of it, trapped under a cap of ice. I can *feel* it. Can you?'

'Yes—'

'But it is very deep.' He seemed excited as his awakened instincts pieced together the story of this land. 'Perhaps the water broke out in a huge gush, as the waters broke out of Breeze's belly when Woodsmoke was ready to be born. Then it flooded over the land, seeking the sea to the north. The water carved out this valley. See how it washed across the ground here, shaping it, and surged around that island . . . Perhaps the land to the south simply collapsed. If you suck the water out of a hole in the ice on a frozen pond, sometimes the ice will crack and fall, under its own weight . . .'

Maybe he was right. But whatever water had marked this land was vanished a long time ago. She saw craters punched into the ancient valley floor, themselves eroded by wind and time.

Thunder was still talking. But his words blurred, becoming an indistinguishable growl. The air was now drenched by a dazzling light that picked out every stray dust mote around her.

'I'm sorry, Thunder. What did you say? I am hot, and the day is bright.'

But Thunder's pink tongue was lolling. 'It is the sky,' he said. 'Look, Icebones. There is nothing wrong with you. It is the sky!'

The sun had grown huge – and was getting larger. With every extension of that pale, ragged disc, the heat and the brilliance around her increased. It was silent, eerie, and profoundly disturbing.

There was a nudge at her side, an alarmed trumpet. Icebones made out Spiral, a shimmering ghost in the pink-stained brilliance. 'Come away! You are in great danger here. Hurry . . . !' Spiral began to barge vigorously at Icebones's flank.

Icebones needed little further urging.

The ground was littered with scree and, unable to see, she stumbled frequently. Her shoulder hurt profoundly, and she felt as if she would melt from the heat. Though she was half-blinded, she could hear as clearly as ever: Spiral's blaring, the scrape of her foot pads over the loose rock, even the scratchy, shallow breathing of the other mammoths further away.

That flaring sun expanded still further. Eventually it became a great disc draped over the sky, its blurred rim reaching half-way to the horizon.

It was horrifying, bewildering, unreal, a new impossible unreality in this unreal world. *The sun does not behave like that.* If I am the frozen dream of some long-dead seer, she thought, then perhaps the dream is breaking down; perhaps this is the light of the truth, breaking through the crumbling dream . . .

But now the heat began to fade, suddenly. There was a soft

breeze, carrying the tang of ice. The light, too, seemed dimmer.

Her thoughts cleared, like a fever dream receding. Here was Autumn, a blocky, ill-defined silhouette before her.

'If that was summer,' Icebones said, 'it was the shortest I've ever known.'

'This is no joke.' Autumn pushed her trunk into Icebones's mouth. 'You're too hot. Come now, quickly.' So Icebones was forced to walk again, in the footsteps of hurrying Autumn.

They reached a tall, eroded rock, crusted with yellow lichen. In its shade there was a patch of snow, laced pink by dust. Autumn reached down, scooped up snow with her trunk and began to push it into Icebones's mouth.

Icebones lumbered forward and let the cool pink-white stuff lap up to her belly. Mammoths did not sweat, and using frost or snow like this was an essential means of keeping cool. Icebones only wished that the snow were deep enough to cover her completely.

When she felt a little better, she staggered wearily out of the ice. Slush dripped from guard hairs that were still hot to the touch of her trunk tip.

The place where she had been standing with Thunder, bathed in light, glowed a bright pink-white. Threads of steam and smoke rose from the red dust. The stink of burning vegetation and scorched-hot rock reached her nostrils.

Above the glowing ground a column of shining, swirling dust motes rose into the air. It was a perfect, soft-edged cylinder that slanted towards the sun – but Icebones had never seen a sunbeam of such intensity, nor one cast by such a powerful and misshapen sun.

Away from the sun itself, the sky seemed somehow

diminished. Close to the zenith, she could even make out stars. It was as if all the light in the world had been concentrated into that single intense pulse.

An overheated rock cracked open with an explosive percussion, making all the mammoths flinch and grumble.

'If we were still standing there,' Thunder said grimly, 'we too would be burning.'

Spiral nudged him affectionately. 'And your fat would flow like water, you big tusker, and we would all swim away.'

But now the shining pillar of light dispersed, abruptly, leaving dust motes churning, and the intense glow dissipated as if it had never been. When she peered up, Icebones saw the sun was restored to its normal intensity, small and shrunken.

'It is a thing of the Lost,' she said. 'This great tusk of light that stirs and breaks the rock.'

'Yes,' said Autumn. 'Somehow they can gather the light of the sun itself and hurl it down where they choose. From the Fire Mountain I saw it stab at the land, over and over, carving out pits and valleys.'

'Like the canal in the Gouge,' Icebones said.

'But now it is scratching the land as foolishly as Woodsmoke trying out his milk tusks. The Lost are gone, and it doesn't know what to do.'

The cloudy deformation of the sun was gathering again, and the light beam was slicing down once more, this time on the higher land to the south, above the escarpment at the head of the valley. Where it rested the rock cracked and melted.

The ground shuddered – a single sharp pulse – and the mammoths rumbled their unease.

Autumn said, 'I think—'

'Hush!' The brief, peremptory trumpet came from Thunder. 'Listen. Can't you hear that? Can't you, Icebones?'

Breeze said impatiently, 'I hear the burning grass, the hiss of the melting rock—'

'No. Deeper than that. *Listen.*'

Icebones stood square on the ground, pressing her weight on to all her four legs, despite the stabs of pain in her shoulder. And then she heard it: a subterranean growl, deep and menacing.

'We have to get to the higher ground,' she said immediately. They were halfway across the valley, she saw, and the eastern slope looked marginally easier to climb. 'Let's go, let's go. *Now.*' She began to limp that way, her damaged shoulder stinging with pain.

The mammoths milled uncertainly.

'Why?' Breeze asked. 'What are we fleeing?'

'Water,' said Icebones. 'A vast quantity of water, an underground sea locked into the ground. Like the great flood that once burst across this land, scraping out the valley you stand in. And now—'

'And now,' said Thunder urgently, 'thanks to the shining tusk, that underground sea is awakening, stretching its muscles. Come *on.*'

At last they understood. They began to lumber across the plain towards the eastern wall, trunks and tails swaying.

The ground above the escarpment cracked with a report that echoed down the walls of the valley, and steam gushed into the air. The vast body of water beneath, vigorous on its release after a billion years locked beneath a cap of permafrost ice, was rising at the commanding touch of the great orbiting lens – rising with relentless determination, seeking the air.

Chapter Seven

THE FLOOD

Though the ground was broken and their way was impeded by half-buried lumps of debris, they all made faster time than Icebones – even the calf, who clung to his mother's tail.

A giant explosion shook the ground.

Her foreleg folded beneath her. She crashed forward on to her knees, pain stabbing through her shoulder.

From the great scribbled scar inflicted by the tusk of light, a vast fountain of steam gushed into the pale sky. Vapour and debris drifted across the sun, turning it into a pale pink smear.

I'm not going to make it, she thought.

And now dust rained down like a dense, gritty snow. Icebones snorted to clear her trunk, and she tasted the blood flavour of the hot, iron-rich dust.

Suddenly she was alone in a shell of murky dust. And the mammoths were no more than crimson blurs in the distance, fast receding.

She supposed it was for the best that the others had not looked back. She had never wanted to become a burden.

She found herself staring at a rock – staring with fascination, for it might be the last thing she would ever see. It was heavily weathered, eroded, pitted and cracked. Its colour was burnt orange, but there were streaks of blue-red on its north-facing surfaces, which had been exposed to sunlight longer. It was made of a lumpy conglomerate, pebbles trapped in a mix of hardened sand.

Pebbles and sand, she thought. Pebbles and sand that must have formed in fast-flowing rivers, and then compressed into this mottled rock on some ocean bed. All of it ancient, all of it long gone.

She ran her trunk fingers over the rock's pocked surface. She found a series of small, shallow pits, a row of them, each just large enough to take her trunk-tip.

. . . *They were footprints*, locked into the surface of the hardened rock. She probed more carefully at the nearest print. It had six toes. No living animal had six toes. Now its kind was lost, leaving no trace save these accidentally preserved prints.

She felt a surge of wonder. Despite the noise, her pain, despite the imminent danger, despite the rock's shuddering, she longed to know where that ancient animal had been going – what it had wanted, how it had died.

But she would never know, and might live no more than a few more heartbeats, not even long enough to savour such wonder.

The dusty debris falling over her was becoming more liquid, she thought, and warmer too. The flood was nearing. The ground shook. She huddled closer to her rock.

But a long, powerful trunk wrapped under her belly.

It was Spiral. The young Cow loomed over Icebones as a mother would loom over her calf. She was coated in red dust, and her guard hairs were already damp.

Icebones said, 'You shouldn't have come back. You'll die, like me. The flood is coming.'

Spiral rumbled, loudly enough to make herself heard over the noise of the water. 'Yes, the flood comes . . . like the tears of Kilukpuk.'

Icebones felt weary amusement. '*You* talk now of Kilukpuk?'

'I'm hoping you'll tell me more of those old tales, Icebones.'

'It's too late. We can't get to the bank.'

'No. But there is an island, further to the north, that might stay above the waters.' She grabbed Icebones's tusks and began to drag her along the bed of the ancient channel.

Icebones tried to resist, digging her feet into the ground, but the pain in her shoulder was too great even for that.

'You must not do this,' she said.

'Icebones, help me or we'll both drown.'

Icebones forced herself to her feet.

To the north, the way the ancient waters had once flowed, the land was covered by scour marks, braided channels, heavily eroded islands, sand bars, the scars left by flowing water. The island Spiral had selected was shaped like a vast teardrop, its steep, layered sides polished to smoothness by ancient floods.

Climbing the island's crumbling walls was one of the most difficult things Icebones had ever done. The strata cracked and gave way, coming loose under her in a shower of rock and pebbles and dust, and each fall brought lancing pain in her shoulder that made her trumpet in protest. But Spiral stayed with her every step, ramming Icebones's rump with her head, as if driving her up the slope with sheer strength and will-power.

At last they reached the lip of the wall. With a final, agonising effort Icebones dragged her carcass on to the island's flat top. She crumpled, falling on to her knees. The surface was smooth hard mudstone, a fragment of the floor of some ancient sea, she thought.

Spiral stood before her, breathing hard, caked with orange dust, her hair ragged: tall and wild, she was a figure from a nightmare. 'You are a heavy burden to haul.'

Icebones gasped, 'You should have left me.'

'Too late for that.'

And now, through the murky, sodden gloom, more mammoths approached: Autumn, Thunder, Breeze, the calf.

Icebones growled, 'What are you doing here?'

'We are waiting for you,' said Thunder. 'Did you think we would go on without you? And when we saw Spiral bringing you here—'

Lightning flashed. The mammoths flinched.

Where the sky tusk had broken the ground, dust and steam still gushed, crimson red, and over the towering clouds of dust and steam, lightning cracked. Now water was beginning to pulse out of the ground, stained pink by the ubiquitous dust.

Instinctively the mammoths gathered closer, nuzzling and bumping.

Icebones was surrounded by the rich smell of their hair, and they loomed over her as if she was a calf. She snorted. 'Some Matriarch. I did not understand the tusk of the sun. I did not hear the movement of the water under the ground until we were in danger. I am the slowest of us all, and have put you at risk.'

Autumn said, 'But *I* understood the meaning of the tusk. And Thunder with his sharp hearing heard the water, and understood, and warned us in time. And Spiral used her strength to save you – just as you have used your strength to aid others of us in the past.'

'But the Cycle teaches—'

'Is the Cycle more important than the instincts of the mammoths around you?'

'. . . No,' Icebones conceded.

'So you have not failed,' Autumn whispered. 'We are Family. We are what you made us. *My strength is your strength.*'

'It doesn't always work like that,' Icebones said grimly. '*Sometimes it is right to abandon the weak . . .*'

Autumn pushed her trunk into Icebones's mouth. 'No more lessons.'

All the mammoths began to murmur, a deep rumble of reassurance as if to soothe a frightened calf. Their rumbles merged subtly, becoming like the single voice of a vaster creature.

Icebones let her self sink into that comforting pit of sound. She felt her doubts and fears and anxieties dissolve – and her sense of self washed away with them. *She was Family*: she heard the world through Thunder's sharp ears, and felt Spiral's tall strength suffuse her own limbs, and Autumn's deep knowledge and unknowing wisdom filled her head, and she shared Breeze's deep love for her calf, who became as precious to her as her own core warmth.

She had never forgotten how bleakly bereft she had felt on

that rocky hillside, when she first woke from her unnatural sleep, bombarded by strangeness – alone, as she had never been in her life. But now a new Family had built around her – *I* had become *We* – and she was whole again.

With a final shuddering tremble, the ground around the great fracture gave way. Layers of rock lifted like a lid. Angry water spilled into the valley, pounding on the eroded boulders, shattering ancient stones that might not have been disturbed since the world was young.

A wall of dirty, rust-brown water fell on them, hard and heavy.

As the setting sun began finally to glint through the remnant haze, the mammoths separated stiffly. They were cold, hungry, bruised, utterly bedraggled.

Water, turbulent and red-brown with mud, still surged around their island. Immense waves, echoes of the mighty fracture, surged up and down the ancient valley.

But already the flood water had begun to recede. Much of it was draining away through the ancient channels to the Ocean of the North. The rest was simply soaking away into the dust, vanishing back into the thirsty red ground as rapidly as it had emerged. The revealed ground, slick with crimson mud and remnant puddles, sparkled in the low sunlight, as red and wet as skinned flesh.

The very shape of this island had changed, its battered walls crumbled away under the onslaught.

The Lost remake worlds, Icebones thought. But they do not stay remade. Soon the things the Lost have built here, all the bridges and pipelines and Nests and the toiling beetles, will collapse and erode away. And when the dust has silted up even their marvellous straight-edged canal, the ancient face of the Sky Steppe will emerge once more, timeless and indomitable.

The Lost are powerful. But the making of a world will forever be beyond them, a foolish dream.

By the light of a fat, dust-laden pink sunset, the mammoths scrambled down the island's newly carved sides, and across the valley floor. By the time they got to the higher ground they were so coated in sticky red-black mud Icebones could barely raise her legs.

'What now, Matriarch?' 'What should we do?' 'Where should we go?'

These questions emerged from a continuing communal rumble, for the voices of a true Family were always raised together, in an unending wash of communication – as if, emerging from consensus, every phrase began with the pronoun 'we'.

'Thunder, you are our ears and nostrils. Which way?'

He stood straight and still, sniffing the wind, feeling the shape of the world. At length he said, 'South. South and east. That way lies the Footfall of Kilukpuk.'

'Very well. Spiral, you are our strength. Shall we begin the walk?'

'We are ready, Matriarch.'

Icebones made the summons rumble, a long, drawn-out growl: 'Let's go, let's go.'

Gradually their rumbles merged once more, as they tasted readiness on each other's breath. 'We are ready.' 'We are together.' 'Let's go.' 'Let's go, let's go.'

Icebones strode forward, ignoring the pain in her shoulder – which, since it now affected only a small part of her greater, shared body, was as nothing. The other mammoths began to move with her, their trunks exploring the rocky red ground beneath their feet, just as a true Family should. Icebones felt affirmed, exulting.

But as they climbed away from the valley, and as Icebones made out the high bleak land that still lay before them, she sensed that they would yet need to call on all their shared strength and courage if they were to survive.

. . . And then, clinging to an outcrop of rock at the fringe of this harsh southern upland, she found a fragment of hair: pale brown, ragged, snagged from some creature who had come this way. She pulled the hair loose with her trunk and tasted it curiously. Though it was soaked through, the hair had a stale, burning smell that she recognised immediately.

The hair had belonged to the Ragged One.

THREE

FOOTFALL

THE STORY OF THE GREAT CROSSING

The Cycle is made up of the oldest stories in the world. It tells all that has befallen the mammoths, and its wisdom is as perfect as time can make it.

But now I want to tell you one of the youngest stories in the Cycle. It is the story of how the mammoths came to the Sky Steppe.

It is the story of Silverhair, who was the last Matriarch of the Old Steppe.

It is the story of the first Matriarch of the Sky Steppe.

It is a story of mammoths, and Lost.

For generations the last mammoths had lived on an Island. Silverhair was their Matriarch.

The Lost were everywhere. But the Lost had never found the Island, and the mammoths lived undisturbed.

No mammoth lived anywhere else. Not one.

But now, at last, the Lost had come to the Island.

Though most of these Lost showed no wish to hunt the mammoths or kill them or drive them away, they kept them in boxes and watched them with their predators' eyes, all day and all night.

Silverhair knew that mammoths cannot share land with Lost.

But Silverhair was old and tired. She had spent all her strength keeping her Family alive. She was in despair, and ashamed of her weakness.

One night Kilukpuk came down from the aurora. And Kilukpuk said Silverhair must not be ashamed, for she had fought hard all her life. And she must not despair.

Silverhair snorted. 'This world is full of Lost. We have nowhere to live. What is there left for me but despair?'

'But there is another world,' Kilukpuk told her. 'It is a place where there will be room for many mammoths. And mammoths will live there until the sun itself grows cold.'

Silverhair asked tiredly, 'Where is this marvellous place?'

And Kilukpuk said, 'Why, have you forgotten your Cycle? It is the Sky Steppe.'

Silverhair knew about the Sky Steppe, of course. She had seen it float in the sky, bright and red – just as her world, which we call the Old Steppe, once floated in our sky, bright and blue. And, indeed, the Cycle promised that one day mammoths would walk free on the Sky Steppe.

But Silverhair was weary and old, for she could not believe even mighty Kilukpuk. She said, 'And how are the mammoths to get there? Will they sprout wings and fly like geese?'

'No,' said Kilukpuk gently. 'There is a way. But it is hard.'

It would be the work of the Lost, said Kilukpuk. What else could it be? For the Lost owned the world, all of it.

Calves would be taken from their mothers' bodies, unborn.

They would be put in ice, and sent into the sky in shining seeds, and taken to the Sky Steppe. That way many calves could be carried, to be spilled out on the red soil of the Sky Steppe, as if being born.

The bereft mothers would never know their calves, and the calves never know their mothers.

This was very strange – typical of the Lost's eerie cleverness – and Silverhair could not understand. 'How will the calves learn how to use their trunks, how to find water and food? If they have no Matriarch, who will lead and protect them?'

'That is the second thing I have to tell you,' said Kilukpuk. 'And this too is very hard.'

And Kilukpuk said that Silverhair's calf – her only calf – would also be taken. For that calf, already half-grown, was to be Matriarch to all the new calves who would tumble from the shining seeds to the red soil. That calf, daughter of the last Matriarch of the Old Steppe, would be the first Matriarch of the Sky Steppe.

'You must teach her, Silverhair,' said Kilukpuk. 'As I taught my Calves to speak, and to find water and food, and to live as a Family. You must teach her to be a Matriarch, so she can teach those who follow her.'

Silverhair spun around and scuffed the ground. 'My calf is all I have. I will not give her up. How can I live?'

But she knew that Kilukpuk was right.

Silverhair listened to Kilukpuk's wisdom. And she passed on that wisdom to her calf. And, when the time came, she gave her calf to Kilukpuk, and the Lost.

For that one sacrifice alone, we know Silverhair as great a hero as any in the Cycle's long course. For if she had not, and if she had not taught her calf well, none of us alive today would ever have been born.

Even though, as is the way of the Lost's clever-clever schemes, many things went wrong, and the calf-Matriarch was kept in a box of cold and dark for much longer than she should have been — so long that before she emerged, generations of mammoths had lived and died on the Sky Steppe . . .

Well, that was how the Great Crossing was made. But the story is not done.

For Kilukpuk taught Silverhair another truth of the Cycle: that sometimes we cannot spare even those we love.

The Crossing was hard and dangerous indeed. And Silverhair's calf would herself have a dread price to pay for making that Crossing.

That calf's name, as you know, was Icebones.

Chapter One

THE HIGH PLAINS

The land was a tortured wilderness: nothing but blood-red rock, rugged, cracked and pitted, under a sky that shone yellow-pink.

And it was dominated by craters.

The largest of them were walled plains, their rims so heavily eroded they were reduced to low, sullen mounds lined up in rough arcs. The smaller craters were sharper, and when the mammoths ploughed their way over rim ridges, their neat circular shapes were clearly visible. In places the craters crowded so close together that their walls overlapped and merged, so that the mammoths were forced to climb over one smooth fold in the land after another, like waves on some vast rust-red ocean.

Icebones listened to the rumbling echoes that the mammoths' footfalls returned from the distorted ground. She sensed giant rubble lying crammed there. She tried to imagine the mighty blows which must have rained down on this land long ago – mighty enough to shatter rock into immense pieces far beneath her feet, mighty enough to make the rock itself rise up in great circular ripples as if it were as fluid as water.

But the land had been shaped by more than the crater-forming blows. In some places the rock had melted and flowed. Craters had been overwhelmed, their walls buried and their interiors flooded with ponds of hard, cold, red–black basalt.

And water had run here, creating channels and valleys. Some of these cut right through the crater walls and even spilled into their floors. The channels themselves were overlaid by the round stamps of craters, and sometimes cut across by more recent channels and valleys.

Dust lay scattered everywhere, piled up against crater walls or inside their rims and against the larger boulders, streaked light and dark. The dust was constantly reshaped by the wind: each dawn Icebones would peer around as the rocky wilderness emerged from the darkness, startled by how different it looked.

It was as if she was walking through layers of time: every-thing that had ever happened to this land was recorded here in a rocky scar or wrinkle or protrusion or dust heap.

. . . Sometimes, toiling across this unforgiving land of rock, thirsty, hungry, weary, sore, Icebones imagined she was *old*: with eroded molars and aching bones, in a place of moist green, surrounded by calves. Sometimes these waking dreams were so vivid that she wondered if *this* time of redness and desolation was merely a recollection. Perhaps this was not the vision of a long-dead prophet of the past, but a memory from the unknown future. Perhaps she *was* that very old Cow, on her last molars, returning to her youth in memory. Perhaps the Icebones she imagined herself to be was only a thing of memory, walking through a remembered land.

But if that was so, she thought dimly, then it must mean she would survive these harsh days, survive to grow old and bear calves . . . mustn't it?

Troubled, she walked on, as best she could, waiting for the dream to end, the memory to disperse – for herself to wake up, old and safe and content.

But the dream, or memory, did not end.

So the days wore away on the High Plains, where land and sky glowed red in a great monotonous dialogue.

One day they found a narrow valley where a pool of water had gathered. Trapped under a thin crust of ice, the water was brackish and briny. But it was the first liquid water the mammoths had encountered for days, and they smashed the ice and sucked it up gratefully.

Woodsmoke worked his way along the pond's rocky edge, exploring the water's deeper reaches. Suddenly a ledge of eroded rock crumbled beneath him. Rock fragments tumbled into the water, quickly followed by Woodsmoke's hind legs. He scrabbled at the rocky ground with his trunk and feet, but the crumbling rock offered little purchase. The calf slid into the freezing water until he was submerged save for his head and forelegs.

He trumpeted, his hair floating in the water around him.

The mammoths came running, water dribbling out of their mouths.

Breeze and Autumn fell to their knees beside the calf. They reached under his belly to lift him out with their trunks. Icebones and Spiral hurried to help – but the calf was too heavy to lift out, and it was impossible to get a purchase on his soaked, slippery hair. As they struggled, the calf's high-pitched bellows echoed from the rocky land around them.

At last Autumn ordered the others back. Carefully she looped her trunk around Woodsmoke's neck, and drew him towards the pond's shallower end. When the water was shallow enough for his hind feet to touch the pond bed, he quickly clambered out.

The calf shook himself to rid his fur of stinking pond scum, and his mother hurried close to nuzzle him. But he was frightened and angry. 'Why are we in this horrible place? Why don't we go back to the valley? There was water and stuff to eat . . .' The mammoths rumbled in unison, seeking to reassure him and persuade him to continue.

Autumn growled to Icebones, 'He thinks we were safe in the Gouge. He can't see that the world is changing, because it has not changed while he is alive. He thinks it will be the same for ever.'

Icebones, disturbed by the incident, wondered if that was true. What if *she* hadn't emerged so suddenly from her mysterious Sleep? What if *she* didn't have her memories of the Island and the Old Steppe, of such a very different time and place? Would she even perceive the changes from which she was fleeing – and which had already cost these mammoths so much?

And as the featureless days wore away, and the mammoths grew steadily more weary and cold and hungry and thirsty, darker doubts gathered.

It seemed audacious, absurd, for her to lead her mammoths across this high, silent, dead place. Perhaps it was simpler to suppose that the fault lay in her own head and heart, and not in the world around her. Perhaps she was leading these mammoths – not to salvation – but to their doom.

But then she would think of the dried mud and bones

around the ponds of the Gouge, and the wide salt flats that bordered the Ocean of the North. This world was indeed changing for the worse – *she was right* – and she must continue to confront that truth, and she must gather her strength of body and mind, and work to bring these mammoths to safety, as best she knew how.

One evening, as the dark drew in, Icebones hauled her weary legs up the shallow rim of yet another crater. She was limping, favouring her damaged shoulder where pain still stabbed.

She reached the summit of a low, eroded rim mountain – and found herself facing a surface so smooth and flat she wondered briefly if it might be liquid water. But her nostrils were full of the tang of red dust. And as she looked more closely she saw rippling dunes, like frozen waves, and sharp-edged boulders littered here and there. There was no motion, no ripple, no scudding wave: this was a lake of dust, not water, and a faint disappointment tugged at her.

Thunder stood beside her. 'How strange. The other wall of this crater is buried.'

Icebones saw that it was true. The smooth, flat lake of crimson dust washed away to the south, submerging the crater's far wall. Perhaps this crater had formed on a slope, and had been partly buried when the dust gathered. Further away she saw fragmentary ridges and arcs poking out of the dust field: bits of more drowned craters. But the dust sea did not extend far. Beyond the submerged craters was more of the broken, jumbled, very ancient landscape they had become used to.

She raised her trunk and sniffed the air. It was dry, cold, and it smelled of nothing but iron dust: no moisture, no life. 'This raised ridge is not a good place to find water.'

'We need rest,' Thunder sighed. 'Rest and peace, even more than we need food. Let us stay here until morning, Icebones.'

Icebones understood: at least here on the ridge no walls of rock loomed around them. Under an open, empty sky, creatures of the steppe could rest easy, if hungrily. 'You are right,' she said. 'We should call the others.'

Night fell quickly here. Shadows fled across the broken land, and pools of blackness grew and merged, as if a tide of dark was rising all around them. The stars burned hard in the blackness, not disturbed by a wisp of mist or a scrap of cloud, and the silence stretched out into the dark, huge and complete, as if concealing greater secrets.

A mammoth broke from the group and padded to the edge of the crater-rim ridge. Though he was just black on black, a shadow in the night, Icebones could smell Thunder.

Trying not to disturb the others, who were clustered around the snoring calf, Icebones followed him.

Thunder held his trunk high in the air, peering over the dust-flooded crater. She stood beside him, trunk raised and ears spread, listening.

. . . And now she thought she heard a thin, high scraping, like the scrabbling paw of some tiny animal, coming from the surface of the dust sea. It was very soft, so quiet she would never have noticed it if not for the high, lifeless stillness of this place. But in the silent dark it was as loud to her as the bark of a wolf.

The scratching vanished.

Then it returned, a little further away.

She rumbled, 'Perhaps it is a lemming.'

Thunder said bluntly, 'No lemming hops from place to place over great bounds as this invisible scratcher does.'

The two mammoths waited on the ridge, side by side, as the night wore away, and the invisible scratcher drifted, seemingly at random, around the dust bowl.

And when the first bruised-purple light began to seep into the eastern sky, they saw it.

An immense sac hovered in the air, just above the dust. It was like the skin of some huge fruit. At first it was pitch black, silhouetted against the dawn sky. It trailed a tendril, more pliant than the branch of a willow, that coiled on the ground like the trunk of a resting mammoth. But as the sac drifted, the trailing tendril scraped along the ground, making the scratching noise she had heard.

Thunder said, 'Is it a bird?'

'It's no bird I ever saw. Look, it has no wings, although it flies . . . I think it is floating like the feathers of a moulting goose, or as seeds are blown on the breeze.'

'What mighty tree will grow when that vast seed falls?'

Now pale dawn light diffused over the dust pool and shone into the heart of the sac, making it glow from within, pink and grey. The floating thing was made of some smooth shining translucent substance, Icebones saw, but it was slack and loose, like the skin around the eyes of a very old mammoth. And its trailing tendril dragged something knotty and silver across the dust, exploring like a trunk, leaving a shallow trench.

Now that the light was striking the sac it was starting to swell and rise, its surface unfolding with a slow, rustling languor. The silver knot scraped over the dust as the tendril slowly uncoiled.

'Perhaps it rises in the day and flies on the wind,' Icebones mused. 'And then it sinks at night and scrapes its silver fruit on the ground.'

'But it has no bones or head,' said Thunder. 'It cannot choose where it travels, as a mammoth can. It is blown on the wind. What does it travel *for*? What is it hoping to find?'

Icebones blew dust out of her trunk. 'That we will never know—'

The sea's placid surface erupted before them. Dunes flowed and disintegrated. A great black cylinder rose, and dust fell away with a soft rustle all around.

Icebones stumbled back, and she made to trumpet a warning. But so profound was her shock at this sudden apparition that her throat and trunk seemed to freeze. And besides, what warning could she give?

The cylinder of black-red flesh, twisting out of the dust, was crusted with hard segmented plates. At its apex was a nostril, or mouth: a pit, black as night, lined with six inward-pointing teeth. Dust was falling into that gaping maw, but whatever immense creature lay beneath the surface seemed indifferent. The great mouth folded around the lower portion of the floating sac. Huge, sharp teeth meshed together with a noise like rock on rock, and the sac's fabric was ground apart effortlessly.

Then the vast pillar twisted and fell back into the dust. It sank quickly out of sight, dragging half the sac and the trailing cable with it.

There were no ripples or waves. The dust ocean was immediately still, with only a new pattern of dunes left to show where the beast had been. The severed upper half of the sac drifted away, tumbling, on breezes that were gathering strength in the morning air.

For heartbeats the two mammoths stood side by side, saying nothing, stunned.

'It was a beast,' said Thunder fervently.

'Like a worm. Or a snake.'

'Do you think the Lost brought it here from the Old Steppe?'

'I don't think it has anything to do with the Lost, Thunder. Did it smell of the Lost – or any animal you know? Did you see its teeth?'

'They were very sharp and long.'

'*But it had six*: six teeth, set in a ring.' Just as the footprints she saw in the ancient outflow-channel had had six toes. Just as the creatures buried in the rock floor of the Nest of the Lost had six leaves and limbs and petals . . .

She stepped forward, sniffing the chill, thin mist pooling over the flooded crater. 'I think our sand worm was here long before the coming of the Lost.' Surviving in the dust, where creatures of water and air froze and died as the world cooled – perhaps sleeping away countless years, as the tide of life withdrew from the red rock of the world, waiting patiently until chance brought it a morsel of water or food . . . 'Perhaps the Lost never even knew it was here,' she said.

'If they had known they would probably have tried to kill it,' said Thunder mournfully. 'We should not seek to cross this dust pool.'

'No,' said Icebones. 'No, we shouldn't do that.'

Now the other mammoths were starting to wake. The dawn was filled with the soft sounds of yawns and belches, and the rumbling of half-empty guts.

Icebones and Thunder rejoined their Family.

Chapter Two

THE BLOOD WEED

The land, folded and cracked and cratered, continued to rise inexorably. There was no water save for occasional patches of dirty, hard-frozen ice, and the rocks were bare even of lichen and mosses. The sky was a deep purple-pink, even at noon, and there was never a cloud to be seen.

Icebone's shoulder ached with ice-hard clarity, all day and all night. She limped, favouring the shoulder. But over time that only caused secondary aches in the muscles of her legs and back and neck. And if she ever over-exerted herself she paid the price in racking, wheezing breaths, aching lungs, and an ominous blackness that closed around her vision.

One day, she thought grimly, that fringe would close completely, and once more she would be immersed in cold darkness – just as she had been before setting foot on this crimson plain – but this time, she feared, it was a darkness that would never clear.

It was a relief for them all when they crested a ridge and

found themselves looking down on a deeply incised channel. For the valley contained a flat plain that showed, here and there, the unmistakable white glitter of ice.

Woodsmoke trumpeted loudly. Ignoring his mother's warning rumbles, the calf ran pell-mell down the rocky slope, scattering dust and bits of loose rock beneath his feet. He reached the ice and began to scrape with his stubby tusks.

The others followed more circumspectly, testing the ground with probing trunk tips before each step. But Thunder was soon enthusiastically spearing the ice with his tusks. More hesitantly, Spiral and Breeze copied him.

Icebones recalled how she had had to show the mammoths how water could be dug out from beneath the mud. To Woodsmoke, born during this great migration, it was a natural thing, something he had grown up with. And perhaps *his* calves, learning from him, would approach the skill and expertise once enjoyed by the mammoths of her Island.

Icebones longed to join in, but knew she must conserve her strength. To her shame the weakness of the Matriarch had become a constant unspoken truth among the mammoths.

Alone, she walked cautiously on to the ice.

The frozen lake stretched to the end of the valley. To either side red-brown valley walls rose up to jagged ridges. The ice itself, tortured by wind and sunlight, was contorted into towers, pinnacles, gullies and pits, like the surface of a sea frozen in an instant. Heavily laced with dust and bits of rock, the ice was stained pale pink, and the colour was deepened by the cold salmon colour of the sky: even here on the ice, as everywhere else on these High Plains, she was immersed in redness.

Soon Thunder trumpeted in triumph, 'I am through!'

He had dug a roughly circular pit in the ice. The pit, its walls showing the scrape of mammoth tusks, was filled with dirty green-brown water.

All of them hesitated, for by now they had absorbed many Cycle lessons about the dangers of drinking foul water.

At least I can do this much for them, Icebones thought. 'I will be first,' she said.

With determination she stepped forward and lowered her trunk into the pit. The water was ice cold and smelled stale. Nevertheless she sucked up a trunkful and, with resolution, swallowed it. She said, 'It is full of green living things. But I think it is good for us to drink.' And she took another long, slow trunkful, as was her right as Matriarch.

Defying Family protocol, as calves often would, Wood-smoke hurried forward, knelt down on the gritty ice, and was next to dip his trunk into the ragged hole. But he could not reach, and he squeaked his frustration.

Autumn brushed him aside and dipped her own mighty trunk into the hole. She took a luxurious mouthful, chewing it slightly and spitting out a residue of slimy green stuff. Then she took another trunk's load and carefully dribbled the water into Woodsmoke's eager mouth.

After that, the others crowded around to take their turn.

When they had all drunk their fill, Thunder returned to his pit. He knelt down and reached deep into the water. Icebones could see the big muscles at the top of his trunk working as he explored. The modest pride in his bearing was becoming, Icebones thought. He was growing into a fine Bull, strong in body and mind.

With an effort, he hauled out a mass of slimy green vegetation. He dumped it on the ice. It steamed, rapidly frosting over. He shook his trunk to rid it of tendrils of green murk. 'This is what grows beneath the ice,' he said. 'I could feel sheets of it, waving in the water like the skirt of some drowned mammoth. I think the sheets are held together by that revolting mucus.'

Spiral probed at the mat with her trunk, the tense posture of her body expressing exquisite disgust. 'We cannot eat this,' she said.

Autumn growled, 'You will if you have to.'

'No, Spiral is right,' Icebones said. 'If we are driven to eat this green scum, it will be because we are starving – and we are not that yet.' She sniffed the air. It was not yet midday. 'We will stay here today and tonight, for at least we can drink our fill.'

The mammoths fanned out over the valley, probing at the ice, seeking scraps of food in the wind-carved rock of the walls.

Icebones came to an odd pit in the ice, round and smooth-sided.

She probed into the pit – it was a little wider than her trunk – and she found, nestling at the bottom, a bit of hard black rock. When she dug out the rock and set it on the surface, it felt a little warmer than the surrounding ice. Perhaps it was made warmer than the sun, and that way melted its tunnel into the ice surface, at last falling through to the water beneath, and settling to the lake's dark bed.

She found more of the pits, each of them plunging straight down into the ice. The smaller the stone, the deeper the pit it dug. Driven by absent curiosity she pulled out the rocks wherever she could. Perhaps the rocks would start to dig new pits from where she had set them down, each in its own slow way. And perhaps some other curious mammoth of the future would wonder why some pits had stones in them, and some were empty.

Close to one valley wall she found a stand of squat trees. They had broad roots, well-founded in frozen mud, and their branches were bent over, like a willow's, so that they clung to the rock wall. But the fruit they bore was fat and black and leathery.

They were breathing trees.

She began to pull the leathery fruit off the low, clinging branches. She recalled how the Ragged One had shown her how to extract a mouthful of air from those thick-coated fruit. Each charge of air was invigorating but disappointingly brief, and afterwards her lungs were left aching almost as hard as before.

Thunder called her with a deep rumble. He was standing on the shore's frozen mud, close to a line of low mounds. She left the trees and walked slowly over to him.

The mud was dried and hardened and cracked. She could see how low ridges paralleled the lake's ragged shore: water marks, where the receding lake had churned up the mud at its rim.

She pointed this out to Thunder. 'It is a sign that the lake has been drying for a long time.'

'Yes,' he growled. 'And so is this.' He swept his tusks through one of the mounds. It was just a heap of rocks, she saw, with larger fragments making a loose shell over smaller bits of rubble. But its shape had been smoothly rounded, and inside there were bits of yellow skin that crumbled when Thunder probed at them. 'I think this mound was made in the lake.'

She tried to pick up a fragment of one skin-like flake. It

crumbled, and it was dry, flavourless. 'Perhaps this was once alive. Like the mats you found under the ice.'

'The lake is dying, Icebones. Soon it will be frozen to its base, and then the ice will wear away, and there will be nothing left – nothing but rock, and dried-up flakes like this.'

They walked a little further, following the muddy shore.

In one place the lake bank was shallow, and easily climbed. Icebones clambered up that way. The land beyond was unbroken, harsh. But it was scarred by something hard and shining that marched from one horizon to the other: glimmering, glowing, an immense straight edge imposed on the world.

Icebones and Thunder approached cautiously. 'It is a fence,' he said.

'A thing of the Lost.'

'Yes. A thing to keep animals out – or to keep them in.'

That made no sense to Icebones. The land beyond the fence seemed just as empty and desolate as the land on this side of it. There was nothing to be separated, as far as she could see.

Thunder probed the fence with his tusk. Icebones saw that it was a thing of shining thread, full of little holes. The holes were too small to pass a trunk tip, but she could see through the fence to what lay beyond.

And what she saw there was bones: a great linear heap of them, strewn at the base of the fence.

The mammoths walked further, peering up and down the fence, trying to touch the bones through the mesh.

'I don't think any of them are mammoth,' Icebones said.

Thunder said tightly, 'The animals could smell the water. They couldn't get through the fence. But they couldn't leave; the world was drying, and they couldn't get away from that maddening smell.'

'So they stayed here until they died.'

'Yes.' And he barged the fence with his forehead, ramming it until a section of it gave way. Then he tramped it flat into the dust.

But there were no animals to come charging through in search of water; nothing but the dust of bones rose up in acknowledgement of his strength.

She tugged his trunk, making him come away.

From the lake came a soft crushing sound, a muffled trumpet.

The mammoths whirled.

Icebones looked first for the calf: there he was, safely close by his mother's side, though both Breeze and Woodsmoke were standing stock still, wary.

But of Autumn there was no sign.

Ignoring the pain in her straining lungs, Icebones hurried stiffly on to the ice. 'Where is she? What happened?'

'I don't know,' Breeze called. 'She was at the far side of the lake, seeking clearer water. And then—'

'Keep the calf safe.'

Thunder immediately began to charge ahead.

Icebones grabbed his tail and, with an effort, held him back. 'We may all be in danger. Slowly, Thunder.'

He growled, but he said, 'Lead, Matriarch.'

Trying to restrain her own impatience, Icebones led Thunder and Spiral across the frozen lake, step by step, exploring the complex red-streaked surface with her trunk tip.

She heard a low rumble.

She stopped, listening. The others had heard it too. With more purpose now, but with the same careful step-by-step checking, the three mammoths made their way towards the source of the call.

At last they came to a wide pit, dug or melted into the ice. And here they found Autumn.

She lay on her side, as if asleep. But her body was covered with broad streaks of blood red, as if she had been gouged open by the claws of some huge beast. Her face, too, was hidden in redness, from her mouth to the top of her trunk.

'She is bleeding!' cried Spiral. 'She is dead! She is dead!' Her wails echoed from the high rock walls of the valley.

But Icebones could see that Autumn's small amber eyes were open, and they were fixed on Icebones: intelligent, angry, alert.

Icebones reached down and touched one of the bloody streaks with her trunk. This was not broken flesh. Instead she found a cold, leathery surface that gave when she pushed it, like the skin of a ripe fruit.

'This is a plant,' she said. 'It has grabbed on to Autumn, the way a willow tree grabs on to a rock.' She knelt and leaned into the pit. She stabbed at the plant with her tusk, piercing it easily.

Crimson liquid gushed out stickily, splashing her face. The tendril she had pierced pulled back, the spilled fluid already freezing over.

The plant closed tighter around Autumn, and the Cow groaned.

Spiral touched Icebones's dirtied face curiously and lifted her trunk tip to her mouth. '*It is blood.*'

Thunder growled, 'What manner of plant has blood instead of sap? What manner of plant attacks a full-grown mammoth?'

'She cannot breathe,' Icebones said. 'She will soon die . . .' She reached down and began to stab, carefully and delicately, at the tendrils wrapped over Autumn's mouth. More of the

215

bloody sap spurted. But the plant's grip tightened on Autumn's body, as the trunk of a mammoth closes on a tuft of grass, and Icebones heard the ominous crack of bone.

At last she got Autumn's mouth free. The older Cow took deep, gasping breaths. 'My air,' she said now. 'It sucks out my air! Get it off. Oh, get it off . . .'

Icebones and Thunder began to stab and prise at the bloody tendrils. The eerie blood-sap pumped out and spilled into the pit, and soon their tusks and the hair on their faces were soaked with the thick crimson fluid. But wherever they cut away a tendril more would come sliding out of the mass beneath Autumn – and with every fresh stab or slice the tendrils tightened further.

'Enough,' Icebones said. She straightened up and, with a blood-stained trunk, pulled Thunder back.

Woodsmoke stood with Breeze a little way away from the pit. He trumpeted in dismay. 'You aren't going to let her die.'

It struck Icebones then that Woodsmoke had never seen anybody die. She wiped her bloody trunk on the ice, then touched the calf's scalp. 'We can't fight it, little one. If we hurt the blood weed it hurts Autumn more.'

'Then find some way to get it off her without hurting it.'

Thunder rumbled, from the majesty of his adolescence, 'When you grow up you'll learn that sometimes there are only hard choices, calf—'

But Icebones shouldered him aside, her mind working furiously. 'What do you mean, Woodsmoke? *How* can we get the weed to leave Autumn alone?'

Woodsmoke pondered, his little trunk wrinkling. 'Why does it want Autumn?'

'We think it is stealing her breath.'

'Then give it something it wants more than Autumn's breath. I like grass,' he said. 'But I like saxifrage better. If I see saxifrage I will leave the grass and take the saxifrage . . .'

Icebones turned to Thunder. 'What else could we offer it?'

Thunder said, 'Another mammoth's breath. *My* breath. Icebones, if you wish it—'

'No,' she said reluctantly. 'I don't want to lose anybody else. But what else . . . ?'

Even as she framed the notion herself, Thunder trumpeted excitedly. '*The breathing trees*,' they shouted together.

'Get the fruit,' said Icebones. 'You and Spiral. You are faster than I am. *Go.*'

Without hesitation the two young mammoths lumbered over the folded ice towards the breathing trees, where they clung to the lake's rocky shore.

Autumn moaned again. 'Oh, it hurts . . . I am sorry . . .'

'Don't be sorry,' said Woodsmoke mournfully.

'It is my fault,' Autumn gasped. 'The plant lay over the pit. It was a neat trap . . . I did not check . . . I walked across it without even thinking, and when I fell, it wrapped itself around me . . . Oh! It is very tight on my ribs . . .'

'Don't talk,' said Icebones. Her voice lapsed into a wordless, reassuring rumble. Breeze joined in, and even Woodsmoke added his shallow growl.

Perhaps the pit had been melted into the ice by a stone, Icebones thought. Perhaps the blood weed, driven by some dark red instinct, had learned to use such pits as a trap. And it waited, and waited . . .

Autumn lay still, her eyes closed, her breath coming in thin, hasty gasps. But Icebones could see that the blood weed was covering her mouth once more.

This blood weed, like the breathing tree, was a plant of the cold and airlessness of the desiccated heights of this world. It was as alien to her as the birds of the air or the worms that crawled in lake-bottom mud – and yet it killed.

'. . . We got it! We got it, Icebones!' Thunder and Spiral came charging across the ice. Thunder bore in his trunk the top half of a breathing tree, spindly black branches laden with the strange dark fruit. He threw the tree down on the ice, close to the pit. 'Now what?'

Icebones grabbed a fruit with her trunk, lowered it into the pit, and, with a determined squeeze, popped it over the prone body of Autumn.

A little gust of fog burst from the fruit.

The tendrils of the blood weed slithered over the mammoth's hair. Autumn gasped, as if the pressure on her ribs was relieved a little. But the weed had not let go, and already the fruit's air had dissipated.

'More,' said Icebones. 'Thunder, hold the tree over the pit.'

So Thunder held out the broken branches while Spiral, Icebones and Breeze all worked to pluck and pop the fat fruits.

With every brief gust of air the agitation of the weed increased. But they were soon running out of fruit, and Autumn's eyes were rolling upwards. Icebones growled, despairing.

And then, quite suddenly, the weed slid away from Autumn. With an eerie sucking noise its tendrils reached up, like blood-gorged worms, to the dark breathing-tree branches above it.

'Let it have the branches, Thunder! But keep hold of the root—'

The weed knotted itself around the branches, moving with a slow, slithering, eerie stealth.

When the last of its tendrils had slid off Autumn's prone form, Spiral and Thunder hurled the tree as hard and as far as they could. The tangle of branches went spinning through the thin air, taking the crimson mass of the weed with it. Its blood-sap leaked in a cold rain that froze as soon as it touched the ice.

Chapter Three

THE ICE MAMMOTHS

They were suspended in dense, eerie silence – not a bird cry, not the scuffle of a lemming or the call of a fox – nothing but bright red rock and purple sky and six toiling mammoths.

There was nothing to eat, nothing to drink.

All of them were gaunt now, their hair thinning. Their ribs and shoulder blades and knees stuck out of their flesh, and their bony heads looked huge, as if they were gaining wisdom, even as their bodies shrivelled.

And day after day wore away.

They came to another lake, much smaller. They walked down to it, slow and weary.

This time the water was frozen down to its base. The ice was worn away – not melted, but sublimated: over the years the ice had evaporated without first turning to water. The mammoths ground at this stone-hard, deeply cold stuff, seeking crushed fragments they could pop into their mouths.

Around the lake they found scraps of vegetation. But the

trees were dead, without leaves, and their trunks were hollowed out, and the grass blades broke easily in trunk fingers, dried out like straw.

Thunder, frustrated, picked up a rock and slammed it against another. Both rocks broke open with sharp cracks.

Icebones explored the exposed surfaces, sniffing. There was green in the rock, she saw: a thin layer of it, shading to yellow-brown, buried a little way inside the rock itself, following the eroded contours of its surface. Perhaps it was lichen, or moss. The green growing things must shelter here, trapping sunlight and whatever scraps of water settled on the rock. But when Icebones scraped out some of the green-stained rock with a tusk tip, she found nothing but salty grains that ground against her molars, with not a trace of water or nourishment.

She flung away the rock. She felt angry, resentful at being reduced to scraping at a bit of stone. And then she felt a twinge of shame at having destroyed the refuge of this tiny, patient scrap of life.

The lake was fringed by dried and cracked mud. Walking there, Icebones found herself picking over the scattered and gnawed bones of deer, bison, lemmings, horses, and they spoke to her of the grisly story that had unfolded here.

But there was hope, she saw. Some footprints in the mud led *away* from the deadly betrayal of the pond and off to the south, before vanishing into the red dust. Perhaps some instinct among these frightened, foolish animals had guided them the way Icebones knew the mammoths must travel, to the deep sanctuary of the Footfall.

Exploring the mud with her trunk tip, Icebones found one very strange set of prints. They were round, like mammoth footprints, but much smaller and smoother. These creatures had come here after the rest had died off, for bits of bone were to be found crushed into the strange prints. And, here and there, these anonymous visitors had dug deep holes – like water holes, but deeper than she could reach with her trunk.

She noticed Spiral. The tall Cow was standing alone on the ice at the edge of the lake, her trunk tucked defensively under her head. She was gazing at a brown, shapeless lump that lay huddled on the rocky shore.

Thunder stood by her, wrapping his trunk over Spiral's head to comfort her.

Spiral said, 'I was working the ice. I didn't even notice *that* at first. It doesn't even *smell* . . .'

That was a dead animal. It was a goat, Icebones thought – or rather it had once been a goat, for it was clearly long dead. It lay on its back, its head held up stiffly into the air as if it was staring at the sky. Its skin seemed to be mostly intact, even retaining much of its hair, but it was drawn tight over bones and lumpy flesh. The goat's mouth was open. The skin of its face had drawn back, exposing the teeth and a white sheet of jaw bone.

The goat had even kept its eyes. Exposed by the shrinking-back of its skin, the eyeballs were just globes of yellow-white, with a texture like soft fungus.

'It must have lost its way,' said Thunder gently.

'It died here,' said Icebones. 'But there are no wolves or foxes or carrion birds to eat its flesh. Not even the flies which feast on the dead. And its body dried out.'

Spiral prodded the corpse with her spiralling tusks. It shifted and rocked, rigid, like a piece of wood. 'Will we finish up dried out and dead like this? And then who will Remember us?'

'We are not lost,' Thunder growled. 'We are not goats. We are mammoth. We will find the way.'

They stayed a day and a night at the pond, gnawing at bitter ice.

Then they moved on.

They frequently came across blood weed.

It was difficult to spot. The weed gave off little odour, and its blood-red colour almost exactly matched the harsh crimson of the underlying rock and dust – which was probably no accident.

The mammoths found bits of bone, cleansed of flesh, in the weeds' traps, but all such traces were old. Even the weeds had not fed or drunk for a long time. Icebones wondered if these plants could last for ever, waiting for the occasional fall of un-wary migrant animals into their patient maws.

Icebones came across a new kind of plant, nestled in a hollow. It was like a flower blossom, cupped like an upturned skull, and its tight-folded petals were waxy and stiff. The whole thing was as wide as a mammoth's footprint, and about as deep. A sheet of some shining, translucent substance coated the top of the blossom, sealing it off. Under the translucent sheet Icebones thought she saw a glint of green.

Cautiously she popped the covering sheet with the tip of her tusk. The sheet shrivelled back, breaking up into threads that dried and snapped. A small puff of moisture escaped, a trace of water that instantly frosted on the petals. A spider scuttled at the base of the blossom.

Icebones scraped off the frost eagerly and plunged her moist trunk tip into her mouth. It was barely a trace, but it tasted delicious, reviving her spirit a great deal more than it nourished her body. She picked the flower apart and chewed it carefully. Despite that trace of green there was little flavour or nourishment to be had, and she spat it out.

She called the others, and they soon found more of the plants.

Each plant sheltered spiders, which made the moisture-trapping lids that allowed the green hearts of the plants to grow. So each flower was like a tiny Family, she thought, spiders and plant working together to keep each other alive.

It was Thunder who came up with the best way to use the flowers. He opened his mouth wide and pushed the whole plant in, lid first. Then he bit to pop the lid, and so was able to suck down every bit of the trapped moisture. But he had to scrape off bits of spider-web that clung to his mouth and trunk, and Icebones saw spiders scrambling away into his fur.

Spiral made a hoot of disgust. 'Eating spider-web. How disgusting.'

Icebones found another plant and, deliberately, plucked it and thrust it into her mouth. 'Spiders won't kill you. Thirst will. You will all do as Thunder does—'

Suddenly Thunder stood tall, trunk raised, his small ears spread.

The others froze in their tracks – every one of them, flighty Spiral, Autumn with her aching ribs, Breeze with her scored back, even restless, growing, ever-hungry Woodsmoke, as still as if they had been shaped from the ancient rock itself. Icebones found a moment to be proud of them, for a disciplined silence, vital to any prey animal, was a characteristic of a well-run Family.

And then she heard what had disturbed Thunder. It was a scraping, as if something was digging deep into the ground.

'But,' Autumn murmured, 'what kind of animal makes burrowing noises like that?'

Thunder said, 'There is a crater rim ahead. It hides us from the source of the noise. I will go ahead alone, and—'

'No, brave Thunder. We are safer together.' Icebones stepped towards the crater ridge. 'Let's go, let's go.'

The other mammoths quickly formed up behind her. They climbed the shallow, much-eroded crater rim.

Icebones paused when she got to the rim's flattened top, her trunk raised.

In the crater basin, heavy heads lifted slowly.

Thunder pealed out a bright trumpet. He hurried forward, scattering dust and bits of rock. Icebones, more warily, clambered down the slope, keeping her trunk raised.

Mammoths — at least that was her first impression. They were heavy, dark, hairy creatures, spread over the basin. She saw several adults – Cows? – clustered together around a stand of breathing trees, digging at the roots. A black-faced calf poked its head out through the dense hairs beneath its mother's belly, curious like all calves. Further away there were looser groupings of what she supposed were Bulls.

As Thunder approached, the Cows lifted their trunks out of the holes they had dug. Their trunks were broad but very long, longer than any adult mammoth Icebones had met before. Their tusks were short and stubby. They huddled closer together, the adults forming a solid phalanx before the stand of trees.

They looked like mammoths. They behaved as mammoths might. But they did not *smell* like mammoths. And as Icebones worked her way down the slope, her sense of unease deepened.

Woodsmoke had wandered away from his mother. Two calves peered at him from a forest of thick black hair. The adults watched him suspiciously, but no mammoth would be hostile to a calf, however strange. Soon Woodsmoke had locked his trunk around a calf's trunk, and was tugging vigorously.

Icebones announced clearly, 'I am Icebones, daughter of Silverhair. Who is Matriarch here?'

The strange mammoths rumbled, heads nodding and bodies swaying, as if in confusion.

At length a mammoth stepped forward. 'My name is Cold-As-Sky. I do not know you. You are not of our Clan.'

Cold-As-Sky was about Icebones's size, as round and solid as a boulder. Her hair was black and thick. There was a thick ridged brow on her forehead, sheltering small orange eyes. She had a broad hump on her back, and when she took a breath, deep and slow, that hump swelled up, as if she carried a second set of lungs there. Her long trunk lay thickly coiled on the rock at her feet. Her voice was as deep as the ground's own songs.

Icebones stepped forward tentatively. 'We have come far.'

'You are not like us.'

'No,' Icebones said sadly. 'We are not like you.' As unlike, in a different way, as the Swamp-Mammoths had been unlike Icebones and her Family. 'And yet we are Cousins. You speak the language of Kilukpuk.'

Just as Chaser-Of-Frogs had reacted to the ancient name, so Cold-As-Sky looked briefly startled. But her curiosity was soon replaced by her apparently customary hostility. 'We speak as we have always spoken.'

Her language, in fact, was indistinct. This Ice Mammoth spoke only with the deep thrumming of her chest and belly, omitting the higher sounds, the chirrups and snorts and mewls a mammoth would make with her trunk and throat. But her voice, deep and vibrant, would carry easily through the rocks, Icebones realised. This was a mammoth made for this high cold place, where the air was thin, and only rocks could be heard.

Cold-As-Sky said now, 'You call yourself my Cousin. What are you doing here? Do you intend to steal my air trees?'

Air trees – breathing trees? 'No,' said Icebones wearily. 'But we are hungry and thirsty.'

'Go back to where you came from.'

'We cannot go back,' Thunder said.

Icebones stepped forward and reached out with her trunk. '*We are Cousins.*'

Cold-As-Sky growled, but did not back away.

Icebones probed at the other's face. That black hair was dense and slippery, and as cold as the rock beneath her feet. She finally found flesh, deep within the layers of hair. The flesh was cold and hard, and covered in fine, criss-cross ridges. She pinched it with her trunk fingers. The other did not react – as if the flesh was without sensation, like scar tissue. The trunk itself was very wide and bulbous near the face, with vast black nostrils.

To her shock, Icebones saw that Cold-As-Sky's trunk tip was lined with small white teeth. The teeth were set in a bony jaw, like a tiny mouth at the end of her trunk.

Cold-As-Sky's mouth was a gaping blue-black cavern. Even her tongue was blue. Icebones touched that tongue now – and tasted water.

Cold-As-Sky growled again, pulling back. 'Your trunk is hot and wet. You are a creature of the warmth and the thick air and the running water.' Her immense trunk folded up, becoming a fat, stubby tube. 'This is not your place.'

Icebones's anger battled with pride – and desperation. '*I tasted water on your lips*. Please, Cousin—'

'And you have water,' Thunder said, stepping forward menacingly.

Cold–As–Sky snorted contempt, a hollow sound which echoed from the recesses of vast sinuses. 'If you want water, take it. Come.' And she turned and began to push her way through the solid wall her Family had made.

Wary, Icebones followed, with Thunder at her side.

They came to the stand of breathing trees. Icebones saw that the Ice Mammoths had burrowed into the hard rocky ground at their roots. One Cow was kneeling, her body a black ball of shining hair, and her trunk was stretched out, pushed deep into the ground.

Icebones probed into one of the holes with her own trunk. It was much deeper than she could reach. But, around its rim, she saw traces of frost.

Icebones imagined those strange trunk-tip teeth digging into the rock and permafrost, chipping bit by bit towards the water that lay far, far below. With such a long trunk, Icebones saw, mammoths could survive even in this frozen wasteland, where the water lay very deep indeed.

'If you want water,' Cold–As–Sky said, 'dig for it as we do.'

Now Autumn walked up, grand, dignified, rumbling. 'You can see that is impossible for us.'

'Then you will go thirsty.'

'*You* have calves,' Autumn said harshly. '*You* are mammoth.'

Cold–As–Sky flinched, and Icebones saw that the Oath of Kilukpuk, which demanded loyalty between Cousins, was not forgotten here.

But nevertheless Cold–As–Sky said, 'Your calves are not my

calves. Your kind has come this way before — a strange ragged-haired one, mumbling—'

Autumn said sharply, '*She* has been this way?'

Icebones said, 'If you will not give us water, will you guide us? We are going south. We seek a great pit in the ground, where the warmth may linger.'

'I have heard its song in the rocks.' Cold-As-Sky stamped the ground and nodded her head. 'You will fall into the pit and its rocks will cover your bones . . . if you ever reach it, for the way is hard.'

'*Which way?*'

Cold-As-Sky turned to the south-east. Icebones looked, and felt the slow wash of echoes from the hard folded landscapes there.

'I can feel it,' Thunder said, dismayed. 'Broken land . . . Great chains of mountains . . . One crater rim after another . . . It will be the hardest land we have encountered yet.'

Autumn said grimly, 'The Footfall of Kilukpuk made a mighty splash.'

'No matter how difficult, that is our trail,' said Icebones.

Woodsmoke had been playing with a calf of the Ice Mammoths, pulling at her trunk as if trying to drag the other out from the forest of her parents' legs. Now Breeze pulled him away. Woodsmoke looked back regretfully to a small round face, a pair of wistful orange eyes.

Autumn said to Cold-As-Sky, 'Why are you so hostile? We have done you no harm.'

'This world was ours,' growled Cold-As-Sky, her voice deep as thunder. 'Once it was all like this. The blood weed and the air tree flourished everywhere, and there were vast Clans, covering the land . . . Then the warmth came, and *you* came.

And we were forced to retreat to this hard, rocky land, where our calves fall into the pits of the blood weed. But now the warmth is dying, and you are dying with it. And soon I will walk on your bones, and the bones of your calves.'

That strange perversion of the rite of Remembering made Icebones shudder. But she said, 'We did not bring the warmth. We did not banish the cold. If you are hurt, we did not hurt you. We are your Cousins.'

It seemed to Icebones that Cold-As-Sky was about to respond. But then she turned away, and the Ice Mammoths returned to their deep holes in the ground.

Icebones said, 'Let's go, let's go.' And, with one determined footstep after another, she began the steady plod towards the south-east, where distant mountains cast long jagged shadows.

Chapter Four

THE DUST

I know it is hard, little Icebones. But you have walked your mammoths around the world. And there is only a little further to go.

'But that last "little further" may be the hardest of all, Boaster.'

Don't call me Boaster! Tell me about the land . . .

And she hesitated, for this land was like nothing she had experienced, either in her old life before the Sleep, or even here in this strange, cold world. For this land had been warped by the great impact which had created the Footfall of Kilukpuk itself.

She stood at the head of an ancient water-carved channel. The ground was broken into heaped-up fragments, as if the water, draining away, had left behind a vast underground cavern into which the land had collapsed. But the fallen rocks were very old, heavily pitted and eroded and covered with dust. And when the mammoths dug deeper into the ground they found it riddled with broad tunnels – but they were dry, hollowed out like ancient bones, as if the water that made them had long disappeared.

All around her there were hills, great clumps of them, grouped into chains like the wrinkles of an ancient mammoth. But the mountains were eroded to a weary smoothness, and they were extensively punctured and smashed by younger, smaller craters.

Thunder, his listening skills developing all the time, said he thought that around the central basin there were – not the single chain of rim mountains that surrounded most craters – *five* concentric rings of mountains, vast ripples in the rock thrown up by the giant primordial splash. Lacing through these rim-mountain chains were vast, shallow channels, apparently cut by water in the deep past. The channels themselves were covered in crater punctures, or pierced by sharper, litter-filled channels.

Around Icebones, the Family were rooting desultorily at the unpromising, hummocky ground. Icebones felt an unreasonable stab of impatience with this little group of gaunt, helpless mammoths.

She thought of the Clan gatherings Silverhair had told her of, when Families and bachelor herds would congregate on great green-waving steppes, so many mammoths they turned the air golden with their shining hair, and for days on end they would talk and fight and mate . . .

But such gatherings had been even before Silverhair's time. This starving group were perhaps the only true mammoths in half a world, and Icebones knew she had no choice but to accept her lot.

Boaster rumbled softly, still waiting for her reply.

'It is a very old land, Boaster,' she said at last. 'And, like an old mammoth, it is ill-tempered when disturbed.'

It is an old world, I think, much disturbed by the Lost.

But now Thunder was calling, his voice a deep uncomfortable growl.

'I must go. Graze well, Boaster.'

And you, little Icebones . . .

Thunder was standing on a slight rise, staring to the south, trunk raised. She saw that a wind, blowing from that direction, was ruffling the hair around his face. 'Can you taste it?'

Peering south, she made out a hard black line that spread right along the horizon, separating the crimson land from the purple sky. The wind touched her face. It was harsh and gritty. She raised her trunk, exposing its sensitive tip. When she put the tip in her mouth she could taste iron.

'Dust,' she said. 'Like the storm in the Gouge.'

'Yes. It is a storm, and it carries a vast cloud of dust. And it is coming towards us.'

Icebones felt her strength dissipate, like water running into the dust. No more, she thought: we have endured enough.

'You are alert, Thunder. We rely on your senses.'

But this time her praise made little impact, for his worry was profound.

The light grew muddled, as if the day itself was confused. Gradually the wind picked up, blustering in their faces and whipping dust devils before it.

The storm front grew into a towering wall, a curtain that was deep crimson-black at its base and a wispy pink-grey at the top, hanging from the sky like the guard hairs of some vast mammoth. Icebones could hear the crack and grumble of thunder, and the ragged wisps at the top of the sheet of air whipped and churned angrily.. It was an awesome display of raw power.

Icebones had decided that the mammoths should not try to move. They were already badly weakened by hunger and thirst and cold. She tried to ensure they rested, gathering their energy, just as the storm did.

The mammoths had nothing to say to each other. They merely stood, bruised, dismayed, waiting for the storm to break on them.

There was a moment of stillness. Even the wind died briefly. Icebones could see her own shadow at her feet.

When she looked up she could see the sun. It shone fitfully through veils of black cloud and dust that raced across the sky, churning and thrashing.

And then the sun vanished, and the air exploded.

Gusts as hard as rock battered at Icebones's face and legs and neck, and the dust they carried scoured mercilessly at her hair and exposed flesh. It was as if she was in a bubble inside the dust, a bubble that was flying sideways through the air. The sun showed only in glimpses between tall, scudding clouds, and lightning crackled far above her, casting deep purple glows through layers of cloud and dust.

She was immersed in vast layers of noise: the crack of thunder, the howl of the air over the rock, the relentless scraping of the dust. Her sound impressions broke up into chaotic shards. She lost her deep mammoth's sense of the land, and she felt lost, bewildered.

And – unlike the storm they had endured in the Gouge – this wind was *dry*, as dry as the dust it carried, and it seemed to suck the moisture from her blood.

The mammoths were around her, and she felt the tension of

their muscles as they fought the storm. But she knew she was burning her last reserves of strength just to stay standing against the pressure of the wind.

Autumn was beside her, trumpeting: 'It will take half a day for this storm to wash over us, for it stretches deep into the southern lands.'

'I did not imagine it could be so bad. If we stay here our bones will be worn to dust . . .'

'We must find shelter.' That was Thunder, his Bull's growl almost lost in the howl of the air. 'There is a crater rim, some way to the south.'

'We must try,' Icebones said. 'But how will we find it?'

'The storm comes from the south. If we head into it, we will find our ridge.'

Autumn rumbled, 'It is hard enough just to stand. To walk into that horror—'

'Nevertheless we must,' Icebones said. 'Thunder, you go first. The next in line grab his tail. If anyone loses hold we stop immediately. Thunder, you will not have to lead for long. We will take turns.'

Thunder said, 'I will endure—'

'We will do it the way I say. And be wary of the blood weed.' Trying to project confidence, she trumpeted, 'Let us begin. Let's go, let's go . . .'

To break their huddled formation, to expose themselves to the wind, was hard. No matter how she tucked her trunk under her face, no matter how tightly she squeezed shut her eyes, still the dust lashed at her as if it was a living thing, malevolent, determined to injure. The calf was deeply un-happy, trumpeting his discomfort into the wind, continually trying to push his way back under his mother's guard hairs.

As if from a vast distance she heard Thunder's thin, readying trumpet cry.

A few heartbeats later, Spiral began to move, her steady footsteps determined, her buttocks swaying. At the end of the line, Icebones, keeping a careful hold on Spiral's tail, followed behind.

They walked into howling darkness. Icebones could tell nothing of the land around her, smell nothing but the harsh iron tang of the dust that clogged her nostrils and mouth. It was a shameful, selfish relief to shelter behind Spiral's huge bulk.

Spiral stopped abruptly. Icebones's head rammed into her thighs.

Icebones felt her way along the line to sniff out the problem.

It was the calf. Wailing, terrified, Woodsmoke had slumped to the ground.

With much cajoling and lifting by the strong trunks of Autumn and Icebones, Woodsmoke finally got to his feet. But Icebones could feel how uncertain his legs were, as weak as if he was a newborn again.

They managed only a few more steps before the calf collapsed once more.

Icebones had the mammoths form up into a wedge shape facing the storm, with one of the adults at the apex, and the calf and his mother sheltered at the rear.

'His strength is gone, Icebones,' Breeze cried through the storm's noise. 'He is hungry and thirsty and I have no milk to give him. We must stay here with him until the storm is over.'

'But,' Thunder growled, 'we *cannot* stay here. This foul dust sucks the last moisture out of my body.'

'We can't stay and we can't go on,' Spiral said. 'What must we do, Matriarch?'

Battered by the storm's violence, blinded, deafened, her own strength wearing down, Icebones knew how she must answer. And she knew that she must test her new Family's resolve as it had not been tested before.

. . . But I am just Icebones, she thought desperately. I am little more than a calf myself. Who am I to inflict such pain on these patient, loyal, suffering mammoths? *How do I know this is right?* Oh, Silverhair, if only you were here!

But her mother was not here. And her course was clear. She was Matriarch. And, like generations of Matriarchs before her, she reached into the Cycle, the ancient wisdom of mammoths who had learned to survive.

'Autumn, Thunder – do you think we could reach the crater rim, if not for the calf?'

Thunder seemed baffled. 'But we have the calf—'

'Just tell me.'

'Yes. We are strong enough for that, Matriarch.'

Icebones said gravely, '*The mammoth dies, but mammoths live on.*'

Spiral understood first. She wailed, 'Do you see what this monster is saying? She wants us to abandon the calf. We must go to the crater rim, and save ourselves, while he dies alone in the storm. *Alone.*'

'No!' Breeze wrapped her trunk around her fallen calf.

Autumn spoke, and there was a huge, impressive sadness in her voice. 'Daughter, you can bear other calves. Others who will grow strong, and continue the Family . . . *You* are more important than Woodsmoke, because of those other calves.'

'Kilukpuk will care for him,' said Icebones. '*If a mammoth*

237

dies young, it is easy for him to throw off his coat of earth, and to play in the light of the aurora . . .'

'There is no aurora here,' Spiral said bleakly.

'Would you sacrifice him, Icebones?' Breeze trumpeted. 'Would *you*, mother, if this was your calf?'

The moment stretched, the tension between the mammoths palpable.

This was the crux, Icebones knew. And Autumn was the key. If Autumn maintained her resolve, then they would abandon the calf, and go on. And if she did not, they would all die, here in this screaming storm.

Autumn sighed, a deep rumble that carried through the storm. 'No,' she said at last. 'No, I could not abandon my calf.'

And Icebones, with a deep, failing regret, knew they were lost.

Breeze clutched her calf, and her sister came close, both of them stroking and reassuring the calf as best they could.

'I am sorry,' Autumn said, huddling close to Icebones. 'I did not have the strength. It is hard to be mammoth.'

'Yes. Yes, it is hard.'

'We have been toys of the Lost too long . . .'

'Let us huddle. Perhaps we will defeat this storm yet.'

But she knew that wasn't possible. And, from the tense, subdued postures of Autumn and Thunder beside her, she sensed they knew it too.

The continent-sized dust storm continued, relentless, cruel, oblivious to the mammoths' despair.

The dust clogged her trunk and mouth, until she was as dry as a corpse. And still the storm went on, so dense she no longer knew if it was day or night. Perhaps she even slept a while, exhausted, her body battling the storm without her conscious control.

I tried, Silverhair. But they just weren't ready to be a Family – a true Family, able to face the hard truths as well as the easy ones . . .

No. *I* was not ready. *I* have failed.

But it hardly mattered now. After a few days, when they were reduced to scoured-clean bones, nobody would ever know what happened here.

She felt a new, hard form beside her. She turned sluggishly, trying to lift her trunk.

She sensed a stocky body, hair that was dense and slick, crimson against the storm's dark light.

'You are Cold-As-Sky,' she said, her voice thick with dust.

The other did not reply.

'There is no water here.'

'No,' said the Ice Mammoth, her voice somehow clear through the storm. 'This land is very old. Even the deep-buried ice has sublimated away.'

'But you live.'

'But I live. I carry water in my throat, and in a hump on my back, enough to let me survive the longest dust storm.'

'My trunk is clogged,' Icebones said softly. 'All I can taste is dust. Cousin, give me water.'

Cold-As-Sky ignored her. '*This* is the truth of this world. This is how it was before the Lost came here. The planet itself is trying to kill you now. You are meant to die. Just as *we* were meant to die. Did you know that?'

Icebones did not reply, wishing only that Cold-As-Sky would leave her alone with her blackness and despair.

But Cold-As-Sky went on, 'It is true. The first of us who

awoke found that all the world was like this high, broken plain. There were no soft green things, no pockets of thick wet air to clog the lungs . . . Only the clean rock and the red sky. And the only water was buried deep in the dust, where it should lie, where it is safe.

'And we were the only living things. We Ice Mammoths, and the blood weed, and the air trees, and the spider-flowers.

'Many calves died, gasping for air as they were born. But we endured. Slowly the trees made the air thicker, and slowly the spider-flowers captured the water. And we Ice Mammoths dug ancient water out of the ground, and broke up the rock with our tusks, and made the red dust rich with our dung.

'You call yourself a Matriarch. I was born knowing that word. And I was born knowing that *we* had no Matriarch to teach us, to show us how to dig the roots of the breathing trees, or to drink the blood of the weed. We had to learn it all, learn for ourselves. And every scrap of wisdom was earned at the cost of a life. What do you think of that? Where is your Kilukpuk now?'

Icebones, enduring, said nothing; the Ice Mammoth's voice, low and harsh, was like the voice of the engulfing storm itself.

'The Lost were already here, huddling in caves. They had shining beetles that dug and crawled and crushed rock, and a great tusk in the sky that burned channels into the ground. But we were more important than any of that. We knew it. *That* is why the Lost made us, and put us here. We broke the land for them. And we had many calves, and we spread—'

'And you changed the world,' said Icebones.

'Yes,' Cold-As-Sky said bitterly. 'Our tusks and our dung made the land ready for creatures like *you*, with your green plants we could not eat, and your thick wet air we could not even breathe . . . And with every scrap of land that was changed there was a little less room left for *us*. Many died – the old and the very young first – and each year there are fewer calves than the last . . .'

'I am sorry.'

'You do not understand,' Cold-As-Sky said bleakly. 'It was our destiny to die. To make the land, and then die away, leaving it for *you*.

'But then the Lost flew off into the sky in their shining seeds.

'The green things started to blacken and die. The ponds of murky water sank back into the ground and froze over. The ancient cold returned. The dust was freed, and the world-spanning storms began again. And we touched each other's mouths, and tasted hope for the first time in memory.'

'And that is why we are dying,' Icebones said.

'*This is not your land. If you live, I die.*'

'We are Cousins, Calves of Kilukpuk,' Icebones growled. 'You know the Oath. Every mammoth is born with the Oath, just as she is born knowing the name of Kilukpuk, and the tongue she taught us. And so you know that if the Oath is broken, the dream of Kilukpuk will die at last . . . But enough. I am weary. I have come far, Cousin, and I am ready to die, if I must. Leave me.'

And, as the dust swirled around her, it seemed she drifted into blankness once more, as if letting go of her hold on the world's tail.

But then something probed at her mouth: a trunk, strong, leathery, cold. And water trickled into her throat.

She sucked at the trunk, like a calf at her mother's breast. The water, ice cold, washed away the dust that had caked over her tongue.

But then, though her thirst still raged, she pushed the trunk away. 'The calf,' she gasped.

She sensed the vast bulk of the Ice Mammoth move off into the howling storm, seeking Woodsmoke.

Chapter Five

THE FOOTFALL

Icebones breasted a ridge, exhausted, her shoulder a clear icicle of pain. She paused at the crest.

She saw that they had reached a place where the land descended sharply. A new vista opened up before her: a land-scape sunk deep beneath the level of this high, broken plain. Within huge concentric systems of rock, she saw a puddle of green and water-blue.

It was a tremendous crater. It was the Footfall of Kilukpuk.

And, even from this high vantage, still suspended in the thin air, Icebones could hear the call of mammoths.

Eagerly, her breath a rattle in her throat, she walked on, step by painful step.

The Family climbed down through crumpled, eroded rim mountains.

On the horizon Icebones made out complex purple shadows that must be the rim walls on the far side of this great crater.

They seemed impossibly far away. And the wall systems were extensively damaged. In one place a fire mountain towered from beyond the horizon, a vast, flat cone. The rim mountains before it were broken, as if rivers of rock had long ago washed them away and flooded stretches of the central plain. Further to the east, the rim mountains were pierced by giant notches. They were valleys, perhaps, cut by immense floods. Everything here was ancient, Icebones realised: ancient and remade, over and over.

Plodding steadily, the mammoths left the terrain of the rim mountains. They reached a belt of land around the central basin itself, a hard red-black rock, folded and wrinkled into ridges and gullies and stubby isolated mesas.

Icebones could hear the broken song of the ground beneath her, feel the deep shattering it had endured, deep beyond the limits of her perception. But since it had formed, this ancient scar tissue had been crumpled and folded and eroded. Every rocky protrusion was carved and shaped by wind and rain, and dust was everywhere, heaped up against the larger rocks and ridges.

But even here they found stands of grass and struggling herbs and trees, and shallow ponds which were not frozen all the way to their base. Already the bony rockscape over which they had struggled for so long, with its killer weed and breathing trees and distorted, resentful Ice Mammoths, seemed a foul dream, and the habitual ache in Icebones's chest began to fade.

After many days' walking over this ridged plain, the mammoths at last reached the basin itself.

Quite suddenly, Icebones found herself stepping on to thick loam that gave gently under her weight. When she lifted her foot she could see how she had left a neat round print; the soil here was thick and dense with life.

All around her the green of living things lapped between crimson ridges and mesas, like a rising tide.

The mammoths fanned out over the soft ground, ripping eagerly at mouthfuls of grass, grunting their pleasure and relief.

This lowest basin was a cupped land, a secret land of hills and valleys and glimmering ponds. Icebones made out the rippling sheen of grass, herbivore herds which moved like brown clouds over the ground, and flocks of birds glimmering in the air. And, right at the centre of the basin, there was an immense, dense forest, a squat pillar of dark brown that thrust out of the ground, huge indeed to be visible at this distance.

Here, all the ancient drama of impacts and rocks and water had become a setting for the smaller triumphs and tragedies of life.

Woodsmoke ran stiff-legged to the shore of a small lake where geese padded back and forth on ice floes. The mammoth calf went hurtling into the water, trumpeting, hair flying, splashing everywhere. The geese squawked their annoyance and rose in a cloud of rippling wings.

Icebones watched him, envying his vigour.

Woodsmoke, shaking water out of a cloud of new-sprouting guard hairs, ran to Breeze. The calf wrapped his trunk around his mother's leg, a signal that he wished to feed. Welcoming, she lifted her leg, and he raised his trunk and clambered beneath her belly fur, seeking to clamp his mouth on her warm dug.

Icebones might have left him to die on the High Plains.

Warily she explored her own feelings. Woodsmoke's death would have left a hole in her that would never have healed, she thought. But she knew, too, that it would have been right – that she would make the same decision again.

Autumn, more sedately, came to Icebones. 'It is a good place. You were right, Icebones.'

Together they walked back towards the foothills of the high rocky plain. At the fringe of the broad pool of steppe there was a stretch of mud, frozen hard and bearing the imprint of many vanished hooves and feet.

Icebones sniffed the air. 'Yes. It is a good place. But look at this. Even here the tide of life is receding – even here, in the Footfall itself.'

Autumn wrapped her trunk over Icebones's. 'We are exhausted, Icebones, and so are you. Tomorrow's problems can wait until we are stronger. For today, enjoy the water and the grass and the sweet willow twigs.'

'Yes,' Icebones said. 'You are wise, Autumn, as always—'

They heard a mammoth's greeting rumble.

Immediately both Cows turned that way, trunks raised.

It was a Bull. He was walking out of the central steppe plain towards them. He was no youth like Thunder, but a mature Bull in the prime of his life, a pillar of muscle and rust-brown hair, with two magnificent tusks that curled before his face. He towered over Icebones – taller than any of the mammoths of her Family, taller than any mammoth she had ever encountered before her Sleep.

He gazed down at her, curious, excited. '. . . Icebones?' His voice was complex, like the voice of every mammoth, a mixture of trunk chirps and snorts, rumblings from his head and chest, and the stamping of his feet. But she recognised the deep undertones that had carried to her around half a world.

'Boaster – *Boaster*!'

Boaster pressed his forehead against hers. Icebones grasped his trunk and pulled at him this way and that. Then she let go, and they roared and bellowed and ran around each other until they could bump their rumps. Then they stood side by side, swaying, urinating and making dung urgently.

He touched her lips, and lifted his trunk tip to his mouth, tasting her. 'It is indeed you, little Icebones.'

'Littler than you imagined,' she said dryly.

'Yes. But *I* am not.' And he swung around, showing her what hung from his underbelly. 'There. Isn't *that* magnificent?'

She realised, awestruck, that he hadn't been boasting after all . . . But she said, 'You will always be Boaster to me.'

He growled. 'You are not in oestrus, little Icebones. Have I missed your flowering? Must I wait? Who took you – not that *calf*?'

Thunder rumbled. 'I am no calf. Would you like me to prove it?' And he raised his tusks, challenging the huge Bull.

But Boaster ignored the challenge. He ran his trunk over the younger Bull's head to test his temporal gland and his ears. 'You need to do some filling out. But you are a fine, strong Bull. Some day our tusks will clash over a Cow. But not today.' And, symbolically, he clicked his tusks against Thunder's.

Thunder backed away, not displeased.

Now more Bulls followed Boaster, fanning out around the Family. Some of them trunk-checked Thunder. 'Ah, Thunder. We have heard of you. The great bird killer!' 'You are just skin and bones!' 'What was it you bested – just a chick, or a full-grown duck?'

Thunder growled and threw his tusks threateningly. 'It was a mighty bird whose wings darkened the sky, and whose beak could have cut out *your* flimsy heart in a moment, weakling . . .' And he launched into the story of his battle with the skua, only a little elaborated. Gradually the other Bulls drifted closer, at first rumbling and snorting their scepticism, but growing quieter and more respectful as he developed his tale.

Autumn walked up to Icebones. 'He will have to defend the reputation he makes for himself. He is not among calves now.'

'He is a strong and proud Bull, and he will prosper.'

'And there is somebody else who is looking rather proud of herself,' Autumn said.

She meant Spiral.

Two of the older Bulls had broken away from the herd, watching each other warily. One of them boldly approached Spiral, trunk outstretched.

Spiral backed away, shaking her head. But she allowed him to place his trunk in her mouth.

The Bull lifted his trunk tip into his own mouth, touching it to a special patch of sensitive tissue there, and inhaled. Immediately he rumbled, 'Soon you will be in oestrus. And then I will mate you—'

'*I* will be the one,' said the other Bull. 'My brother is weak and foolish.' And he nudged his brother with his forehead, pushing him aside.

But now another Bull emerged from the herd, a giant who even outsized Boaster, with yellowed tusks chipped from fighting. 'What's this about oestrus? Is it this pretty one? Ignore these calves, pretty Cow. See my tusks. See my strength . . .'

Spiral turned and trotted away, trunk held high. The huge tusker followed her, still offering his gruff blandishments, and the younger Bulls followed, keeping a wary distance from the tusker and from each other.

'She has barely met an adult Bull in her life,' Autumn said. 'Yet she plays with them as a calf plays with lumps of mud. She always did relish being the centre of attention.'

'But the attention of Bulls is better than to be a toy of the Lost.'

Now Boaster was tugging at Icebones's tusks. She saw sadly that Boaster, too, was distracted by the scent of imminent oestrus that came from Spiral – that part of him longed to abandon Icebones and her dry belly, to run after the other Bulls and join in the eternal mating contests. But, loyally, he stayed with her, and his manner was urgent, eager.

'Icebones, come. There is something I must show you. Bring your Family. Come, please . . .'

She rumbled to the Family a gentle 'Let's go', and began to walk at Boaster's side.

After a time, the various members of her Family disengaged themselves from their various concerns, and formed up into a loose line and trotted after her: Autumn alongside Breeze, who shepherded Woodsmoke, and then came Spiral, still followed by her retinue of hopeful Bull attendants.

The only one who did not follow was Thunder, who was already becoming immersed in the society of the Bulls. Icebones felt a stab of sadness and turned away.

Boaster walked easily and gracefully, his belly and trunk swaying, and his guard hairs shone in the sunlight, full of health. But he walked slowly alongside Icebones, in sympathy with the battered, exhausted mammoth who had come so far.

It took days to walk into the centre of the basin.

The land opened out around Icebones. This tremendous crater was more than large enough for its walls to be invisible, hidden by the horizon. Soon Icebones would never have guessed that she was crossing a deep hollow punched into the hide of the world.

It was full of life. Icebones saw the tracks of herds of horses and bison, and the burrowing of lemmings, and the nests of birds. But folds of ancient, tortured rock showed through the rich lapping soil. And in the stillness of the night, beneath the calls of the wolves and the rumblings of contented mammoths, Icebones could sense the deep fractures that lay beneath the surface of this hugely wounded land.

After a few days the central forest came pushing over the horizon. Soon it was looming high over their heads, a dense mass of wood, topped by foliage that glowed silver-green in the light.

'I don't understand,' Icebones said to Boaster. 'Mammoths are creatures of the steppe. We like the dwarf trees that grow over the permafrost – willows and birches . . . What interest have we in a tall forest like this?'

'But it is not a forest,' he said gently.

Now Breeze came crowding forward. '*It is not a forest,*' she said. 'Icebones, can't you see? Can't you feel its roots? *It is a tree* – a single, mighty tree!'

Icebones walked forward and peered at the 'forest', and she saw that Breeze was right. There were no gaps to be seen in that dense mass of wood. Its single tremendous trunk was supported by huge buttress-like roots. And when she looked up, she saw that the trunk ran tall and clean far beyond the reach of any mammoth, and the tree's foliage was lost, high above her – lost in a wisp of low cloud, she realised, shocked.

'It is a tree higher than the sky,' she said. 'All the trees here grow tall. But this is the mightiest of all.'

Boaster growled. 'If it could talk, it might be called Boaster too – what do you think, Icebones? But this is a special tree. Its fruit draws in air.'

'It is a breathing tree.' She described the trees they had encountered on the High Plain.

'Yes,' Boaster said. 'But this is their giant cousin. This Breathing Tree is a mammoth among trees.' He touched her trunk. 'I know how hard your journey was. But this Tree shows that the mightiest of living things can prosper here . . . If the Tree survives, so will we.'

She moved closer to him and wrapped his trunk in hers. 'The journey was hard. But you gave me strength when I had none left.'

He pulled away, puzzled. '*I* inspired *you*? Come with me.' He tugged at her trunk. 'Come, come and see.'

They walked a little away around the Tree's vast cylindrical trunk. It was like walking around a huge rock formation.

And suddenly, before her, there were mammoths.

There were huge old Bulls with chipped tusks, bits of grass clinging to the hairs of their faces, giant scars crossing their flanks and backs. And fat, slow Cows, round-faced calves running at their feet. And young Bulls, their adult tusks just beginning to show like gleams of ice in rock folds. And leaner, loose-haired mammoths whose journey here looked as if it had been as hard as Icebones's.

Around her was the sound of mammoths: the click of tusks, the dry rustle of intertwined trunks, the hiss of their hair and tails – many, many mammoths.

'Can you smell them?' Boaster asked gently. 'Can you *hear* them?'

Icebones was stunned. 'Where do they come from?'

'They came from all over this little world. They were abandoned by the Lost, and they were helpless, just as your Family was. If they had stayed in their Lost cages, they would have starved or submitted to the cold – but they didn't know what else to do.

'But your Family was different. *They had you.* And when you made your decision to bring them here to the Footfall, I knew I had to follow you, with my bachelor herd. Not that I didn't have to crack a few tusks to make them see sense . . .

'And then, with our calls and stamping, we spread the word to all the mammoths who can hear. Some were reluctant to come, some didn't understand, and some were simply frightened. But none of them faced so hard a journey as you.

'And one by one, Family by Family, they began the great walk, from north, south, west, east . . .'

'All of these mammoths are here because of *me*?'

Autumn was at her side. 'Because of you, Icebones, Matriarch. Your achievement was mighty. You walked your mammoths around the world. You walked them from the highest place of all, the peak of the Fire Mountain, to the deepest place, this Footfall. It is an achievement that will live for ever in the songs of the Cycle.'

Weak, overtired, hungry, thirsty, Icebones tried to take in all this – and failed. She wished Silverhair could see her now. She would, at last, be proud.

But there was room in her heart for a stab of doubt. She recalled the fringe of the crater basin, the dried mud there where the tide of life had receded. Could it be that she had drawn these mammoths here on a promise of life and security that, in the end, would not be fulfilled? Perhaps what she had achieved was not an inspiration – but a betrayal.

But now Breeze came trotting up to her, her manner urgent and tense. 'Thunder is calling from the edge of the steppe. Can you hear him? Icebones, he says *she* is coming.'

Icebones immediately knew who she meant. And she realised that, whatever her triumph in bringing the mammoths here to the navel of the world, she must gather up her strength for one more challenge.

For, out of the harsh High Plains, the Ragged One was approaching.

Chapter Six

THE BREATHING TREE

Icebones – still limping, still favouring the shoulder she now suspected would never properly heal – liked to walk beside the Tree. Around it the air was dense with the life of the long summer. A great misty fog of aerial plankton, ballooning spiders and delicate larvae drifted over the land in search of places to live.

She stroked the Tree's deep brown bark and listened to the currents of sap that ran within it, considering its mysteries. She sensed how this Tree was dragging heat and water up from the world's depths.

And, slowly, as she began to understand its purpose, she came to believe that this vast Tree was the core of everything . . .

It took many days for the Ragged One to cross the Footfall.

And she was not alone. She had entered the crater with a mysterious herd of her own. And as she crossed the plain more mammoths were joining her. A determined force was trekking steadily towards the Tree, and Icebones.

Autumn and Boaster stayed with her, her closest companions.

Boaster said, 'You do not have to face this *Ragged One*, little Icebones. Let me drive her off with a thrust of my tusks.' And he dipped his head and lunged at an imaginary opponent.

She stroked his face fondly. She knew that though she was slowly regaining some of her health, she would never be as strong as she had been before. She had left her strength and youth, it seemed, up on the High Plains.

But she knew it was her duty to face the Ragged One.

Autumn and Boaster knew it too, of course.

Autumn growled, 'It would help if we knew what that wretched creature wanted. I'm sure it has nothing to do with being mammoth.'

Boaster rumbled, 'It is disturbing how many here think back nostalgically to the days when the Lost ran our lives for us. That is why those addled fools follow her.'

Icebones said, 'But the way of the Cycle is often harsh. Even we, on the High Plains, turned back from confronting the final truth . . . I cannot blame these others.'

She spotted Breeze, who had come into oestrus. She was walking fast, holding her head tall. Her eyes were wide amber drops. She was being pursued by a large, grizzled Bull, his tusks scarred and chipped. Dark fluid leaked from his musth glands and down his face, and he dribbled urine as he walked.

A little further away, two younger Bulls were challenging each other, raising their tusks and shaking their heads. But they both must know that whoever won their battle would not gain access to Breeze while the battered old tusker claimed her.

Breeze and the victorious tusker began a kind of dance. She would walk away, glancing over her shoulder, and he would follow, rumbling. But then he would hold back, as if testing her willingness and desire, and in response she slowed.

Beyond this central pair and the two young competing Bulls was a ring of more males, eight or ten of them – some of them massive, many sporting savage scars and shattered tusks. Further away still more Bulls watched the central couple jealously, standing still as rocks.

The whole circle of Bulls, young and old, was held in place around Breeze, trapped by invisible forces of lust and jealousy and fear.

'It is the consort,' Autumn observed. 'So the ancient dance continues.'

'As it should,' Icebones said.

Boaster growled and pawed the ground, his huge trunk swaying. A sad unspoken thought passed between Boaster and Icebones: she had still not come into oestrus, and they both feared now that the dryness at her core would never be broken.

Autumn, oblivious to this, said, 'I only wish that Spiral could find some happiness too.'

Icebones understood her regret. Spiral had come into oestrus soon after Icebones's mammoths had arrived here in the Footfall. She was tall and handsome, and the Bulls could tell from her complex scents that she had borne healthy calves before. But though Spiral had attracted an even larger consort retinue than Breeze, in the end she had brayed at her winning suitor and fled, refusing his advances.

'She will come to no harm,' said Boaster. 'She is proud and difficult, but she is beautiful.'

'Ah,' Autumn said, rather grandly. 'But she wrestles with problems you may not imagine, child . . .'

'Just as,' came a muddy voice, 'you big hairy animals can barely imagine the troubles *I* have.'

Icebones turned. A squat creature was waddling towards her, its peculiarly naked skin covered in drying mud. It raised a small stubby trunk.

Icebones limped forward, inordinately pleased. 'Chaser-Of-Frogs!'

The Mother of the Swamp-Mammoths looked up at Boaster with small black eyes and burped proudly. Boaster trumpeted, startled, and he backed away from the stubby form.

Chaser-Of-Frogs said, 'Without me, you know, these clumsy oafs would be blundering around that Gouge still.' She reached up with her trunk and probed at Icebones's belly. 'But your journey was hard too. You are a bag of skin. And,' she said more gently, probing at Icebones's dry dugs, 'you have other problems, I fear.'

Icebones gave a brief rumble of regret. But she insisted, 'What of you, Chaser-Of-Frogs? I thought you would never leave that muddy pond.'

'My Family have found a new pond now.' She raised her trunk towards a shallow lake nearby.

Icebones heard and smelled more Swamp-Mammoths burrowing gratefully into the muddy pond floor. Their wet backs gleamed in the sun like logs, and their protruding eyes blinked slowly. Mammoths stood around these new arrivals, trunks raised in curiosity, and a clutch of ducks swam away indignantly.

There were perhaps a dozen Swamp-Mammoths in the lake.

Icebones said softly, 'This is all?'

Chaser-Of-Frogs said grimly, 'We both knew how it would be, Bones-Of-Ice. Most would not follow. Of those who set out, those who died first were the old and the young, our calves . . . It was hard, Bones-Of-Ice. So hard.'

Autumn rumbled, 'We faced the same choice – and failed – and our bones would now be scoured by the dust storms of the high plain, our line extinct, if not for good fortune . . .'

'*The mammoth dies, but mammoths live on,*' Icebones said softly.

But now Boaster stiffened. He was looking to the north, his tusks raised, and he trumpeted.

There was a sound of feet, purposefully walking. And on the northern horizon a black cloud hugged the ground, like the approach of a storm.

Icebones, with deep reluctance, turned that way. When she raised her trunk she could smell a tang of blood and staleness.

It was no storm. It was mammoth: a great herd of them, and they walked through the billowing crimson dust raised by their own powerful footfalls.

Calves ran squealing in search of their mothers. Bulls broke off from their jousting and backed away, grumbling. Even Breeze's consort circle was broken up.

'It is as if a cloud has come across the sun,' Autumn said.

But Icebones stood straight. For, in the lead of the marching mammoths, grey hair flying wispy in the wind, was the Ragged One.

It was time. Relief flooded Icebones.

One more trial, Icebones. Just one more. Then you can rest.

She gathered her strength.

The Ragged One trumpeted, her loose hair wafting around her strange grey-pink face. She was gaunt, her ribs protruding beneath her sparse hair. Her face was scarred, her tusks badly chipped.

'So, Icebones,' the Ragged One said, 'you survived. And you did not kill any more mammoths on your journey.'

Before Icebones could reply, Autumn raised her trunk. 'Spiral,' she said softly. 'Daughter – is that *you*?'

From behind the Ragged One, Spiral stepped forward, head held high, her beautiful tusks gleaming.

Autumn rumbled her dismay.

Icebones growled to the Ragged One, 'Say what it is you want here. And say what you have promised these mammoths who follow you.'

'That is simple,' the Ragged One said. '*I have told them I will bring back the Lost.*'

Icebones immediately sensed the hopeful, longing mood of the mass of mammoths who had followed Icebones – and, to her shock, she even sensed a stirring of doubt in Boaster, who stood at her side.

For a heartbeat she felt giddy, weak, as if she might fall. This was a dangerous moment indeed: a moment that could decide the future of the species, here on this rocky steppe – and all that she could bring to bear was her own failing strength.

Spiral called thinly, 'The Lost gave us life, Icebones. What have you to offer us but a jumble of myths, suffering and death – as my own sister died, as *we* nearly died?'

There was a great rumbling from the mass of mammoths behind her.

'I have nothing to offer you,' Icebones said. 'Nothing but the truth, and dignity.'

The Ragged One snorted contempt. 'I cannot eat truth. I cannot drink dignity.'

Autumn demanded, '*How* do you imagine you will call back the Lost from the sky?'

The Ragged One walked up to the giant Breathing Tree. Its mottled bark loomed above her like a wall. Grunting, she slashed at the bark with her tusks.

The gouged wood leaked a blood-red sap.

'I am one mammoth, with a single pair of tusks. But I can cut and slash. And when I am exhausted, another will come and cut after me, and then another, and another . . . It might take a season, a whole year. But we are mammoths, and we are strong. And we will destroy this Tree, as we can destroy any other.'

'You are a fool,' said Autumn. 'How will that help you bring back the Lost?'

'You are old and your mind is addled,' said the Ragged One. 'You are the fool. Look at this Tree. Smell it. Hear its roots worming into the earth. Is there another such Tree in the whole of the world? No, there is not. *Because this Tree is a creation of the Lost* – their mightiest work, destined to outlive the Nests, and the beetle things that toil and burn. And if we destroy the Tree, the Lost will wish to restore it – *and they will return.*'

A wave of excited trumpeting rippled through the crowd of her followers, and the noise was briefly deafening.

Before the Ragged One's intense anger and determination, Icebones felt weak, like a figure in a dissolving dream. But she knew she must act. 'I will stop you.'

'And if you try,' hissed the Ragged One, 'I will kill you.'

'Then that is what you will have to do, for I will oppose you to my last breath.'

'Why?' Autumn asked. 'Icebones, it is only a tree.'

'No,' Icebones said. 'I have thought deeply on this, and I believe I understand the Tree's true importance – *as do you, Cold-As-Sky*. Show yourself now.'

Out from the crowd beyond Spiral, a squat, rounded form shouldered her way: mammoth, yes, but with a hump and covered in black, sticky hair, and with small feet and tiny pointed ears, and a pair of eyes that glowed orange.

The mammoths around her recoiled, rumbling uncertainly.

'I am here, Icebones,' said the Matriarch of the Ice Mammoths. 'I followed your Ragged One. I come here despite the thickness of the air, and the stench of water and your fat green growing things . . .'

Icebones said, 'Cousin. You saved my Family on the High Plains. And yet now you seek to destroy a world.'

Cold-As-Sky said harshly, 'I come not to destroy, but to make the world as it once was.'

'I don't understand any of this,' Autumn said.

Icebones spoke loudly enough for every mammoth in the Footfall to hear.

'This one is right, that the Tree is a gift of the Lost – their last gift to this world. But the Lost have gone, and the Tree remains. And now its meaning has nothing to do with the Lost, but with the Cycle – *with us*.

'When Longtusk led his Family away from the advancing Lost and over the great bridge, he reached a land of ice, where nothing could live. But Longtusk had heard of a place called a *nunatak*. It was a refuge, a place where heat bubbled from the ground, keeping back the ice, and green things lived, even in the depths of winter. There the mammoths survived.'

'These are fables for calves,' said the Ragged One sourly.

Icebones walked up to the Breathing Tree and stroked its

261

cut-through bark. 'Like Longtusk's Family, we are stranded in a world of ice. But this Footfall is our *nunatak*.' She stamped her feet, challenging the mammoths. 'Listen to the song of the rocks. Feel how the ground is shattered and compressed. This is the deepest pit in the world, where the rock has been pushed far down – so far that the inner heat of the world, which lies beneath the plants and soil and rocks, is close. Can you feel it? Can you hear the mud that bubbles, the liquid water that gurgles?'

There were rumbles of doubt and surprise among the gathered mammoths. Icebones could hear them pawing at the ground, listening for the secret songs that welled there.

'The heat is deeper than any of us could reach,' said Icebones. '*But the roots of this Tree will reach deeper than any mammoth's trunk.* Even yours, Cold-As-Sky. One day this Tree will draw up the heat of the world. It will breathe rich air, and weep water – and the world will live.'

'One day?' Boaster asked wistfully.

'Not yet,' Icebones said gently. 'This Tree, mighty as it towers over us poor mammoths, is but a sapling. Can't you tell, Boaster?'

The Ragged One trumpeted desperately, 'If we destroy the Tree, the Lost will return.'

'No,' Icebones said. 'You showed me yourself how the Lost abandoned this world. Wherever they have gone, it has nothing to do with us. But if you destroy the Tree, you destroy yourselves – and your calves, and their calves after them.' She raised her tusks. 'This is the truth. If I am the only one opposed, then you must kill me first.'

There was an expectant silence, a forest of raised trunks.

Icebones stood alone. She had done all she could. And so she waited in the thin, high sunlight, with the tang of red dust strong in her nostrils.

The small world spun around her, and heat gathered in her head.

Autumn came to stand behind Icebones.

Breeze joined her.

And even the calf faced the crowd of mammoths, his tiny tusks upraised as if he was ready to take them all on.

'We are your Family, Icebones,' Autumn said. 'On that long journey, *I* became *We*. And now we stand with you.'

'And me,' growled Boaster, adding his massive presence. Icebones touched his trunk with affection and gratitude.

Chaser-Of-Frogs came waddling up, scattering drying mud. 'None of you is as handsome as me. But Bones-Of-Ice taught me we are all Cousins, and she spoke the truth – and that truth saved me. I am proud to be your Family, Bones-Of-Ice. *I* become *We*.'

Autumn trumpeted, 'Spiral. Join us.'

But Spiral, standing close to the Ice Mammoths, postured and pranced, as if for an invisible audience of Lost.

But now Thunder emerged from the crowd. He approached Spiral. Another young Bull followed him, unknown to Icebones.

Thunder called, 'I recall how it was for you on that distant Mountain, Spiral. The Lost pampered you and praised you – *but they took away your calves.*'

'It is true,' Autumn said. 'Daughter, you recall the Lost with affection. But in truth they hurt you as no mother should be hurt.'

Spiral trumpeted, 'Leave me alone – oh, leave me alone!'

The other Bull stepped forward. His tusks, though still

immature, were long and smooth – and they made neat curls that were, Icebones saw, an exact match of Spiral's own. He walked awkwardly up to Spiral. He reached out with his trunk, and probed her mouth and trunk tip and breasts. 'But *I* cannot leave you alone,' he said thickly. 'Have you forgotten me, mother?'

Spiral stood stiff and silent, eyes wide. Then she cried out, pain mixed with joy, and wrapped her trunk around her son's face.

Icebones pealed, 'This is how it is to be mammoth: mother with calf, Families together, herds of Bulls strong and proud. We have no need of the Lost. All we need is each other. Join me now. Join my Clan.'

And, like an ice floe slowly melting, the group beyond the Ragged One lost its cohesion. One by one mammoths broke away from the disciplined mass, to join Icebones and her Family.

Spiral came lumbering stiffly to her mother, her trunk still wrapped tightly around the head of the calf that had been taken from her long ago. Autumn embraced her daughter gruffly.

A massive tusker came up, dribbling stinking musth. He tried to get close to Breeze, whose oestrus smell was still powerful. Curtly Autumn shielded her daughter from his attention.

A part of Icebones was amused that even now the deeper story of life went on.

Thunder joined Icebones. She nuzzled his mouth affectionately. 'Well done,' she said. 'You have made the difference, I think . . .'

'I thought it would work,' Thunder said softly.

'What do you mean?'

'I thought Spiral might have run off to join that ranting fool. I found the calf two days ago. I thought he might come in useful. So I kept him distracted until now.'

Icebones was astonished. 'How can you think in such a devious way?'

'Just be glad I am on your side,' Thunder said modestly.

Cold-As-Sky snorted. 'But what of us, Icebones?' The Ice Mammoths were breathing fast, their blue tongues lolling. To them, Icebones recalled, the thin, clean air of the Footfall was dense and clammy and much, much too hot. Cold-As-Sky said, 'If I join you, I die. If the Tree makes your world, it destroys ours.'

Autumn turned on the Ragged One. 'You see why they followed you? Even these strange creatures cared nothing for the Lost, for your dreams. *All they wanted was to smash the Tree*, for they understood its importance, as Icebones did. You are a fool – you let them use you—'

Icebones touched Autumn's trunk to still her.

Thunder said unexpectedly, 'But you need not die, Cold-As-Sky.'

The Ice Mammoths inspected him suspiciously.

In brief phrases – illustrated with much stamping and growling – he told them of the Fire Mountain, where he had been born. 'It is high,' he said. 'Higher than your High Plains, the highest place in all the world. No matter how hard this Tree breathes, that Mountain's summit will still be a place of cold and thinness and ice.'

Cold-As-Sky said to Icebones, 'Is this true?'

Icebones glanced at the Ragged One. '*She* knows it to be true. We walked to the summit, and saw breathing trees . . . Yes, you could live there, Cold-As-Sky.'

'But it is half a world away.'

Now Breeze's calf stepped forward. 'I will lead you,' said Woodsmoke brightly. '*I* have walked half the world. I will show you how.'

Breeze cuffed him affectionately but proudly, for he stood tall and determined.

Cold-As-Sky rumbled, and her Ice Mammoths clustered around her.

Then, hesitantly, Cold-As-Sky stepped forward and stood behind Icebones. Her Family followed.

The Ice Mammoths smelled of ice and iron.

At last the Ragged One was left isolated.

It is done, Icebones thought. Her sense of relief was overwhelming, leaving her weak.

'You have defeated me,' said the Ragged One bleakly.

'No. We are not Bulls battling over a Cow. There is no defeat, no victory. Be with our Family.'

'You don't understand,' said the Ragged One. 'You have never understood. *I* cannot become part of your *We*.'

'That isn't true—'

'But it is, in a way,' said Chaser-Of-Frogs.

'This muddy thing is right, Icebones,' said Cold-As-Sky, ignoring Chaser-Of-Frogs's bristling. 'She is mammoth, yet she is not – *just as we are*.

'I told you we have our own legend, our own memories. We know we were set down on a world where nothing could live – nothing but ourselves, and the blood weed and other plants which feed us. And we recall the first of us all – *for those first had no mothers*.'

Chaser-Of-Frogs said grimly, 'I hate to ally myself with one so ugly as this, but our memory is the same. In the beginning there were no mothers. There was no Cow, no oestrus, no consort dance, no mating . . .'

'Then how did you come to be?'

'The Lost made us,' Cold-As-Sky said simply. 'They took the bones of mammoths who died long ago, and ground them in the blood of others – remote Cousins called *elephants* who lived in the warm places. And, out of the mixing, came—'

'Us,' said Chaser-Of-Frogs sourly.

'It was not enough for the Lost that they brought mammoths to this place,' said Cold-As-Sky bitterly. 'They had to make us into things of their own.'

Icebones asked, 'But *why*? Why would they do this?'

Autumn growled, 'Perhaps they were in musth, and sought to impress their females.'

'No,' said the Ragged One. 'They loved us. They loved the *idea* of us. That is what I believe. They wanted to remake us, to bring us back from the extinction to which they almost drove us, to give us this new world where there would be room for us to browse.'

Autumn walked up to the Ragged One and ruffled her sparse, untidy hair. 'If it was love, they loved us too much,' she said gruffly.

'And that is why you sought to wreck the world,' Icebones said, understanding at last. 'That is why you wanted the Lost back so badly. *Because they made you.*'

'Enough,' said Autumn. 'Give this up. Join us now.'

The Ragged One hesitated, agitated, distressed. She reached out to Autumn, raising her trunk – and, briefly, Icebones believed it might be possible.

But then the Ragged One trumpeted wildly. She pushed past the Ice Mammoths and lumbered away.

Icebones made to go after her, but Autumn held her back with her long, strong trunk. In a moment the Ragged One was lost among the mammoths — and Icebones sensed that she would never see her again.

The mammoths began to disperse.

'It is done, Icebones,' Autumn said. 'The shadow of the Lost is gone at last. This is our world now.'

'Yes. It is done . . .'

And the last of Icebones's strength drained into the red dust. The colours leached out of the world, and her head filled with a sharp ringing. She would have fallen, if not for the support of her Family.

A watching human would only have seen the mammoths gather, heard nothing but an intense and mysterious rumbling and growling and stamping and clicking of tusks.

She would never have known that the destiny of a world had been tested, and determined.

Chapter Seven

THE DREAM OF KILUKPUK

The Song of Oestrus disturbed Icebones, startling her awake.

She sniffed the air querulously.

It was cold and damp. The sun was dim, or so it seemed to her. Perhaps another winter was coming, though it seemed no more than heartbeats since spring was done.

But then the seasons were shorter on this hard little world. Or were they longer? She could not recall.

Time flowed strangely here, like water, like blood. Sometimes it seemed that her life had fled as rapidly as the fleeting summers, for here she was, suddenly a last-molar, barely able to chew the softest grass any more, her senses and her memories as eroded as her teeth.

Ah, but sometimes she thought she was young again, young and *imagining* how it would be to be a broken-down old mammoth, here in this green hollow, the navel of the world.

Young dreaming of old age, or dotard dreaming of youth? Perhaps, in the end, it made no difference. Perhaps there was no past or present, young or old; perhaps life was just a single moment, a unity, like a pebble taken into the mouth to ward off thirst, inspected by the tongue from every angle . . .

Anyhow, whether the world was growing cold or not, *she* certainly was.

She lumbered towards the Breathing Tree.

Soon she was wheezing with the effort of the walk, and her shoulder ached, never properly healed from its ancient injury. Close to the Tree's roots, where hot air gushed and warm water flowed, the Swamp-Mammoths had made their wallows. She would find some company there, and perhaps would try a little grass, or even a willow bud. And she would ruminate a while with Autumn. Ah, but poor, stolid Autumn was long dead, and she had forgotten again.

She saw a herd of caribou. They preferred to live out their lives at the fringe of the great forests of warmer climes, but came to the steppe to breed. They crossed a stream, splashing and pawing at the water, so that sunlit droplets rose up all around them. Their movements were hasty, nervous, skittish, like horses.

She found the source of the oestrus call. On a small rise a Bull had mounted a young Cow, laying his trunk over her back and the top of her head, and gripping her hips with his forelegs.

When he lumbered away from her, the Cow's song was loud, a series of deep swooping notes repeated over and over, rising out of silence then fracturing into nothing. Soon more Cows joined her to celebrate, trumpeting and making urine together, and they reached out crisscrossing trunks to explore the ground, seeking the strong smell of the mating.

But Icebones's battered old trunk could smell nothing, and

the oestrus songs were fuzzy in her hearing – and even her heart felt only the smallest pang of jealousy. She, of course, had never come into oestrus, not once in her long life since she had woken from her strange, half-forgotten Sleep on that remote mountainside. It didn't seem to matter any more. Perhaps her heart had grown calluses, like the broken pads on her feet.

She walked on, labouring to breathe, heading for the Tree.

There were mammoths everywhere. They walked steadily through long grass that swirled in their wake. One of them stopped to graze, and the swaying grass fell still at the same time as the rippling of his hair.

There was a sense of stillness about the mammoths, Icebones thought: of meditation, patience, their calmness as solid and pervasive as the crimson rock beneath her feet. All creatures of the steppe knew stillness.

Where the mammoths walked, ground-nesters like plovers and jaegers flew up angrily if they threatened to step in their nests. But snow buntings and longspurs were making their nests of discarded mammoth wool. And in the winters the snow-clearing of the mammoths exposed grass for hares and willow buds for ptarmigans, and the wells they dug were used by wolves and foxes and others, and even now the insects stirred up by the mammoths' passage served as food for the birds.

It was as it had always been, as the Cycle proudly pro-claimed: *Where mammoths walk, they bring life*. It was right, and it was good.

The mammoths reached out to her with absent affection. But they were strangers to her.

Of course they were. By comparison with their spindly liquid grace she felt like a lump of earth, grey and dull. These were mammoths shaped by this new world. The grass grew from the blood-red dust, and the mammoths ate the grass, so that the red dust of the Sky Steppe coursed in their veins. Changing, shimmering, these new mammoths moved past her like tall shadows, shifting, growing stranger with every new generation.

And none of them were her children, or grandchildren: not one.

Taken from her mother on the Island, she had devoted her life to a quest for Family. Well, she had succeeded. She had built the mammoths into a Family, into Clans. But now the Sky Steppe was taking them away.

. . . Icebones.

She stopped, struggling to raise her heavy old trunk. The calling voice had been unfamiliar, and it had seemed to come neither from left or right, nor before or behind.

The colours leached out of the world. She felt herself sway.

Icebones. Icebones. '. . . Icebones.'

She looked up. A Bull stood before her – little more than a calf, no taller than she was, his tusks still stubby and untested.

'Woodsmoke?'

'No,' he said patiently. 'Woodsmoke was the mate of my grandmother, Matriarch. I am Tang-Of-Dust. You recall – as an infant I loved to roll in dust dunes and—'

'Ah, Tang-Of-Dust.' But his smell was indistinct, his form in her eyes only a wavering outline. 'Always eat the tall grass,' she said.

'Matriarch?'

'You are what you eat. That much is obvious to everyone. And the tallest grass dreams of touching the sky, of reaching the aurora. So that is what you must eat . . .'

Here was a pretty stand of tussock grass. Forgetting Tang-

Of-Dust, she bent to inspect it. The tall thin leaves grew as high as her shoulder, rising out of a pedestal of old leaves and roots. Between the tussock clumps burnet grass grew. This sported round red flower heads that swayed gracefully in the breeze. There were other plants scattered more thinly, like ferns and buttercups and dandelions, and many clumps of fungus, some of them bright red or white, their colours a startling contrast to the deep green of the grass.

Just a stand of grass. She couldn't even smell or taste it. All she could do was see it, as if with age she was turning into one of the Lost. But it was beautiful, intricate, like so much of the world.

She was still herself. She was Icebones, daughter of Silverhair. Nothing would erode *that* away: the last thing she would retain, even when the world had worn away like her molars.

She said, 'He went away, you know.'

'Matriarch?'

'Woodsmoke. He was born on the great Migration – did you know that? I suppose wandering was in his blood . . . At first it wasn't possible, of course. The world away from the Footfall just got too cold for anything to live. Anything like us, anyhow. But gradually that changed, and off he went. But they say that where his dung fell, grass and trees grew, and the animals and birds that live on them followed. Isn't that wonderful, Woodsmoke? As if life is spreading out from this deep warm place. He never came back, of course . . .'

'Yes, Matriarch,' the calf said respectfully. But he was growing impatient. 'Matriarch, *it has changed*. In the sky.'

She grumbled, '*What* has changed?'

'The blue star that flies near the sun.'

She squinted, compressing failing eyes.

The calf was right, she saw. The familiar blue spark had been replaced by a sliver of silver light.

. . . And now, quite suddenly, the silver grain winked out – vanished completely, as if it had never been. Its small brown companion, abandoned, sailed alone in the sky.

She raised her trunk but could smell nothing, hear nothing. How strange, she thought.

Tang-Of-Dust asked, 'What does it mean?'

'I don't know, child.'

'They say that the Lost went there. To the blue light.'

'It might be true,' she said. And she wondered where they had gone now.

'Some say the Lost were insane. Or evil.'

She lowered her heavy head. 'No, not evil, not insane . . . But not like us. In many ways they were arrogant and foolish. But the Lost brought life here. Think of that. We existed a long time before the Lost came, and we will exist for a long time now that they are gone. Theirs was just a brief moment of pain and change and death – but in that moment they gave us a new world. Even if this world is nothing but a dream of Kilukpuk . . .' She slumped forward, to her knees, and her trunk pooled in the dust. 'And, I suppose, by redeeming us, the Lost redeemed themselves. Isn't that wonderful?'

The calf reached out uncertainly. 'Matriarch. Are you ill?'

Her belly settled on to the dust, and she closed her eyes. 'Just tired, Woodsmoke. In a moment we will talk—'

But now there was an explosion of pain in her chest. She gasped and fell forward.

She saw legs all around her, a forest of them, as if she was a newborn calf surrounded by her mother and aunts. That was absurd, for she could hardly be more different from a calf.

She closed her eyes again.

A memory of old age, or a dream of youth? But she tasted blood – or perhaps it was the dry dust of this red world – not a dream, then . . .

Or perhaps the dream was over.

'Icebones . . . Icebones . . .'

Icebones.

She tried to lift her head, to open her eyes, but could not. And yet she thought she saw a mammoth before her: a vast mammoth with dugs the size of mountains, and feet that could stamp great pits in the rock, and tusks like glaciers, and a voice like the song of a world. A mammoth who shone, even though Icebones's eyes were closed.

Do you know who you are?

'I am Icebones, daughter of Silverhair.' That much remained. 'I am very tired.'

You know who I am?

'Yes. Yes, I know who you are, Kilukpuk.'

It's time to go, little one.

'But my Family needs me.'

Now I need you. And Icebones felt a trunk wrap around her head and probe into her dry mouth.

She was lifted up, shedding her body as every spring she had shed her winter coat.

'I am not fit, Matriarch . . .'

No one is more fit than you. And no one paid a greater price than you. The Lost brought you here, in your Sleep, across a vast gulf. And in that gulf a hard light shines. And you were – damaged.

And Icebones knew Kilukpuk meant her dry womb. 'That is why I have no calves.'

But every mammoth who lives is your calf. You saved your kind in every way it is possible to be saved: you gave them life, and you gave them back their selves.

'Will there be soft browse? My molars aren't what they were.'

I will show you the softest, sweetest browse that ever was.

'There is no aurora here. Where are we going?'

To where Silverhair is waiting for you. No more questions, now.

The great shining mammoth drew away.

Effortlessly, Icebones followed. And the small red world receded beneath her, folding over on itself until it became a crimson ball splashed with green and blue, before it disappeared into the dark.

EPILOGUE

Ice still swathes much of the northern ocean, and the southern pole. But the ice is receding. In the ancient highlands of the south the flooded craters and rivers and canals glow blue-green once more. Much of the land is covered by dark forest and broad, sweeping grasslands and steppe – but the primordial crimson of the dust still shines through the green.

This will always be a cold, dry place. This world is too small, too far from the sun. But life is spreading here, year by year: life first brought here by vanished, clever creatures with silver ships and toiling machines, but life now finding its own way on the hard, ancient plains, led by the stately beasts whose calls echo around the planet.

But those calls will never be heard on the summit of the Fire Mountain. That obstinate shoulder of rock still pushes out of the thickening air, just as it always has. From its barren summit the stars can be seen, even at midday.

Here, in the thin air, not even the hardy Ice Mammoths venture. Here, nothing grows.

Nothing, that is, save a solitary dwarf willow, a single splash of green–brown against the ancient crimson rock. Against all odds, the willow's windblown seed has found a trace of water here, high on the Fire Mountain: enough to germinate, and survive.

Just a trace of water, trapped in the buried skull of a mammoth.

DEEP FUTURE
Stephen Baxter

Deep Future takes you on a dazzling ride to the limits of time and space. Along the way Stephen Baxter looks at our place in the universe, considers the possibility that we are in fact alone, and wonders whether that fact gives us the right to inherit everything. He also looks at how we might strive to overcome the limitations of the physical universe and win the deepest future.

Stephen Baxter has brought his trademark narrative flair and imaginative brilliance to the latest ideas in physics and cosmology and produced a breathtaking guide to our possible futures.

'Gripping – but more than a little disturbing – essays and speculative writing. Stephen Baxter has been hailed as the natural successor to Clarke, Asimov and Heinlein for the hard science in his novels . . . Read, be awed and amazed at our deep future, but be prepared to lose sleep.' *SFX*

'A thoroughly engrossing read!' *Starburst*

'State of the art futurology' Dave Langford

£6.99 • A Format Paperback • 0 57507 286 5

All Gollancz titles are available at your local bookshop or from the following address:

Mail Order Department
Littlehampton Book Services
FREEPOST BR535
Worthing, West Sussex, BN13 3BR
telephone 01903 828503, *facsimile* 01903 828802
e-mail MailOrders@lbsltd.co.uk
(Please ensure that you include full postal address details)

Payment can be made either by credit/debit card (Visa, Mastercard, Access and Switch accepted) or by sending a £ Sterling cheque or postal order made payable to *Littlehampton Book Services*.
DO NOT SEND CASH OR CURRENCY.

Please add the following to cover postage and packing

UK and BFPO:
£1.50 for the first book, and 50p for each additional book to a maximum of £3.50

Overseas and Eire:
£2.50 for the first book plus £1.00 for the second book and 50p for each additional book ordered

---

BLOCK CAPITALS PLEASE

name of cardholder _____

address of cardholder _____

delivery address
(if different from cardholder)
_____
_____

postcode _____   *postcode* _____

☐ I enclose my remittance for £_____

☐ please debit my Mastercard/Visa/Access/Switch (delete as appropriate)

card number ☐☐☐☐☐☐☐☐☐☐☐☐☐☐☐☐☐☐

expiry date ☐☐☐☐   Switch issue no. ☐☐

signature _____

prices and availability are subject to change without notice